PE

Rachel Silver grew up in Jerusalem, studied Anthropology at University College, London, and has written for television and the national press. Her first play, *Trapping the Antelope*, was staged at the Young Vic in 1986. She has since published four books, including most recently *The Girl in Scarlet Heels* (Century, 1993) and *Where Their Feet Dance* (Century, 1994). Rachel now lives and works in west London.

RACHEL SILVER

MADSON

PENGUIN BOOKS
BBC BOOKS

PENGUIN BOOKS
BBC BOOKS

Published by the Penguin Group and BBC Worldwide Ltd
Penguin Books Ltd, 27 Wrights Lane, London w8 5tz, England
Penguin Books USA Inc., 375 Hudson Street, New York, New York 10014, USA
Penguin Books Australia Ltd, Ringwood, Victoria, Australia
Penguin Books Canada Ltd, 10 Alcorn Avenue, Toronto, Ontario, Canada m4v 3b2
Penguin Books (NZ) Ltd, 182–190 Wairau Road, Auckland 10, New Zealand

Penguin Books Ltd, Registered Offices: Harmondsworth, Middlesex, England

First published 1996
1 3 5 7 9 10 8 6 4 2

Copyright © Rachel Silver, 1996
All rights reserved

The moral right of the author has been asserted

◼◼◼™ BBC used under licence

Set in 10/12 pt Linotype Sabon
Typeset by Rowland Phototypesetting Ltd,
Bury St Edmunds, Suffolk
Printed in England by Clays Ltd, St Ives plc

Except in the United States of America, this book is sold subject
to the condition that it shall not, by way of trade or otherwise, be lent,
re-sold, hired out, or otherwise circulated without the publisher's
prior consent in any form of binding or cover other than that in
which it is published and without a similar condition including this
condition being imposed on the subsequent purchaser

With thanks to Ian McShane,
Colin Shindler, Charlotte Allum and
Joey Silver

CHAPTER ONE

'We have decided unanimously that the errors in procedure demonstrated by the appellant, howsoever
caused, were fatal to the prosecution case. His conviction was therefore unsafe and unsound. We can make
no other order than that the conviction be quashed and
that John Peter Madson be allowed his immediate
release. You are free to go.'

The words of the Appeal Court judge echoed through
his head as John Madson emerged into the blinding light
of an autumn morning. He could hardly dare to believe
it as he stood on the broad stone steps, bewildered, but
triumphant. After eight years in a prison cell with only
his cherished law books for company and the horror of
his wife's brutal death to preoccupy him, here he was
taking his first steps as a free man.

He stood musing for a moment, his vision hazy with
the excitement, a confusion of images playing before his
eyes. He was now nearer fifty than the man of forty he
had been when convicted, but his hair was not yet grey;
he presented a handsome figure against the severe stone
facade of the institution he was leaving, his face chiselled
and earnest, his piercing eyes intelligent and thoughtful.
People in sombre suits hurried down the steps, brushing
past him, pressmen clicking their cameras, others
waving notebooks to catch his attention, calling out
their questions. None of it reached him; all he could
take in was that he was out. Free to begin a new life.
Free to find out the truth.

A familiar figure reached out and touched his arm. Elaine Dews had been Madson's prison visitor; she had made time for him, believed in him, written letters to the right people. In her sensible tailored suit she was every inch the wife of the Whitehall civil servant now moving towards retirement at the top of his profession.

'John, you did it! You're free!' Tears glistened in the corners of her eyes. She hugged his arm, carried away with the joy of their success.

Madson glanced down at her and smiled vaguely. Quickly realizing the state he must be in, she began to steer him firmly down the steps towards the bustling street. 'We should get to the hospital,' she began, as he glanced furtively around, as if seeking the prison guards who always accompanied him. She wanted to help him make the transition from purgatory to real life. With no home or work to go to, and a son seriously ill in hospital, it was not going to be simple. If I can just get him through this mob, she thought, the car's just around the corner.

'Madson!' Madson turned sharply at the aggressive command. They had reached the bottom of the steps, and he looked straight into the angry face of DI Dennis Rourke, who stood, feet apart, glaring at him. You won't get away with this, the throbbing vein in his large red face seemed to declare.

John Madson looked at the short, stocky man who had effectively put him away on a false charge, and strangely felt nothing; his capacity to hate was all but dried up. At this particular moment he had no wish to confront the rogue policeman, who was apparently driven to persecute him. No, he wanted to think, to get away, to make his own plans and decisions. DI Rourke, however, was having none of it. 'So,' he turned to Elaine with a sneer, 'Madson's now a brief . . .'

'He's a free man,' Elaine retorted angrily. She sighed inwardly and hoped that John would not be drawn into a full-scale shouting match right here, in front of the press.

But Rourke continued to taunt, 'You think he's a hero, don't you, Mrs Dews? He's not a hero.'

'He did eight years on your evidence, Inspector Rourke.' Surely this could be classed as harassment. 'Eight years!' she reiterated. 'Now let us through.' Taking Madson by the arm she began to move away.

Rourke continued unabashed, 'I was called out by Elizabeth Madson on three occasions, all for domestic violence.' He lowered his voice to a malevolent growl. 'What's the matter, Madson? Nothing to say. You weren't short of the verbals in there.'

Madson turned silently to face his old adversary, who still stood squarely on the steps. He looked with revulsion at the man who had put him away, now middle-aged and slightly overweight; he certainly intended to find out the truth about his arrest and conviction. Madson turned abruptly, and to Elaine's intense relief, without saying a word, he began to walk with her towards the city traffic roaring along Fleet Street.

Elaine strode ahead thankfully, weaving her way hurriedly through the traffic to reach her large, safe Audi on the other side of the street. As she beeped her remote control to unlock the doors she looked round for Madson – he was not there. But quickly spotting him, she smiled. There he was marooned on the traffic island, while cars, buses and taxis swept relentlessly by. After eight years away from it all, it must certainly be hard to negotiate the dreadful London traffic. She crossed back to rescue him, and he gave a rueful smile at his inability to carry out this simple manoeuvre.

*

Euphoria was short lived. The hospital was stark and institutional, and it smelt of carbolic, reminding Madson unpleasantly of prison. He and Elaine sat waiting on uncomfortable plastic chairs in a narrow corridor. Madson tapped his toe nervously, waiting for a doctor to come and inform them of the current condition of his twenty-two-year-old son Rob. He was aware that Rob's chances were not very good. If only he had been around as his son grew up, perhaps Rob would not have got involved with drugs and would not be lying in a coma in intensive care. But he could only suppose; in the circumstances, it had all been beyond his control. Now the best he could hope for was to make up for lost time.

A young Asian woman doctor walked towards them along the corridor. With a frown of concern on her face she led them silently to a window in the partition wall. Robert Madson looked thin and drawn, his pallor matching the regulation white hospital sheets on which he lay. Madson could not discern any sign of life. He looked up inquiringly at the doctor. 'He has full physical function but he is still in a coma,' she confirmed. 'The cocktail of drugs your son took, Mr Madson, is the equivalent of a stroke for a man in his sixties. Until he comes round we can't say whether there has been any progress.'

This was really exactly what Madson had expected, but somehow he had hoped that there would have been some change for the better. With a heavy heart he asked the doctor if he might go in and sit with the boy for a while. Elaine nodded at the doctor and said she would wait outside. Dr Chakiri led Madson into the intensive care unit. Once inside he could hear the regular bleeping of the heart monitor machine Rob was hooked up to and watch the drip going into him. Madson drew up a chair beside the comatose figure and sat down; his hand reached out to touch the long, pale, but reassuringly

4

warm fingers of his son's hand. He looked down at the boy with a great sadness; tears welled in his eyes. 'Rob ... It's me ... Dad ... Rob ...' he murmured. There was no response, not even a flicker of an eyelid. Only the sound of the machinery with its regular, methodical bleeping.

Slowly Madson became aware that he was being watched, and he looked up to find that a dark-haired girl of about twenty had entered the room and was looking at him inquisitively.

'John?' she suggested shyly. 'I'm Sarah.'

They shook hands awkwardly. This was his daughter-in-law. He hadn't thought much about her before now, but his immediate emotional reaction was to blame her to some extent for Rob's condition. What kind of life could they have been having to lead to this? Sarah looked very slight in her faded jeans and T-shirt. Could she have been taking drugs too? Yet she too looked young and vulnerable, and his heart went out to her as she gazed at Rob with such love and concern.

'I wanted to visit you, but Rob always said no,' Sarah said at last into the embarrassing silence.

'No, I said no,' he replied.

Madson was a proud man. His relationship with his son had deteriorated from the moment of his arrest. He couldn't bring himself to believe that the boy, then nearly fourteen, had ever thought his father guilty of the brutal murder of his mother. But it had been the young Rob who had discovered his mother's butchered and bloody body. Madson had written frequently to his son while the boy was growing up, living with his maternal grandparents. Over the last year or two Rob had visited his father in prison and the two had at last forged a bond. With this relationship still in embryonic form it had not seemed appropriate to Madson to meet

5

Rob's new wife. There was too much ground still to cover.

'I was talking to your friend outside. You won.' Sarah smiled nervously. 'I'm glad.'

Madson turned back to look at Rob, changing the subject. 'Do you see any change?' he said.

'The doctors don't think so,' she said at last, rather lamely.

He looked at her speculatively. But she just shook her head. There was not really much more that could be said on the subject of Rob's condition; they could only wait and hope. For a time they both stared in silence at Rob breathing shallowly.

Sarah wondered whether Madson had been able to make any plans as to what he would do on release from prison. Had he anywhere to go?

'Where are you going to stay?' she offered, her voice slightly high with nerves. From the look of surprise on his face it was clear that he had not thought about it.

'I didn't like to think about it,' he confessed. 'In case . . .'

She realized what he was saying: he had not made plans as he had not been able to think of failure.

'You're welcome to stay at our flat for a while, if you'd like.' She smiled encouragingly.

He accepted immediately, grateful to have this arranged so easily. 'Thanks,' he said. 'There's somewhere I've got to go first.' He was too shy to tell her that he wanted to visit his wife's grave.

He left with Elaine, and Sarah remained keeping vigil beside Rob's bed.

Soon they swept smoothly in through the ornate gates of the vast Kensal Green cemetery in Elaine's well-padded car, which purred to a halt in the car park.

'I'll wait here,' began Elaine tentatively, 'and take you to the flat afterwards.'

'You gave me fifty pounds, I can take a cab,' he said decisively.

'A cab.' Elaine laughed, her normally restrained Manchester accent coming to the fore. 'I'll drive you. Go on; I'll wait.'

He smiled gratefully and got out of the car, picking up the roses he had bought. Madson began to walk slowly along an unkempt muddy pathway. Tall trees overhung the pathway and made the autumn day gloomy and sinister. He stopped to get his bearings and then turned left past some old graves, mostly overgrown with grass and weeds. At last he came upon the more recent graves. He stopped beside one, bent down and cleared away some dying dahlias, and then placed his own roses by the simple marble slab. He touched the stone with his hand, running his fingers gently over the engraving, reading it as if it were Braille: 'Elizabeth Madson 1953–1987'.

Madson sat down beside the grave and lent back against an ancient stone, his legs drawn up, resting his arms on his knees. He contemplated the grave, thinking of the woman who had been his wife, and who now lay here. He thought of the man he had been, the glamorous life he had led as a professional gambler.

He pulled a battered pack of cigarettes from his overcoat pocket and lit one. Taking a deep drag of the cigarette he looked up at the sky. Sitting here he felt a strange peace, and yet he felt exhausted, old. It was hard to come to terms with the trauma of the event that had split and destroyed his family.

The memory of the night of his arrest came rushing back to him. It had been a successful night, and he had celebrated until the small hours in the richly decorated club bar with champagne and several tall blond croupiers. He had crept back into the small hotel in Pembridge Square which had been home since his separation at 5 a.m. and tiptoed up the staircase to his room. Later that morning, the radio alarm had jolted him awake and he had dialled Elizabeth's number on the bedside telephone, remembering his promise to take Rob to choose a new football kit. The phone just rang and rang. He remembered giving up and dropping back to sleep. The next thing he knew he was being shaken roughly awake and dragged from his bed. 'John Peter Madson, I am arresting you for the murder of your wife, Elizabeth Madson,' boomed the voice of the then DS Rourke.

Rob had discovered his mother's body that morning, slashed and red with blood, in her bed. Madson could still hear the judge's voice as he passed sentence on him: '. . . the jury has found you guilty of the murder of your wife, Elizabeth Madson'. The deep gravelly voice had reverberated through his mind over and over again as the doors clanged behind him in the first prison he had been sent to. He had sat on the prison cot numb with shock. 'Having listened to all the evidence in this trial I am bound to say I find myself in total agreement with the verdict. You are an evil and violent man, and you should not return to society for a very long time. You will go to prison for life.'

Sitting there by Elizabeth's grave, he thought about all the work that he had done over those years, poring over law books and case notes, taking a law degree through the National Extension College of London University. He had been driven to prove his innocence, to gain an appeal hearing, to get himself out of that prison and back into real life. Now that he had won his appeal, he intended to find out who the culprit really was and why he had not been arrested and then convicted.

Startled by the sudden flutter of a bird taking flight he realized guiltily that Elaine would still be waiting for him. He had no idea how much time he had spent by the graveside, but he got to his feet and hurried back through the clearing towards the path.

Madson stood outside a neglected council block in west London checking the address on the scrap of paper that he pulled from his trouser pocket. Elaine had dropped him off and left him to see Sarah on his own. She said she would be in touch the next day to see if there was anything she could do; right now what he most needed was a rest.

The first thing that caught Madson's eye once inside the cramped second-floor flat was an old photograph of a young Robert – must be about six he estimated – flanked by his two smiling, youthful parents. He picked it up from amongst the clutter of cards and candles on the mantelpiece and examined it more closely; tears pricked the back of his eyes. 'Sorry about the . . .' Sarah said into the air, vaguely indicating the limited size of the flat. The size of the flat didn't matter to him; Madson was grateful to have been invited to stay. It was something else that had been bothering him, an issue which had to be raised. 'Doctor Chakiri said you couldn't tell them what drugs Rob took.' The words came tumbling out, there was no tactful way to put it.

'I don't know. He took whatever he could get his hands on.' Sarah sounded flustered, but he could not stop now. 'What about you?' he asked, looking her straight in the eye. She looked hesitant. 'What are you on?' he repeated.

'Me?' Sarah looked away from him nervously.

'Nothing ... Not recently ... Can't afford it.' She looked about for something to distract him, and her eye fell on the note pad by the telephone. She looked back at Madson. 'There was a call for you: Gordon Berry.' Picking up the note pad she went over and handed it to him. 'He left you his number. I'll just go and make us some coffee.'

Madson thanked her for taking the phone message. He still wasn't satisfied; however much she didn't want to discuss it, he wanted to know whether they were both doing or even both dealing in drugs. He followed her into the kitchen.

'Look,' he said carefully, 'I don't want to interrogate you like this but I've got to know. What was he using?'

'I've told you I don't know!' she almost screamed, turning away from the coffee cups to face him. 'Why don't you believe me?'

'Because you're living with him,' Madson said, stating the obvious in an attempt to calm her down. It did at least have the effect of getting some information from her.

'That's why he never told me! Can't you understand? He kept all that private, secret ... He shut me out.' Her voice had begun to crack.

'You weren't dealing,' Madson persisted.

'No!'

'So how did you make a living?'

Sarah, rattled, began to feel angry. She had done her best. Rob's addiction had been impossible to control; not only that but it had reduced them to penury. She decided to tell Madson the truth. 'We didn't make a living. We're being evicted.'

'What?'

Sarah picked up a sheet of paper from the top of a

heap on the tiny kitchen table, and waved it at him despairingly. 'Look, it's an eviction notice! We haven't paid the rent for months.' A tear dripped down her nose. 'You still want to stay here?'

Gordon Berry stood in the doorway of his rundown office, speaking into his mobile phone. At thirty-three he cut an attractive if rather down-market figure, his well-developed body poured skilfully into a sharp designer suit, his short red hair standing up slightly on his head. 'The couple we pulled back belonging to Lombank – got to be forty per cent of book value. I suggest auction . . .' From his base under the railway arches Berry, an amiable ex-con, now ran a legitimate car repossession business.

'I can arrange delivery to Trent Auctions, Dagenham. Yeah, the best for the shape these motors are in. Yes. Yes.' He caught sight of Madson walking towards him up the cobbled road, and quickly signed off and stowed the phone in his jacket pocket.

'JP!' he enthused as they embraced. 'I was at court, half eleven. I was told you'd already been made Lord Chancellor – you impressed them so much representing yourself at the appeal! And now it's down to serious money. Eight years' compensation.'

'All in good time,' nodded Madson calmly; this would not be his first concern. Berry, he realized, was one thing in prison, big bear-like and useful in a corner, but he wondered suddenly, whether he might prove to be a liability out of jail. But he put the thought from his mind; Berry was clearly genuinely pleased to see him, and, if he let himself admit it, it cheered him up immensely to see Berry.

Berry led Madson into a garage, with a small make-shift office screened off to one side. There they found

Berry's Uncle Donald, an enigmatic chap somewhere in his fifties. Berry introduced them and then, turning to Madson, revealed, 'You've got a soul mate here. Donald did a five on bent evidence.'

'Oh yes?' Madson turned and nodded at Donald with interest.

'Grimm's bloody Fairy Tales,' Donald acknowledged ruefully.

'How are you off for cash then?' Berry turned back to Madson, changing the subject. 'You'll need something,' he concluded, without waiting for a response, and whipping out his wallet he thrust five hundred pounds in fifty-pound notes into Madson's reluctant hand.

'No, Gordon.'

'A loan . . .' suggested Berry persuasively, with a generous smile. 'Your credit's fine.'

Uncle Donald looked impressed at his nephew's generosity, but then, he thought it was the right thing to do in the circumstances. And Gordon knew what he was doing; Donald always left the financial side of things for him to handle. He turned to his nephew, 'I'm off to do the Isleworth job.'

'And this time,' joked Berry, 'no excuses, right? No grandmothers having heart attacks! Just bring the bugger back here.'

As Donald disappeared out of the door Berry took Madson by the arm and led him back towards the office to get his car keys. 'I've arranged a little present for you,' he muttered mysteriously.

'What's that?' he inquired cautiously. He knew Berry only too well.

'Won't bite.' He laughed. 'Well, she might.'

Oh God, thought Madson with a sigh, Berry's idea of a little treat could mean only one thing. But the lad was looking so pleased with his plan that it would have taken a hard man to put him off.

Berry parked his car outside a block of flats in Olympia, and gestured Madson out of the car. 'Go on,' he urged. 'It's flat 26.'

Madson got out of the car rather stiffly but, by this time intrigued, he headed for flat 26. Perhaps it would be all right.

A young girl with dyed blond hair and smudged red lipstick answered the door. 'John? Come in,' she said brightly. 'Gordon tells me it's eight years and never been kissed!' Madson took one look at the thick make-up concealing what was probably a very young girl. Changing his mind, he began to wonder how he could refuse without hurting the girl's feelings. Meanwhile she had led him into a large front-facing room containing little save a vast ancient double bed.

'Look . . .' he began.

'My name's Mandy. Come on,' she said, as she sat down and began to bounce on the pink nylon eiderdown.

'Look, I'm sorry. I'm not in the mood,' he blurted out, still standing up.

She responded huskily, 'Now there's a challenge.'

'It's not a challenge. I mean it.'

'Why don't you take the weight off your feet, and tell me about your mood? Go on, sit down,' she continued patting the place beside her persuasively. Madson looked at her regretfully, thinking that perhaps he should make an attempt to comply. He sat down. After all he had been in prison for years and had all but forgotten what sex felt like. He had often thought of former girlfriends while sitting in his cell, remembering the glamorous clothes they wore, the smart restaurants they had frequented, the musky Yves St Laurent scent one had always used, how she had worn the smoothest stockings on her long legs. He never thought about his former wife; not only had they been acrimoniously separated, but her brutal death had had the effect of shutting off the phase of his life that he had shared with her. Only his son brought any of these memories back. He came back sharply to the present. Mandy was staring at him quizzically; then she slid down on to the floor and gently began to undo his flies. Somehow it was a disembodied experience. He didn't really feel like it; this young girl in her sad microscopic skirt wasn't right. Suddenly he thought of Rob and Sarah. This girl must be about the same age as they were, she could have been his daughter. She took out his cock and carefully stroked it for a time, but nothing happened – it remained limp and vulnerable. With a sultry pout she raised her head and kissed Madson on his stomach and then his chest, squirming herself on to his lap and kissing him softly on the mouth.

Madson zipped up his trousers, 'Let's have a cup of tea,' he suggested.

'It isn't me, is it?' she asked nervously.

'No, it's not you.'

'Right,' Mandy bounced back cheerfully. 'Polly put the kettle on . . .'

Gordon Berry had waited for him in the car outside and grinned wickedly as Madson got back in and they drove off at his usual rapid pace back to Notting Hill.

'All right, JP?' he smirked.

'It was great.' Madson smiled back reassuringly at his friend.

'I mean, that was the only thing on my mind when I got out.'

They drove in companionable silence for a few minutes.

'Still going to join the law-and-order mob?' Berry queried as they drove round the Shepherd's Bush roundabout.

'If I can.'

'They won't want you, that lot,' he said with dislike, narrowly missing a rusting B-reg Vauxhall which hooted indignantly as he skimmed into the Holland Park exit. 'A convicted criminal.'

'On forged evidence,' Madson reminded him curtly. 'Sentence overturned. Self-made lawyer.'

'Think they care? Forget it, JP. You'll need a job.'

Madson reflected that he was probably right, but he had Elaine's connections; her husband Richard had already spoken to someone on his behalf. There was also the Polish woman solicitor who had once visited when Elaine had been away. He intended to use every possible contact he could think of. He felt very determined.

'I'll be all right,' he said at last to Berry.

'You say that like it's simple. Things weren't easy when I came out. Jobs are scarce. People are poorer. The rackets are tougher. Cops less bent. Well, most of them. And everything costs. Anyway, four years inside sobered me up. And Cheryl says she'll leave me if I go back inside. So that's why I joined Uncle Donald's repo business. I thought what am I good at? Bit of dialogue, bit of slapping, only when necessary of course. So here I am.'

DI Rourke parked his white Ford Sierra in one of the few empty spaces in the car park behind the dull concrete office building which housed the Organized Crime Squad. His thick blond hair stood on end from a day spent running his hands through it with frustration, on his face an expression of displeasure and irritability. Getting out, he slammed the door, and then noticed an ugly scratch all down the offside of his car. It certainly had not been his day.

Rourke took the lift to the third floor. In the large open-plan office he headed directly for a wall lined with old metal filing cabinets. Pulling out a drawer he began to riffle through the thickly stuffed files. He glared in turn at each of the labels. Somebody must have filed the Madson case in the wrong year – and anyway why on earth wasn't information from 1987 on computer. On the other hand, he realized it was probably better for him that it wasn't. He found the right file at last, a mass of papers bulging out of it, only just held together by the thick elastic band, and took it over to his desk to examine it. He flipped through and at last came upon an old photograph of Madson clipped to the top sheet of a batch of case notes.

A voice from behind startled him. 'I hear Madson's turned himself into a brief.' It was Burridge, his commanding officer.

Rourke wheeled round to face him. 'Yes, sir,' he said. He had always been against the idea of open-plan offices; there was simply no privacy, no door. Rourke did not want to appear rattled by Madson's early release.

'Could be trouble,' Burridge continued relentlessly.

Rourke looked down at the pile of notes. 'There's nothing he can do, no records, nothing here,' he challenged.

Burridge was severe. 'I've been having a word with the Chief about your promotion; you might have trouble with the selection board.'

'I thought you said it was just a rubber stamp.'

'That was before Madson walked.'

It was not looking good, Rourke reflected, but he stood his ground, glaring at his superior officer.

Burridge sighed. The man was not thinking straight. It occurred to him that Rourke and Madson were actually rather alike – both difficult men of a certain age, both with broken marriages behind them. Perhaps, he thought irreverently, they ought to go out for a pint together – they might get on.

'Remind me,' he said at last. 'Who was on the case with you?'

'Johnny Aston.'

'Well,' concluded Burridge with some force, 'you're both DIs, Dennis. Bury him or you'll both be back with the Met.' He swung round abruptly and left the office, leaving a rather agitated Rourke, who continued to glare at his retreating back and then slumped back into his chair and began to go through the papers in Madson's file again, more carefully.

Berry drove Madson back to his home in Notting Hill, still badgering him about the compensation he must sue for.

'I'm not thinking about that yet,' said Madson. He thought he had better put a stop to this; he was not ready for all that yet, he was only just out of prison and had more pressing things on his mind. There was a six-year statute of limitations on compensation, so there was ample time.

Gordon and Cheryl had a small, two-up, two-down council house on the local estate. With all the children's paraphernalia lying around and the thick carpet richly patterned with swirls, it generated warmth and friendliness. In the kitchen Gordon took a couple of beers out of the fridge, and put together some bread and cheese for sandwiches on the table. As they sipped the cold beers straight from the can Gordon pulled out a Buddhist emblem on a leather thong from his trouser pocket and waved it vaguely at Madson. 'It's a Phra,' he said rather sheepishly, 'Buddhism. God directing good luck to you through it. I know it seems silly, but Cheryl wanted you to have it. Hang it round your neck for a few days, then lose it.'

The Phra did seem a bit cranky, Madson thought, but it was a touching gesture. He put it on and smiled. 'Gordon, believe in something, anything . . .' He thought of Rob in hospital, and decided to check in on Rob again before going back to Sarah's flat. As he was about to leave, the door burst open and Cheryl, a striking blonde, and their two young boys bounded in. Laden down with shopping from Tesco's in Portobello, Cheryl was a bit flustered and bad-tempered from the trip with the children, but she was pleased when she saw that he wore the Phra.

'Gordon's talked so much about you, I feel I know you as well as he does,' she smiled.

'It's really nice. Thank you. I'll wear it.'

Madson walked down the bleak hospital corridor feeling depressed. He had not been able to discern any change in Rob's condition, and the pale face of his son haunted him as he thought of the hopes he had had for this new beginning. He yearned for Rob to wake up, he ached with guilt about his son and the events that had led him to this place. As he reached the hospital reception area, he realized that there was one thing that he could begin to sort out. Surrounded by miserable and ill patients and visitors, he lifted the receiver of a convenient pay phone, put a coin in and punched in the number.

'Is Mr Gardner there?' he inquired.

'Mr Desmond or Mr Walter Gardner?' the reception-ist replied crisply.

'Mr Walter.'

'Mr Walter. Who shall I say is calling?'

Madson put the phone down. The man was still prac-tising then, the solicitor who had defended him at his original trial. Walter Gardner had unaccountably, even deliberately let him down, and he intended to find out why.

CHAPTER TWO

The diminutive bathroom window opened awkwardly at an angle to reveal a blaze of sunshine heralding a promising day. Madson attacked his stubble with a pink plastic ladies' razor which was all he could find in the flowery bathroom. As he nicked his chin and blood dripped down on to his vest he made a mental note to get to a chemist's shop. Stanching the flow with a torn-off piece of toilet paper he considered his plans for the day.

Deliberately blinding himself to reason, he intended to go out and get himself a job in the law. He hoped to persuade a solicitor he had met once, when she visited him in prison, to take him on as a clerk. The first rung on the ladder glowed for him like a beacon in the dark.

He had returned to Sarah's flat that night full of remorse. 'I'm sorry. I came on much too strong,' he apologized.

Sarah was not entirely mollified by this; she had listened to too much well-intended advice and criticism from everyone she knew to feel at ease with him. She had done her best, searched every corner of the flat in the hope of discovering where Rob stashed his drugs, but to no avail. She felt it was she who was being judged and criticized, not Rob, and that others like Madson felt superior, sure that they would have been able to sort it out. Of course, at the time, nobody had come forward to help her sort things out.

Madson reassured her that things would be all right.

Rob would come home, Sarah could nurse him and Madson would find them a new flat. It could be done.

But that first night, Madson himself would have liked some reassurance. Sarah had made up a bed for him in the spare room, a small single bed placed against the wall. Despite the pretty design on the bedcover, Madson had felt uncomfortable with this arrangement. He had spent too many years in a prison cell to appreciate a small single bed in a narrow room against a wall. Pulling the bed to a more satisfactory position in the centre of the room, he glanced out of the window. He pulled aside the muslin curtains and, opening the window wide to get a better view, breathed in the cool night air. From this window in the council block he had a stunning night-time view of the lights over the Hammersmith flyover. Mundane, even ugly, by day, it had a magical quality that night, the lights along the flyover seeming to go on for ever, car lights streaking into the distance like comets. Madson lit a cigarette, and leaned out, puffing gently, taking in the atmosphere of the dark starlit night, and the heady notion of being back out in the world of freedom.

Dennis Rourke sat in the front seat of an unmarked CID squad car, a DS driver beside him and one other plain-clothed officer in the back. The radio crackled as they sat silently waiting in the car park, busy with early morning shoppers hurrying back to their cars with their purchases.

It had been a long wait, and Rourke was growing impatient, almost ready to explode. A seedy character could be seen hanging around on the corner by a trolley park with a brown paper bag in his hand. He looked around nonchalantly, passing the time.

Suddenly another car pulled up beside Rourke's,

almost completely obstructing their view of the warehouse entrance. Rourke snarled angrily as DI Aston leapt out and slipped into the CID car behind Rourke. 'Who told you I was here?' he complained in a low voice, full of irritation.

'One of your office nonces,' said Aston.

'I can't talk to you now, this is about to go off.' It was really not the time or the place to bring up their shared involvement in the Madson case. Rourke was very peeved. Aston remained cool. 'We can chat till it does. I've been trying to get you all day . . .'

'Derek? Any sign?' said Rourke into his walkie-talkie, ignoring the problem of Aston for a moment.

'Nothing,' came the flat response from the walkie-talkie.

'Second anything moves, get on it,' Rourke commanded into the machine.

'Yes, yes, affirmative,' crackled the reply.

Aston tried again. 'I heard Madson won his appeal.'

'I was there,' answered Rourke dryly.

'And you didn't bell me?'

Rourke was busy looking out of the window into his wing mirror, trying to concentrate; something looked like it was beginning to happen.

'It's nothing . . .' he said vaguely to Aston.

'Nothing? When he goes for compensation our evidence will be re-examined . . .'

'Shut up!' Rourke was finding this extremely irritating when he was trying to concentrate. He bent forward intently as he spotted a black BMW coming gradually into view up the road. It turned into the supermarket forecourt, and their walkie-talkie immediately spluttered into action. 'Target eyeballed. We are seeing three – that is three men in target vehicle, approach premises. We are off! Off! Off!'

The shiny BMW looped around and began to head for the man with the bag. It swerved and stopped.

'Get him out!' Rourke flung over his shoulder as they revved up the car. The DS in the back gave Aston a push and they took off in a flurry of screeching tyres, leaving an astonished Aston sprawling untidily in the street.

Outside Hearnley & Partners, at 2 Temple Place, Madson waited patiently on the pavement in the early morning breeze, casually watching a news-vendor selling papers beside the nearby Temple Station. In a smart city suit and white shirt, he was dressed to impress, though slightly nervous. He felt sure Miss Ostrowska would be willing to help, remembering her piercing intelligence and radical legal views. Her prison visit was still fresh in his mind, though it had taken place nearly two years previously.

The pretty cherub-like face of Magda Ostrowska came into view, and Madson caught up with her just as she was about to go in through the gate.

'Hello,' he said, startling her.

Magda looked at him puzzled. 'Hello?'

Madson was disappointed. It had been some time ago, but she was a friend of Elaine's, and she had been so clear in her support of him.

'You don't remember me?' he said at last, concealing his disappointment. She clearly did not remember him. 'Two years ago.'

'I'm sorry, I don't remember . . .' she concluded in her soft, Polish-accented English, and made as if to go.

But Madson was persistent. 'My prison visitor, Elaine Dews, was ill . . . you came once, instead of her.' To his intense relief, as he looked at her, light began to dawn.

'John Madson! You're the prisoner with the Open University degree in law?'

'Not Open University, National Extension Degree, London University.'

'I've just been reading about you.'

He was pleased by this, but he began to feel embarrassed and unsure how to continue. Magda broke into his reverie. 'You've been waiting for me?'

'Yes,' he said with relief.

'So what can I do for you?' She was obviously keen to get on with her day.

'I wondered . . .' he hesitated. 'Could I take you for a coffee?'

'You didn't think of phoning first?' she suggested, but gently; she found herself relenting. He remained silent and she looked at him for a moment longer, dissecting the invitation for a problem. Then with a shrug, she smiled. 'I've got a nine-thirty appointment. There's a place near here where we could get a quick coffee.'

They walked through the Embankment Gardens down to the Embankment itself, where there was a permanently moored boat which served as a café, drifting in the rippling water of the Thames. As they walked, and talked about his case, Madson began to feel more confident.

'So you won. Impressive,' Magda said.

'I reckoned I was the best-motivated lawyer I could hire,' he boasted jokingly.

She responded with irony, 'A triumph of British justice.'

But Madson didn't want to see the irony, he was in earnest. 'Law doesn't have a lot to do with justice.' He was determined she should be clear on his view. 'The legal system in this country almost destroyed me. And it does it to others like me. I've got my degree. I want to practise law. And to do that I need help.'

She looked at him with surprise. The law was a conservative profession. How could he propose to take such a step? None the less she was interested in his reasoning.

'You were a professional gambler. Then you were a convicted criminal,' she reminded him. 'You really think you can practise law?'

She raised an inquiring eyebrow, stopping at the first step on to the quivering gangplank to catch his reply.

'Yes.'

'And you've just come from eight years in prison.'

'I was innocent.'

She turned to face him. 'This may be irrelevant, but the legal profession is very conservative. With your background ... I'm sorry but what you want ... it's impossible.' Madson looked away. Sitting in his prison cell he had rehearsed this meeting in his mind many times: he would be confident, determined, and she would agree to help. Now his heart sank with disappointment, but he was resolute. 'To serve eight years for a crime I didn't commit without going mad. I thought *that* was impossible.'

His determination was almost frightening, she thought, her interest aroused as they walked in silence to one of the round café tables to order their coffee. They sat sipping espresso, and exchanging pleasantries for a short time. Against the backdrop of the blue water they stood out, an attractive couple looking tense in their well-cut dark suits, she tall and willowy with long delicate hands, her hair swept neatly into a blond knot at the back of her neck, he in contrast dark and saturnine.

As they walked back to the office, Madson tried again to persuade her of his value, but it was an uphill task. She was still circumspect about Madson, his situation, and his dogged determination that what he wanted could be possible.

'Just a moment,' she cut into his monologue. 'You must realize, Hearnley & Partners is one of the most prestigious law practices in the country.'

He took a deep breath. 'I know. And it's stagnating. Sir Ranald himself is over seventy, Nigel Alwyn is sixty-five. The St Jermyn brothers are well over fifty and George Lodge is forty-four.' Looking at her intently, he raced rapidly on without allowing her to interrupt. 'You're the only one under forty and they won't make you an equity partner because you're a woman.'

This was something of a sore point for her, of which she did not need to be reminded.

'Also the practice is ninety per cent commercial,' he continued rapidly, keen to make his point before she retreated to her meeting. 'I've seen the statistics. Crime is the growth area. And I know a lot of criminals. I could be useful to you.'

'Stop there.' She held up her hand firmly; they had reached Temple Place. 'I have to tell you, Mr Madson, you won't even get an interview. And it's nine twenty-eight.'

'Lunch?' he pleaded. His intention was to gain her confidence.

'Only ever have a sandwich. Unless a client's buying,' she said, but she smiled.

'I'll buy.'

'I'll have a low-cal. chicken salad on whole wheat. No mayonnaise,' she said with mock severity.

As they stood laughing in the sunshine outside her office, a silver Rolls-Royce pulled up at the kerb beside them. A uniformed chauffeur leapt out and opened the passenger door to allow Sir Ranald Hearnley, the head of the practice, to emerge.

He was in a hurry. He had always been flustered in the mornings, and as he reached his late seventies he found that it had begun to make him bad-tempered.

'Magda . . .' he called in greeting as he spotted her, pleased to be able to speak to her first thing.

'Good morning, Sir Ranald.'

'I'm going to look at the papers on the Dorman pension fund fraud. Do you have those SFO depositions about the Horton case?'

'I'll look them out for you,' she said smoothly, thinking she had better get her secretary on to it. 'This is Mr John Madson, Sir Ranald Hearnley.' Perhaps, she thought, it was a fortuitous moment to make the introduction; after all, he would have read about the case in the *Times* law reports that morning and would have been impressed that the man had represented himself so successfully at his appeal.

Sir Ranald shook Madson's hand. 'Are you counsel in the Grayford enquiry?' He had not recognized the name.

'No, sir.'

Magda cut in quickly, 'Mr Madson's not a counsel, but he's well acquainted with the law.'

'Then you're not in good company.' Sir Ranald had returned to his morning fuss. 'Some chap served me a writ at breakfast. I forget to post him a letter, and he served me a writ.' With that Sir Ranald headed off through the ornate gate towards his office. Magda turned to follow him.

'Chicken salad on whole wheat,' Madson called flirtatiously.

'No mayonnaise,' she reminded him as she disappeared through the door. He grinned.

*

The relative success of his first meeting with Magda left him feeling buoyed up and cheerful. He whistled a tune to himself as he walked along the street to Embankment station. Presumably the London Underground would still be there after eight years. The Bakerloo Line was entirely unremarkable. Ancient trains still clattered through the deep grimy tunnels. For the first time since his release he felt surprisingly at home. But as the train swung recklessly towards Paddington his spirits fell. He doubted whether he would find much change in his son's condition; however, he felt compelled to go to the hospital, to be there with Rob.

Bright light glared in through the window, bouncing off the glossy white surfaces of the hospital room. Madson sat beside the pristine bed, searching Rob's body urgently with his eyes for any sign of awakening. But there was none. Rob remained in a deep coma, his breathing reassuringly regular, but unchanged. Madson's eyes remained fixed on his son while the minutes ticked seamlessly by; he glared intently, as if willing Rob to rise up and walk.

Elaine Dews was pruning roses in the extensive gardens surrounding the Dewses' substantial mock-Georgian East Sheen property. Over one arm she carried a wooden basket in which she had collected several elegant stems of yellow roses with which she intended to make an arrangement for the hall. In her right hand she held a pair of secateurs with which she was cutting back the dead flowers. Then the housekeeper, Mary, appeared in her cosy gingham apron, and directed Madson round to the back of the house.

Elaine and Madson embraced cautiously. She was sympathetic, for she realized how serious Rob's condition was; she had seen many young drug addicts in her years as a prison visitor.

'How's Rob?' she said, taking Madson's arm.

'Not good.' He was cryptic.

'Can I do anything?'

'No. Nobody can.' He had not come to discuss Rob, and indeed he felt there was nothing to say. He was beginning to expect the worst.

Elaine led him towards the house. And they walked up to the broad stone steps of the terrace in silence.

As they went in through the French windows Elaine remarked that she had heard from Magda that morning.

'It's all right. She just wondered why you didn't phone her first.'

'I thought if I phoned her she'd put me off,' Madson confessed. Elaine smiled at his honesty.

The living-room was elegant, like its mistress, with its polished parquet floor, lavish Persian rugs and chesterfields, and antique paintings and furnishings garnered from country-house auctions, which were a particular passion with Elaine. She indicated for Madson to sit down, and then disappeared through the door to arrange for coffee to be brought in.

'It's a beautiful house, Elaine.' Madson looked about him, taking in the quality of the paintings.

'I was born in a two-up, two-down outside Bolton,' pointed out Elaine sensibly. 'I hope you'll have some coffee with me,' she added as the housekeeper appeared with a tray.

'Look,' she said, as she poured the coffee, 'I wish you'd talked to me before bursting in on Magda.'

'I've lost eight years. I feel I can't lose a second more. She can help me.'

Elaine was firm. 'She says she can't. She says she told you that.'

'I think she can.' Knowing that Elaine could speak up on his behalf, he was not going to take no for an answer. He simply needed to be given a chance. 'And I want you,' – he hesitated, it was a big favour he was asking – 'I want you to help me convince her that she can.'

Elaine was silent. She busied herself for a moment, handing Madson his coffee, and offering a plate of biscuits, which he refused. Well aware that her husband did not like her to become too involved in these matters, she wondered how best to handle it.

'Richard and I . . .' she began. 'I trust his judgement. As the people in the Treasury and the Cabinet trust it. He's met some of the prisoners I visited – when they got out. He always says prisoners seem to have more problems outside than in. He worries that my prison friends, when they get out, will become dependent on me.'

'I won't,' said Madson flatly.

Elaine remained calm. 'There's another side to dependency. It's called manipulation.'

'What's that got to do with me? What I'm talking about is becoming independent.'

She tried to explain gently: 'There may be other uses for the degree, but with your background you're not going to get an articled clerkship with a firm of solicitors.'

'I never said an articled clerk,' retorted Madson. 'There's something called an "outdoor clerk", the lowest rung on the ladder. If I have to, that's where I start.'

Elaine sighed. 'I still don't see how I . . .' She leaned forward, watching him with concern. And Madson looked at her earnestly.

'I know Magda likes you. If you give her a ring before I go back, say I can do it, she's bound to be impressed.' He grinned. 'That's not manipulation, is it?'

30

Elaine smiled back, giving in to him. 'OK. What do you want me to tell her exactly?'

Madson whistled quietly under his breath as he hurried across the courtyards of Inner Temple swinging a bag of chicken sandwiches. He passed the imposing facade of Temple Hall, turned down a cobbled alley peopled with serious faces in black suits and emerged on Temple Place, opposite the gracious exterior of Hearnley & Partners.

Seated on a comfortable leather sofa under the stern eye of an elderly receptionist in blue spectacles, Madson admired the 1930s oak panelling and the crystal chandelier. He looked about; clearly Magda was going to be late. Idly he picked up a well-thumbed copy of the *Economist* from a side-table and began to read an obscure article on economic cooperation between Israel and the Gulf States.

Disturbed by the noise of a door opening, he looked up and saw a couple of articled clerks chatting quietly as they walked along one of the corridors leading towards reception. He watched as a bald solicitor of about sixty came down the magnificent wooden staircase with a handful of mail. The man exchanged pleasantries with the receptionist, who thawed visibly. Madson was mesmerized by the atmosphere of this place, the people, the ambience. This was a place he would like to be a part of; this was what he would like to do, work in a place like this. In the middle of his reverie a door opened close to the reception area and Magda came out to speak to him.

'I'm sorry,' she said anxiously. 'I'm going to have to cancel.'

Madson's face fell; words failed him. Over Magda's

shoulder he could see a rather striking red-headed girl in her twenties seated before Magda's desk.

'What kind of problem means you can't eat a sandwich?'

She hesitated but knew that it meant a lot to him; she had just had Elaine on the phone pressing his cause.

'I shouldn't say . . . I'm in court in forty-eight hours and I've just lost my key defence witness,' she said desperately, nodding over at the girl in her office. 'She's been got at!' And then, more dramatically and in an almost impenetrable Polish accent, 'Nobbled!'

Madson sat in silence, more dejected than he could ever have believed. He was desperate to talk to Magda and she had fobbed him off with a reluctant witness. It tipped him over the edge.

'Nobbled?' he roared. 'That doesn't surprise me. All in a day's work for you. Witness changes her mind. Police do nothing. You lose your lunch. Some poor bastard goes down, but you get your fees.' His voice rose again. 'So everything's fine.'

'Look, I'm sorry. Give me a call next week some time . . .'

'Next week?' Madson stood up furiously, thrusting the bags of sandwiches at her. 'Here! Don't worry. There's no mayonnaise,' he said, as he stormed out of the door.

The receptionist was unmoved; she had seen it all many times before. Difficult client she said to herself as Magda retreated to her office.

Outside Hearnley & Partners Madson stopped, and turned to face the building, realizing with sudden panic what he had done. This was his best hope of employment within the legal profession, and he had lost his temper and fled like a child. As he walked away, it was clear to him that he had blown it totally, not only with Magda, but probably with Elaine too.

CHAPTER THREE

As he sat in despair on a bench near the Embankment Gardens, Madson caught sight of the plump red-headed girl he had seen in Magda's office crossing the road and hailing a cab. She jumped in, but not before Madson had dashed across the busy street and hailed the next cab.

'Follow that cab!' he roared at the driver, who put his foot on the accelerator and smiled. But Madson was watching the first cab intently, completely failing to see why the cabby thought it funny.

They followed the taxi until it stopped outside a large old pub on the Harrow Road. Madson watched as the girl paid and disappeared into the pub. Paying off his cab, Madson followed her inside.

From a vantage point by a convenient pinball machine Madson could see that she had gone straight to the bar and was ordering a gin and tonic. She took her drink with relief and drank it back in a couple of rapid gulps. Then she exchanged a few words with the barman and disappeared up the dark back stairs. He began to follow her up the stairs, only to discover that the old-style inn accommodation had been turned into bedsitters. He had no idea which of the identical numbered doors, 1 to 9, the girl had gone through.

Madson sighed and headed back downstairs to the bar. He considered his options: Berry was always full of ideas.

By the time he had fought his way through to the

phone and found Berry's number his head had begun to spin in confusion; it was a long time since he had faced a crowd in a pub. He pulled himself together as Berry answered with a cheery, 'Yes?' He shouted the name and address of the pub and a quick summary of the situation into the receiver over the noise of the pub, hoping that Berry would come to help. He was not far, he estimated, from Berry's Recovery.

Berry turned up barely ten minutes later. He winked at Madson, who was by this time ensconced in a corner seat reading the early edition of the *Evening Standard*, and then swanned confidently over to the bar.

'Scottish double, with half an American dry.'

Berry took a satisfying slug of the whisky, making a show of smacking his lips with satisfaction, and began to talk to the barman.

'Had a very pleasant chat the other night,' he confided. 'Redhead, lives above. Didn't get her name.'

'Didn't you?' the barman sounded wary.

Berry slipped a ten-pound note unobtrusively out of his wallet and into the barman's hand. 'Have a drink yourself.'

The barman looked around before pocketing the money. 'Leila. Leila Halkin,' he whispered.

'What's her room number?'

'Room 6. But don't you tell her I told you,' he warned.

'Never . . .' Never had Berry looked so innocent.

Five minutes later, the red-headed girl, Leila, left the pub and walked up the street a few yards searching for a taxi. Berry followed her out of the door only moments later and crossed the road to where Donald was waiting in the Jaguar, and climbed in.

'Follow that tart,' he said quickly as Leila jumped

into a taxi cab. Donald pulled out smoothly into the traffic.

Leila's taxi stopped outside Kilburn Park tube station. Donald pulled up opposite minutes later, with some difficulty, as there were a large number of buses and cars blocking the way. Berry could just make out the red hair and the sensible skirt of the girl, as she bought a paper from a booth outside the tube entrance. The girl then stood on the pavement, looking uncertainly from left to right.

'On the game?' suggested Donald.

'Too classy dresser.' Berry shook his head; Donald never did have much idea about these things.

'It's all the class ones now,' Donald insisted, unabashed.

'That's not a pross,' said Gordon decisively. At that moment a Mercedes drew up beside the girl and a short man in a sharp suit sprang out.

'She's got a client,' pointed out Donald, rather pleased with himself. Ignoring him, Berry watched as the pair had an animated conversation, perhaps an argument. At last the two parted, Leila disappearing into the tube station and the man getting back into his car.

'Follow him,' said Gordon nodding at the man, confirming what they both instinctively felt, and Donald pulled out casually after the Mercedes.

Madson sat once again in the white hospital room. There was still no change in Rob's pallor, no hint of an eyelid flickering back to life. But this time Madson took his son's right hand in his and stroked it softly. Today he felt less agitated, more able to carry on. He had a plan, and he could trust Berry to do the legwork.

*

The Mercedes drove up the winding approach road to an industrial area at quite a pace. From a distance Berry and Donald could see some rather unappealing two- and three-storey factory units; large and functional.

Still some distance behind they watched the Mercedes pull in and park outside a concrete two-storey unit, and the man Leila Halkin had talked to got out. By this time Berry and Donald had pulled in beside another unit, far enough away, they supposed, not to be noticed. The man unlocked the door and went in. Donald waited a few minutes until he was confident all would be clear and then cruised carefully by, taking note of the sign outside, which read, 'Frank Banford Enterprises'.

'Frank Banford,' mused Donald. He glanced round at Berry. 'Don't we know that name?'

'I don't. Do you?'

Donald looked thoughtful.

Rourke walked grimly down the uncarpeted stairs of the Organized Crime Squad. Passing the crowded canteen, he left the building by a back door and walked quickly across the car park. Aston was waiting in a dark blue Montego; Rourke got into the front seat beside him.

'I was a bit busy the other night,' he apologized.

Aston had not taken offence. 'You got the collars?' he inquired reasonably.

'Yes,' Rourke confirmed crisply, intent on dealing as quickly as possible with the subject he had come to discuss. 'This Madson . . . ,' he began, 'you and I, we'll find a way.'

'Find a way to do what?' Aston found his attitude rather menacing.

'We have to sort this out,' Rourke said grimly.

Aston was having none of it. 'I don't have to sort him

out. I was just warning you, we may be involved in a suit for compensation.'

'Look,' Rourke began angrily. 'I'm five years away from my pension. That little shit sticks his nose in where it's not wanted and my pension's gone.'

'He just wants his compensation like all the rest,' argued Aston.

'No!' Rourke almost shouted. 'Not like all the rest. This one's clever. Thinks he's a brief. He's coming after us, I know he is.'

'So?' Aston shrugged in an attempt to soothe him.

'So we do him first.' Rourke had not been placated.

'You're overreacting . . .' said Aston, slightly frightened by this.

'I'll do anything it takes,' Rourke growled in a low voice. 'Just wait.'

Aston for a moment saw Rourke, his colleague and drinking mate of many years' standing, as a loose cannon. Rourke had always been that bit more involved in their cases than his other colleagues, particularly once his marriage had failed. Now Aston looked with some concern at his fellow officer.

Donald carried a tray containing three large whiskies over from the bar of a decaying Mile End pub to a table in an alcove by the dusty front window. He sat down beside Berry and placed a drink in front of the cop who sat uncomfortably opposite them.

The officer looked at Donald suspiciously. 'We're getting our wires crossed,' he remarked. 'You used to be my snout – now I'm supposed to feed you?' He was incredulous.

'First time for everything,' said Donald cheerfully, taking a swig of his Scotch.

Berry took over. 'We're not requesting access to CID

files or computers, just your street knowledge,' he said reasonably.

'I don't know . . . ,' the policeman hesitated.

'One day you may want to whistle me up,' Donald interjected. 'And you know I'll come,' he said persuasively.

The policeman shrugged and put down his empty glass with a clatter.

'A bloke, maybe a whoremaster, or whatever. Anyway, he's got a factory unit, King's Cross industrial park.'

'Frank Banford?' The police officer rolled the name around on his tongue and stared at the ceiling for a moment as if checking a computer directory in his mind. 'Jeff,' the policeman said at last. 'Jeff Banford is due up any day at Southwark Crown Court, extortion. He's got a cousin. I think his name may be Frank.'

Sitting in the intensive-care waiting-room that evening, watching his motionless son through the glass partition, Madson was disturbed by the sharp tone of a telephone ringing near by. A uniformed porter popped his head round the door and pointed to a telephone in an adjacent office.

'Mr Madson?'

Madson nodded. He went into the outer office and picked up the receiver. 'Yes?'

'The factory unit, Frank Banford Enterprises . . .' Berry was speaking on the crackling airwaves of his mobile phone, as he and Donald sped through the streets of north-west London.

'Yes?' Madson asked again.

Berry was pleased with himself. 'Frank Banford is cousin to Jeff Banford. Due up shortly at Southwark Crown Court, extortion.'

'So?'

'So,' said Gordon eagerly, 'Frank nobbles the witness for his cousin's trial.' Madson thought about it for a moment, and then smiled.

Berry waited alone in the car, a hundred yards away from the factory unit that was Frank Banford Enterprises. Most of the units were in almost total darkness and the King's Cross industrial zone appeared spooky and uninviting by night. Only the pinpoint glow of security devices pierced the gloom, and the two spinning lights of a helicopter passing overhead to its destination in Docklands. Berry jumped as Donald tapped on his window; he had not noticed the figure walking towards him from the shadows of the factory unit. He reached over and opened the door, and Donald slid in.

'Christie Total Circuit CDS. Touch pads – infra-red,' Donald whispered.

Berry studied the building briefly. 'Suppose we went in, and all the alarms went off – how long before cops or security got here?'

Donald looked thoughtful.

Five minutes later Berry stood beside the unit reception area where there was a large red fire extinguisher. With a resounding crash he brought the heavy fire extinguisher down hard and smashed their way through the frosted glass of the office door. The door exploded into thousands of tiny glass pieces, and Berry and Donald crunched their way through into the room.

Piercing alarms inside and outside the building began to scream loudly. Behind them the street door was hanging at an angle from a single hinge. Unmoved by this racket Berry and Donald began to go through the office files systematically, removing all files and books that looked relevant.

Berry picked up a phone from the desk and dialled Sarah's number. She answered on the first ring.

'Yes,' she said breathlessly.

'Is JP back?' Berry inquired.

'John?' she said, slightly uncertain. 'He's still at the hospital.'

'Tell him there's a load of paperwork. We're sending two boxes over.'

Donald was meanwhile piling the boxes high behind Berry, finding yet more files. Berry raised his eyebrows – he had thought they had got the lot. Sarah could hardly hear him above the shriek of the alarms.

'Right,' she shouted down the line. 'Right, I'll tell him.' She rang off in confusion.

With the alarm bells still ringing Berry and Donald loaded up their car with the two overflowing boxes and unhurriedly clambered into the car. Donald pulled out at a moderate pace and turned left away from the factory units and out towards the main road.

The police arrived several minutes later, in their well-marked vehicles, lights flashing, sirens sounding. Uniformed constables spilled out into the night only to find the building empty, the bird flown.

The ticking clock on Sarah's mantelpiece showed 2 a.m. Madson sat at the table in a state of deep concentration, going carefully through the contents of the boxes Berry and Donald had provided. Sitting here in the small flat he felt almost the comfort of a familiar situation, for he had often sat up at night studying by torchlight in his prison cell. He was determined that by morning he would know what Banford was up to.

At last he picked out a pile of invoices and, as if dealing a pack of cards, he placed them in a pattern on the table. Then, still concentrating, he picked out several and fanned them out, like a strong poker hand.

Sarah got up at eight that morning, which was early for her, and padded out barefoot and yawning into the hallway, in an old blue towelling dressing-gown, to put the kettle on. To her surprise she found Madson wide awake in the kitchen, making breakfast. His eyes were grey with tiredness, and he still wore yesterday's clothes.

'John,' she said, as she rubbed her eyes, still slightly stupid from sleep. 'Didn't you go to bed?'

He looked at her. He was driven by the will to succeed. Having endured eight years behind bars he could not bear to waste a moment longer. He had to have all his answers immediately. It would be a long time, he reflected, before he would be able to sleep peacefully again.

'I was looking . . .' he explained badly, '. . . looking for something . . .' he waved at the piles of paperwork.

'Did you find it?' she asked sympathetically, her heart going out to him. He looked exhausted.

'I think so,' he said wearily, taking a thoughtful sip of tea.

Later that morning he and Berry sat in a workmen's café on Portobello, over a meal of bacon sandwiches and steaming tea.

'It's a long fraud,' Madson explained as Berry ate greedily. 'Banford is pulling a long fraud.'

'What's that then?' asked Berry through a mouthful of bacon, dropping some out of the side of his mouth.

Madson elucidated. 'You set up maybe hundreds of companies. All paper companies. You establish credit for each of them, buying goods, paying your bills promptly. Then, after a while, for each of the companies you give the big order for a lot of goods. They're delivered. You disappear with the goods, flog them elsewhere.' He pulled out a paper and showed it to Berry, who by this time had finished his sandwich and wiped his hands clean on his jacket.

'Maybe a hundred companies,' he continued, indicating the list on the right-hand side of the paper. 'He's at it in a big way.'

This was too complicated for Berry, who wore a puzzled frown as he tried to comprehend the information on the paper. Finally he turned to Madson with a grin.

'Did I do good?'

Madson nodded at him. 'You did good.'

Frank Banford's Mercedes stood outside his factory unit, alongside two other cars and a Christie security van.

Inside Frank Banford angrily watched the Christie security man resetting the control panel. He did not know why he was bothering to have it done, for the police had, infuriatingly, arrived much too late. A couple of his workers checked out the damage, while a bald glazier replaced the glass in the damaged door.

Unreasonably, Banford vented his fury on the glazier. 'You any idea how much those infra-red detectors cost me? And what's the point?' he rambled. 'Hairy-arsed coppers couldn't get here in time!' The glazier ignored him, concentrating on his work. He had seen all sorts.

At that moment a motor-cycle courier arrived clad in

black leathers and helmet, and the glazier was saved further harassment. The courier, a po-faced Berry, handed Banford a large brown envelope addressed to him and then a clipboard for him to sign.

Banford began to open the envelope as Berry left. The phone on Banford's desk rang, and he picked it up. 'Yes?'

'Is that Frank Banford?' Madson spoke into the phone in Sarah's flat.

'Yes.'

'You had a package delivered recently?' Madson was enjoying this.

'Just now.' Then it clicked as he looked at the sheet of paper he had just pulled from the envelope, and his jaw dropped. 'Jesus!'

'Don't worry,' Madson said reassuringly, 'I've got the originals. I'm just about to send them off to a friend in the Fraud Squad.'

'What do you want?'

'You're putting pressure on a witness not to testify at your cousin's trial. Tell the witness to testify.' Madson hung up, a smile on his face.

Later the phone rang at Hearnley & Partners. Magda was talking with a great sense of relief to Leila Halkin. The witness had unaccountably changed her mind, and Magda was keen to get on with the case; she did not have much time left to prepare. She picked up the phone slightly distracted.

'Yes?'

'Put him through,' she sighed. Madson would clearly not be put off easily. 'Yes, hello.'

'That witness of yours,' Madson's voice flowed loud and confident down the line.

'She's changed her mind. She's going to testify.'

Staring in amazement at the bubbles in the heavy crystal paperweight, she took in the implications of what Madson was claiming.

'Lunch tomorrow?' Madson ventured into the silence.

Looking up at the red tresses of her restored witness, she found it hard to believe.

'Sandwich? Low-cal. chicken salad on whole wheat?' suggested Madson.

She gave up. 'No mayonnaise,' she almost laughed, hanging up the phone and wondering how he had managed it. And also feeling that it might be better not to know, if she wanted to maintain her own integrity as a lawyer.

Finding that he had smoked the last of his packet of cigarettes, Madson left the flat and went down to the street, looking for a tobacconist's. He smiled inwardly as he walked along, thinking of his lunch the next day with Magda.

Rourke was waiting, and intercepted him. Madson jumped.

'I want to remind you of a few facts, Madson,' Rourke said in a low, threatening voice, getting close up to Madson and attempting to grab his lapel.

'You're an ex-con,' he growled. 'You did eight years of a life sentence. You think you're a proper brief now, don't you, now you've conned the Appeal Court,' he taunted, his voice rising. 'Well I've got news for you, you little scumbag. I'm on your case.'

Madson looked grim; he stood stock still, unable to utter a word. Rourke turned on his heel and walked back to his CID car.

Sarah appeared distraught at the entrance to the building, her face white. She caught sight of Madson.

'John . . . The hospital just called.' He turned to follow her back inside.

At the hospital Madson and Sarah strode purposefully down the corridor, Sarah almost running to keep up. They were uneasy, and fearful, aware that the doctor might not have told them everything over the telephone. They rushed round the corner and into the intensive care unit, where they saw the young Indian doctor standing with a couple of nurses by Rob's bed. Rob's body was covered with a sheet, the machines no longer bleeping.

'I'm very sorry,' began the doctor, 'the cardiac arrest team got here in seconds. We couldn't save him . . .' They left Madson and Sarah alone with Rob's body to say their farewells.

Madson sat down beside the head of the bed, and carefully pulled back the sheet to reveal Rob's face. He stroked his son's cheek tenderly. Then he took the weeping Sarah in his arms.

CHAPTER FOUR

The funeral took place on a grey and damp morning at Kensal Green cemetery. Madson stood beside Sarah on one side of the newly dug grave, and Elizabeth Madson's elderly parents, the Lewises, stood on the other. They avoided eye contact.

Madson looked across at his wife's grave and sighed; this double tragedy was simply unbelievable, too terrible to take in. What, he thought, was the point of freeing himself from prison if his son was lost. He had harboured great hopes of their renewed relationship. He had planned to make up for lost time; he and Rob would have got to know one another again as adults. He had imagined them both cheering in the stands at a football match, having a pint in the pub, taking a fishing trip together. Now he glanced round at Sarah. She looked stunned; she shivered slightly in the cold air and he reached out and put his arm round her shoulders.

The priest finished the service and stood in reverent silence for a moment; then he exchanged a brief word with the Lewises and departed. Tears rolled down Mrs Lewis's wrinkled face; she had looked after Rob when her daughter was found murdered and son-in-law had gone to jail. She had never approved of Madson, and now it was all over, for Rob as well as for her daughter.

Madson moved round the grave and approached the Lewises. 'I know you don't want to talk to me but you may want to speak to Sarah,' he suggested.

Peter Lewis hesitated – he knew his wife's views on the subject. 'No, we'd rather not.'

'I think she needs it,' Madson urged.

'I'm sorry.' He looked at the ground; he blamed Sarah for Rob's addiction.

'I'm sorry too. I'm sorry about everything,' Madson said calmly.

Lewis put in abruptly, 'It's a bit late now.'

'I know. Look, I've never really had the chance to thank you. For looking after Rob when I was inside.'

Lewis spat angrily, 'With you as his father ... and that girl ... as his wife, he never had a chance!'

Madson walked back round the grave, now heaped with dark clods of earth, to rejoin Sarah, who looked exhausted and wore a defeated expression.

'I heard that,' she said to Madson in a squeaky voice, holding back her tears.

'They made sacrifices,' Madson reasoned kindly, 'bringing up Rob. They loved their daughter. She dies. Now her son dies. I'm the common factor.' He shrugged.

'I'm not ...' Tears began to well in Sarah's eyes. 'I heard him ... he said Rob never really had a chance.'

'Sarah, come on,' Madson said gently, but he could see that Sarah was going to break down and cry.

'This farce of a Roman Catholic funeral ...' Sarah began, pointlessly tilting at windmills. 'Rob hated religion! Especially Catholics. Especially that Catholic school they put him in. Those priests made his life hell. It's like we've given him back to his tormentors to be buried!'

Madson took her firmly by the arm, as the tears spilled down her cheeks.

In the imposing panelled courtroom Judge Jonathan Haldane sat behind his antique podium. He was tired of listening to witnesses giving interminable evidence in a case about the importation of hard-core pornography; he stifled a yawn. Corrupting the young, he thought to himself with distaste, wetting his thin lips with his tongue and unobtrusively glancing at his watch. He had plans for the evening.

He summed up, looking sternly at the defendant with a well-practised frown. '... You have introduced into this country material which threatens the moral fabric of our society. These publications have the undoubted potential to corrupt, and I am thinking particularly of the impressionable young that it is our duty to protect ...'

Soon after, Judge Haldane was peacefully ensconced in his leather office chair; he leaned back, stretching luxuriously in his white open-necked shirt. Behind him his ancient manservant was fussily folding and packing away the judge's robe and carefully arranging his peri-wig on a stand.

Haldane swivelled round to face him. 'Phone Donald Rawlinson, Queen's Counsel,' he commanded. 'Tell him I won't be free for dinner.' He paused unpleasantly on a high note – today's hearing had rather got him going. And now he planned another, more pleasurable enter-tainment. He stroked the leather of his chair, his hand damp with anticipation. 'I shall be busy tonight,' he remarked cryptically, looking down his nose at Jenkins.

'Very good, my lord,' nodded Jenkins, as he padded out.

Sarah's flat looked bleak and empty that evening. Most of their packing had been done and a row of black bin bags stood ominously on the bare floorboards of the hall. They would soon be forced to move out and had not yet found other accommodation. Sarah sat at the kitchen table drinking tea with Madson.

Madson sipped his tea, and studied Sarah. 'D'you want to talk about Rob?' he offered.

'No,' she said blankly.

He left her to think for a moment while he drank his tea, and then tried again. 'You're not on your own you know . . .'

Sarah looked up at Madson. The sense of devastation and abandonment was overwhelming; she felt that she only existed as an empty shell, a husk. Her skin felt dry and old. The hair that once had tumbled in bright curls now hung lankly to her shoulders. She got up, picking up the empty cups and taking them over to the sink. Leaving them there, she went back over to the table to sit with Madson; he was grieving too.

On one side of the table amongst a clutter of old letters and postcards lay a small tin box. She reached across, opened it, and carefully rolled herself a joint. Lighting up, she took a deep puff, inhaling an anaesthetizing quantity of the drug. She offered the joint to Madson.

'Do you have to smoke that stuff?' he snapped in response. He had tried to get her to talk about Rob; he wanted to help her, but deep inside he was tense and angry. And he had seen too many people in prison resort to smoking dope instead of dealing with their problems.

'Why not? It relaxes me. Try some?' She reached out to him again.

'There's a cop breathing down my neck. I don't want to give him any excuse to bust us!'

'That's your problem, not mine.' She was beginning to argue back at him, her own feelings of helpless anger at the waste of Rob's life coming to the fore.

'Get rid of it,' he growled.

She looked at him for a moment, dissolving again into misery; it was clear there was nothing either of them could say that would be right.

'I'm sorry . . .' Madson apologized.

'We've no milk,' said Sarah into the ensuing silence. 'I'll go to the corner . . .'

'I'll do it,' Madson offered.

'No, I'll do it . . .' she said, scrambling to her feet and picking up her purse. A walk to the shop might clear the tense atmosphere.

The library in Judge Haldane's house was lit by flickering candlelight. Beautiful leatherbound law books filled floor-to-ceiling bookcases. The room smelt musty, which, together with the aroma of smoke and melting wax, gave it a feel of belonging to a different era. A youth in an ill-fitting schoolboy outfit knelt incongruously on a deep purple velvet-covered prie-dieu, next to a large carved antique desk. A gold candelabra with six candles lit up the desk and cast a flickering light over the malevolent face of Haldane, who was dressed only in a heavy silk dressing-gown.

Haldane looked down at the boy lustfully. 'Put your cap on straight,' he scolded, taking his sadistic role seriously. Pete at seventeen had fled from abuse at home in Barnsley to what he hoped would be a new life in London. The desperate state of the job market for the young and unskilled had led him on to the streets.

Pete reached up silently and adjusted his cap.

Haldane reached out and touched the boy's youthful chest, sliding his hand longingly down the firm skin. 'The prefect tells me you've been a wicked boy,' he murmured unpleasantly.

'You're not going to beat me.' Pete raised his head

and looked at Haldane in alarm, fear reflected in his soft blue eyes. 'Last time you bloody hurt me.'

Haldane continued to caress the trembling torso. 'We'll discuss this,' he said quietly. 'Get up to your dorm. I'll be with you in a minute.'

Pete got up from his knees and moved quickly towards the door. Haldane was blowing out the candles, slowly, ritualistically, one by one.

'I mean it,' begged Pete. 'You don't hurt me . . .'

That night Sarah lay fully clothed on her bed staring blankly at the ceiling. She was unable to summon the energy to undress, and it all seemed so pointless. Music crackled sadly from the radio, one of the few things which had not yet been packed up. She finished the last of the second joint she had found in Rob's old tin, and began to feel oddly disembodied, as if the world was a long, long way away, very mellow. She did not know when she fell asleep.

Madson lost himself in an old copy of Smith and Hogan, *Criminal Law, Cases and Materials*. Studying at the kitchen table, elbows supporting his head, he made a concerted effort to memorize a particularly complicated criminal case. A small tranny on the fridge echoed the sound of 'The World Tonight' on Radio 4. He had intended to listen to a whole programme on the criminal justice system, but had somehow missed it. He ploughed on with his case, but with the weight of the day on his back found it almost impossible to concentrate.

'The Home Office agreed the prison population figures were continuing to rise, and were now the highest for seven years.' He pricked up his ears and raised his head to take in what the voice on the radio was saying.

'Members of the Prison Governors' Association said

that the large number of remand prisoners was the main reason for overcrowding. The current total of prisoners in British jails as of 1 April was 51,239 . . .'

'Minus one!' Madson found himself saying out loud to the radio, and then looked about quickly in case Sarah had heard. It was the end of a long and emotional day, but he did not feel able to surrender himself to sleep.

The phone rang in the depths of Haldane's house in the early hours of the morning; still awake he padded into the library in his dressing-gown to answer it in the dim pink light of sunrise.

'Yes?' he inquired.

'It's me, Pete,' the voice came down the line in a high-pitched hysterical moan. He was in such pain from his session with Haldane that he had not been able to sleep, and he meant to hurt back.

'What do you want?' Haldane responded calmly.

'You. I want you,' his voice rose higher still, and he banged his fists on the glass sides of the Bayswater phone booth, dislodging a shower of erotic calling cards. 'You bastard!' he yelled. 'You nearly killed me. I told you not to hurt me. I warned you . . .' He trailed off, temporarily spent of energy and slightly confused by the can of beer he had drunk to give himself dutch courage.

'You warned me?'

'I'm not stupid like you think,' said Pete, screwing up the courage to make his threat. 'I know everything about you,' he continued slowly. 'I know where you live. I know what you've got in your bedroom. I've got you. And I'm going to make you pay. Or I'm going to the newspapers.' He paused triumphantly.

Haldane remained controlled. 'So,' he said calmly. 'I might have guessed. How much?'

But Pete was not going to let him get out of this yet, he wanted him to suffer. 'I haven't decided yet ... my lord,' he said sarcastically. 'And don't bother trying to find me. I've moved,' he said quickly before slamming down the phone without giving Haldane the chance to reply.

Judge Jonathan Haldane sat without moving for some minutes, a frown of concentration on his face.

Later that morning he picked up the receiver and dialled Ranny's number. His old friend was the one person who would be able to solve this discreetly.

Madson sat nervously in reception at Hearnley & Partners. The morning after Rob's funeral, a day that he had intended to spend comforting Sarah and finding a new flat to live in, there had been an early call from Magda. Sir Ranald Hearnley wished to see him. Despite his private sorrow, this was not an invitation to be ignored. He struggled to suppress his hopes in case they were dashed. Magda came bustling in from her office wearing a smart navy blue suit. 'I'm sorry it's such short notice. How was everything yesterday?'

'It was like a funeral,' Madson said shortly, getting up awkwardly from the low seating.

'How's Sarah?'

'As you might expect.' It was kind of her to ask, but there was not much to be said on the subject. Also he was eager to see Sir Ranald and find out what he had to say.

'He didn't say why he wanted to see you, so he may not be offering a job,' Magda warned, reading his mind.

'Right.'

As they climbed the polished wood staircase up to Sir Ranald's office and the various conference rooms, she offered further advice: 'Be careful with him. Let him do the talking. Don't launch into long explanations. He never listens to anybody. Just answer his questions, as briefly as possible. OK?'

'Yes.' Madson nodded as they reached the door.

Tall but slightly stooped with age, and with white hair, Sir Ranald must have been closer to eighty than the seventy-odd years he owned up to. Madson felt both impressed and daunted by the power of the man, in roughly equal measures.

Sir Ranald gestured for Madson and Magda to sit down. 'You seem to have a good friend in Miss Ostrowska,' he said with good humour. 'She's told me all about you. And of course I read the papers about your appeal. You'll sue for compensation, of course?'

'Yes. Eventually.' Madson agreed.

'We would be happy to represent you.' Madson was pleased and surprised. Sir Ranald, paused for a moment, considering the situation. 'Of course, you got a law degree in prison. Remarkable.' He seemed genuinely impressed. 'I believe you propose to practise law.'

'Yes.' Carefully adhering to Magda's instructions, Madson did not like to elaborate. Having accomplished his law degree by correspondence course at her majesty's pleasure, he had never had the experience or encouragement of a tutor. To some extent he regretted this. Madson suddenly felt like a young student gamely attending his first interview with a firm of solicitors.

'It's a novel concept,' Sir Ranald continued, in a voice like raked gravel. 'You do understand the difficulties?'

Madson nodded earnestly.

'In order to practise law you'll need to take the legal practice course,' he explained, apparently disregarding the fact that Madson, a former convicted criminal, would have rather more obstacles than that to overcome.

'I know.'

'And you'll have to go before the education casework committee. Have you chosen your referees?'

'Not yet.' Where was all this leading, Madson wondered.

'I understand you're a good chap at finding people. Witnesses and so forth.' At last he was getting to the point.

'I like to help.' Madson answered noncommittally.

'As it happens, I have a friend who needs help.' Sir Ranald leaned forward confidentially. 'I wondered if you might be useful to him.'

'I'd like the chance,' Madson said eagerly, without thinking to ask for further details.

Sir Ranald then began to explain. 'A close friend of mine, a judge, Mr Justice Haldane. I was at Harrow with his older brother. Terrifically accomplished, a charming man, an outstanding High Court judge. He rang me early this morning. He seems to have got himself into some kind of trouble. And he has asked me if we ever use a private inquiry agency. Of course I thought of you – finding this witness for Magda.' He hesitated. 'You'd be doing me a great favour if you could see him . . .'

Magda walked Madson through the Inns of Court to find a bus or taxi on Fleet Street. They paused by Temple church and wandered in to have a look at it, something which Magda had not done before. They walked down the aisle admiring the stained glass windows. Stealing a glance at him as they walked Magda reflected that he was one of the most interesting men she had met for some time: in an impossible situation he had struggled to pull himself up, working hard to achieve it. She admired his tenacity. 'I never asked you,' she said, pondering Sir Ranald's request, 'who tried your original case.'

'Judge Harley-Roberts.' With a shudder he recalled the stern voice sending him down for life.

'The worst of the lot,' she sympathized. 'Stupid, bigoted, prejudiced. Mind you, the firm makes a fortune out of his cases going to appeal!'

Madson was still too tense to find this amusing. Instead he took her seriously and found himself railing against the system. 'They're all the same. They go to the same schools and universities, they come from the same social background.' Magda looked at him, not very surprised by this outburst. She too felt rather alienated in a male, élitist profession; and she was not only a woman, but foreign. 'Without their robes and wigs,' Madson continued, 'they'd be nothing – just like the rest of us!'

'Would you want to become a judge?' she queried, sending him up gently.

'Yes,' he replied, to her astonishment. 'I'd be brilliant.'

'You probably would,' she said thoughtfully, reconsidering her opinion of him yet again.

Later that day Madson found himself ensconced in the lawcourts in Judge Haldane's office. A manservant poured tea into delicate cups and offered a tin of biscuits. He watched the judge as he carefully selected a slim biscuit from the tin. The man looked slightly fussy and mannered; he was perhaps sixty, with thinning greyish hair. He held his teacup carefully between his thumb and forefinger.

'There are ways of conducting this discussion – euphemism, white lies, half truths, items passed over vital to the picture,' he paused. 'I won't do that.'

Madson assessed Haldane as he sat nibbling his biscuit. It was clearly some kind of sexual indiscretion.

'I've always been of the opinion that my sexual preferences are nobody's concern but my own,' Haldane spoke in a matter-of-fact voice. 'When we met he told me he was twenty-two. Now he claims he is seventeen. I'm not a seducer of the young. I saw him in Soho two months ago. He was no innocent. He came to my house on five occasions. I don't need to tell you that what is perfectly legal is sometimes nevertheless not acceptable in the public eye. If this gets out . . .'

Madson nodded. Strangely he began to feel some sympathy for the judge. This was the kind of thing that was the lifeblood of the tabloids. Haldane handed him a fuzzy Polaroid of Pete which had been snipped jaggedly in half and was now simply a head-and-shoulder shot. The naked shoulders spoke ominously of the bottom half.

'I don't know his surname. He's slightly built, comes from the north somewhere. He phoned me last night, told me he wanted money or he'd go to the newspapers. Presumably the tabloids, but you can't always be sure these days, can you?'

'How much does he want?' asked Madson, discounting what was presumably a joke and getting down to business.

'He hasn't said.'

'Why don't you go to the police?' Madson suggested, wondering if the judge had not told him the full story, if there was something even more salacious to it.

'I can't take the risk,' Haldane replied, confirming Madson's suspicions. 'I realize I'm in an extremely vulnerable position, Mr Madson. I also understand that you will have an unflattering opinion of the English judiciary. The fact is I need your help. Will you help me?' He looked Madson straight in the eye.

Given that he wanted a job at Hearnley & Partners

– and that with a criminal conviction in his past he was not likely to gain employment elsewhere – Madson did not have much choice but to agree.

'Yes,' he replied, keeping his negative opinion of Judge Haldane to himself.

Clutching her pink copy of *Loot*, the 'Flats for Rent in West London' page folded outwards, Sarah walked up a dreary, litter-strewn street in Ladbroke Grove. Groups of lads hovered in doorways, a jug-faced pit bull barked sharply and pulled at its chain. Consulting the details she had scrawled beside the advert, Sarah checked that she had the right house. She pushed open the gate and rang the doorbell. A bald man of indeterminate age with tattoos on his arm, his T-shirt stretched over multiple beer bellies, opened the door.

'Mr Hunter?' asked Sarah nervously.

'Yeah?' Looking her up and down, he realized she had come to see the flat and stood aside to allow her to pass. In the gloom of the hallway he directed her down to the basement; a pungent smell of damp enveloped them as they descended the narrow staircase. There was very little natural light, one of the bedrooms was more of a cupboard under the stairs, the kitchen was filthy and totally unmodernized, the telephone was a broken old pay phone and there was no heating. Sarah felt at a loss for words, but to her intense relief Madson arrived just then to join them.

'You like it? Plenty of punters out there.'

Emboldened by Madson's arrival and infuriated by Hunter, Sarah waved her copy of *Loot* in the air, stabbing her finger at the advert.

'I want to read you your advert,' she said. '£210 weekly. Large, two-bedroom modern flat, Ladbroke Grove area, phone and all services –'

'Listen,' Hunter cut in. 'You don't want it, so clear off.'

But Sarah was too annoyed to feel threatened by him. 'You listen,' she replied. 'You've wasted our time.'

'Get out of here . . .' Hunter snarled.

Tense, both Madson and Sarah stood stock still. Then Hunter gave Sarah a sharp push towards the stairs. Madson turned on him blazing. Hunter leapt back in anticipation of a blow, but Madson remained quite still.

'Don't touch her,' he barked. 'Apologize, Mr Hunter. Now.' It was Madson's turn to be menacing.

Sarah was frightened of what he might do. 'John. No,' she cried. 'Don't. Leave it.'

Fortunately Hunter had by this time got the message and began to mutter an apology. 'Maybe it needs a bit of a clear-up . . .' echoed up the staircase as Madson and Sarah made their exit.

Portobello Road was alive with its usual multi-ethnic buzz of activity. Reggae music blared from open fronted music shops gaily painted in green, red and yellow. Fish and vegetables were spread out invitingly on the stalls. Harassed single mothers with dark roots to their straw-coloured hair struggled out of Woolworth's and Tesco's, trailing shopping trolleys and screaming toddlers. A few people stood about on the pavement eating takeaway food from foil containers with large plastic spoons.

Madson consulted his Polaroid of Pete and approached a suitable young man in denims, every available spot pierced with silver rings, but the lad shook his head. He did not recognize Pete. He directed Madson vaguely on towards a gay video shop on the corner of Lancaster Road. No one knew him there either, but a helpful shop assistant pointed him up the road to a former pub which now served as a wine bar.

Once again it proved a dead end; the clientèle of this bar in their tight leather trousers and salon haircuts were too affluent for the likes of Pete. These were media men, meeting friends and jotting down the numbers of new contacts in their Filofaxes. The music was so loud that it proved impossible to make himself heard, but Madson showed the Polaroid to a few regulars at the bar in the hope of a lead, but without success.

Madson's minicab pulled up outside Berry's Recovery. Seeing his friend, Berry sauntered out to greet him with a twinkle in his eye. 'Just the geezer I was looking for. Got a nice motor for you, JP.'

Madson smiled. 'I don't need a car. I need to talk to you, Gordon.'

Regardless, Berry steered him towards some cars parked under the arch of his garage.

'A man without wheels is a man without dignity,' he continued. 'Besides, he's a bloody pedestrian. Beautiful motor. Look at that bodywork. Twenty thousand on the clock, one lady owner. Only ever drove it to church Sunday morning. Trouble is she couldn't keep up her payments,' he gloated wickedly.

He slid into the sleek Rover, pressed a button which wound down the windows, revved the engine and turned the car smoothly out from between the parked cars into the mews.

Madson followed him. 'I don't want to buy it, Gordon.'

'Triumph of British engineering,' Berry crowed, ignoring Madson's admonitions. 'You can have it for a day or two till I need it. And for Christ's sake watch where you park it. There's some right nut cases out there.'

'It's very kind of you, Gordon. But what I'm really looking for is a rent-boy.'

'Blimey.' Gordon's eyebrows shot up. 'You've changed since you came out. You tried the Meat Rack?'

'Yes.' Madson was serious. 'And Soho. And Notting Hill. Needle in a haystack. Any other ideas?'

'Yeah.' Gordon was sidetracked again. 'Here, cop this.' He pulled a mobile out of his pocket and tossed it to Madson, who caught it.

'A man is also without dignity who cannot communicate . . .' He trailed off, looking at Madson for a positive response.

'Thanks.' Madson smiled fondly. 'Gordon, the rent-boy?'

'I know a bloke who'll give you a great blow-dry for a fiver . . .' Berry teased, with a twinkle in his eye. Madson had at last gained his attention.

CHAPTER FIVE

Adrian was the sort of hairdresser who liked the sound of his own voice. An old queen with a number one haircut and an outrageous line in satin shirts, he kept his regular clientèle of blue- and pink-rinsed old ladies spellbound and content. The small Chippenham Road salon was dusty, its pale orange paintwork peeling, the cane furniture sighing with neglect. A picture of George Michael was sellotaped above the cash desk, competing with one of Princess Diana in full ball gown and tiara on the opposite wall.

'It's a personal thing,' Adrian confided. 'Wouldn't touch them now. Rent-boys. Of course you want to rescue them off the street. So you bring them home, and there's a couple of weeks of seeing them getting fit again. Then they start to take over the house, and bring in their friends – and you start to make concessions.' He looked over at Madson for a sympathetic response, and then continued pulling out curlers and drying the hair of an elderly customer.

'Then they say, "no more sex", because you're just like the rest of them. Then a few things start to go missing. Then one morning you wake up to what's hap-pened. And you throw the little bugger out. And you feel rotten with yourself, and stupid, and you know within three months you'll do the same thing over again!' he concluded with mock horror as he expertly fluffed out another curl.

The mere mention of a rent-boy got this man's

interest, thought Madson with amusement; perhaps he ought to get his own hair cut here and enjoy the conversation on a regular basis. 'He was picked up in Notting Hill,' he prompted.

'Yeah, you said.' Adrian thought for a moment, eyeing the George Michael poster lustfully. 'There's a café,' he said at last. 'Bella Café, Dorset Lane, near Portobello, a lot of those boys hang out there. Steer clear of the shepherd's pie,' he added for good measure.

'Thank you,' said Madson getting up and gratefully slipping a fiver into Adrian's pocket.

Adrian smiled at his reflection. 'Lucky with the teasy weasy,' he joked, prodding the old lady's hairdo, causing her to smirk with pleasure, 'unlucky in lust!' Madson headed out with relief to Berry's Rover.

Beside the majestic wrought-iron gates on the Notting Hill side of Kensington Gardens, Rourke and Aston licked at their Mr Whippy vanilla ice creams. Beyond them dogs romped through the park, and the twang of arrows could be heard coming from the field behind Kensington Palace. Rourke, who had been trying to bring up the subject of Madson once again with Aston, was glad of the chance of a quiet word. The case, and their involvement in it, had been going round and round in his head, day and night.

'Eight years ago, Madson murdered his wife.'

Aston looked at his colleague. Surely he must have realized by now that they should leave it alone, wait for the inquiry if there was one. Certainly there was nothing to be gained by pursuing the poor man. But he thought better of interrupting.

'All right,' – Rourke could not leave it alone, though he could plainly hear the thoughts running through Aston's mind – 'maybe we didn't have more than a ninety per cent case,' he shrugged, 'so we added a bit. So what?'

Aston licked his ice cream, and then bit off a chunk of chocolate flake and chewed it. 'Is there a B side to this record?' he inquired.

'He sues, and all our original evidence will be up for re-examination. Everything,' he emphasized heavily.

But Aston had reached the end of his tether, it was becoming impossible to work with Rourke, let alone relax together on a hot day. He glanced longingly at the people around them lying on the grass, and then looked back at his friend with irritation.

'Dennis, this is one of those moments in a friendship you always hope won't happen,' he said intently. 'I don't give a toss!' He emphasized each syllable to make himself clear.

'I don't believe you're saying this.' Rourke was desperate. At the same time he felt hurt and betrayed. Aston had worked alongside him for many years; he had always made the decisions, Aston had always followed. This disagreement was incomprehensible to him. Aston tried once again to offer advice.

'You want to stick one on Madson? You'll end up in more trouble than the mess he got you into at the original trial. Walk away, son. Forget it.' He gave Rourke a hard despairing look. He chucked the remains of his cornet into a convenient litter bin, and strode off to his car without a backward glance.

Furious, Rourke threw his dripping ice-cream cone high into the air and with some force; it fell with a hard plop into an area marked 'Dog toilet – please encourage your dog to use this space.' A woman with a great Dane glared at him.

*

That evening Madson helped Sarah dry the dishes in the small kitchen. Sarah washed despondently, her hands in thick yellow rubber gloves, the sink overflowing with careless bubbles.

'Are you all right?' Madson asked, as a plate Sarah had been washing accidentally crashed to the ground.

'Don't keep asking that,' Sarah answered with annoyance. 'It just slipped. What am I supposed to say,' she continued as he bent to pick up the pieces. 'He's dead, buried, everything taken care of. So I'm just fine . . . ?'

Madson threw the broken plate in the rubbish bin, and then picked up his teacloth again.

'Just leave them to drain . . .' she said irritably. 'They'll dry better.'

He put down the cloth. He had thought that it would be a good idea to try and talk to her, find out more about her, and about Rob. There was so little that he did know. He felt deeply that he would like to know more, to salvage some of what he had missed.

'Let's talk about you,' he suggested.

'Me? What's there to talk about?' she pondered. Then she began to talk, the whole story spilling out. 'I was just a normal girl with a good job as a graphic designer and then I met Rob and suddenly I'm in love and I'm married. I mean,' she continued, eyes glazing over, 'he seemed like a nice boy, kind and loving and attentive, and I felt sorry for him, wouldn't you? Mother dead, dad in prison. And you can't blame him if he likes the occasional joint, I mean who doesn't?' She opened her eyes widely and looked at Madson. 'Then it's not occasional, then it's not a joint, then there's needles in the bathroom and suddenly the nice boy you married has turned into a junkie and the guy I felt sorry for has sold my Apple Mac to feed his habit so I can't get work any more and he's busy injecting anything he can find.'

'I'm sorry,' said Madson, inadequately.

'Why? It was my life.'

'What did your parents say?' Madson wondered.

'Oh I gave them up because they didn't like Rob,' she said nonchalantly. 'Then I gave up my friends because Rob didn't like them. He said he wanted to look after me. Just like you.' The world was heavy on her slight shoulders.

'Me?' Madson queried.

'I know how you feel. You lost your chance to help Rob. So you get this fixation you've got to help me. You've just come out of jail. You're the one who needs help,' she said harshly.

A glass she was washing cracked into two pieces in her gloved hands. She threw the pieces into the bin with one hand and then rinsed all the soap suds down the sink. Not a good day for the crockery Madson reflected, but at least she had begun to talk, to let out all the hurt.

Late that night Berry and Donald sat in the Fox and Feathers on Lonsdale Road. Madson carried over pints of bitter for them all from the bar. He sat down and began to explain about the need to find Pete, the black-mailing rent-boy, and about the information he had gleaned from Adrian at the hairdressing salon. He felt sure they would help him, and they nodded agreement as he outlined his plan.

'The Bella Café, near Portobello. If we could cover the hours of seven to midnight . . .' He hesitated. Donald opened a packet of pork scratchings thoughtfully.

Berry turned to Donald. 'Watches, Donald,' he suggested. 'Three of us take our turn, under two hours apiece.' He turned to Madson. 'Donald was in the navy for six months . . .'

'You're always sending me up,' complained Donald goodnaturedly. 'What happens if the bloke walks into the café?' he wanted to know.

'You make amorous advances, cash in hand,' grinned Berry.

'God almighty!' his uncle exclaimed, jerking perilously backwards in his seat.

'You'll have my portable,' Berry concluded as he drained his glass. 'Dial 999!'

With a reluctant Donald in tow, Berry reached the café soon afterwards. With its blue wooden facade and hand-written special offers stuck up in the window, the Bella Café did not look much above a transport cafe. Perhaps they would do a good egg and chips thought Donald, cheering up. Inside a number of young gay men sat drinking mugs of tea at Formica tables; bottles of ketchup and HP sauce abounded. Some of the men looked up and giggled as Berry entered, and he quickly decided to leave Donald to take the first shift. Handing Donald the mobile phone, he winked at the Irish proprietor and departed, leaving Donald alone to order his egg and chips.

At the Organized Crime Squad Rourke had deliberated long and hard over what to do about Madson. Clearly, he thought, some action was necessary. Damn Aston and his complacency. He called two of his detective constables into his office; they could be temporarily spared from the Brampton warehousing case. Poole was a hefty lad in his twenties, with a face reminiscent of a prop forward; Lear was thin and nervous with a prematurely receding hairline. They sipped the inevitable cups of tepid tea and waited for Rourke to get to the point. They had hoped to get off early to meet a colleague at the local pub. If Rourke did not release them soon it would be too late.

'We've two loyalties in this squad, one to the squad, and one to each other,' Rourke began carefully, stopping momentarily to make sure they were listening. 'I want to talk about the second, right?'

'Yes, guv,' nodded Lear.

Rourke rambled pleasantly on for some time. He suggested that as there was no rush on the current case to which they were assigned, they could reasonably do some work for him, 'on the quiet'. He raised an eyebrow, as if expecting dissent, waited a moment, and then concluded, 'And I expect you to help me.'

'Who is it?' ventured Poole.

Rourke took the cue gratefully; clearly they would carry out orders without a great deal of questioning. 'His name's John Madson. Does a con with the Appeal Court. Now he's out, and he wants to play games. I've got to teach him a lesson. And you'll help me. Cost you nothing. A little effort.' He smiled. 'Yes?'

They both nodded quickly, half-listening, still hoping to make it to the pub.

'I have to see the Guvnor,' Rourke concluded, and then got up and left them.

'What was all that about?' said Poole as they got up, and stretched their limbs.

'I believe he said "loyalty".' Lear shrugged.

'That's a concept from the past.'

'Confidential, he said.' Lear looked at Poole. 'Sounds dodgy.'

'So?' asked Poole, fed up with the whole thing. They had both had an arduous day. 'Let's get to the pub. Mine's a double.'

Lear nodded. 'Just watch your back,' he said.

*

It was after midnight when Madson reached the wooden door of the Bella Café. He could see through the windows that there were only about half a dozen people left in the all-night venue. He met Berry coming out.

'No sign of your northern lad,' he said regretfully.

'Did you ask?' Madson had hoped for a lead.

'Didn't need to.' He shook his head. 'I don't recommend the mixed grill.'

'Thanks, Gordon,' he threw at the already retreating back. He turned and entered the café. At the counter he ordered a black coffee, and joined a party of young lads at the nearest table.

'Hi,' he began.

A blond boy wearing eyeliner and lipstick misread the signals and eyed him up, sensing work.

'Hello,' he purred.

'I'm looking for someone.'

'You don't like me?' the boy mewed in mock disappointment.

'He's a bit younger than you,' smiled Madson, partly joining in the game.

'How cruel!'

'His name's Pete.' Madson stated the name clearly, looking about him to see if any of the lads had recognized the name.

'Pete?' piped up a shabbily dressed youth with a mohican haircut. 'Why didn't you say so? Dark curly hair, body like a Greek god?'

'Could be . . .'

'Won Wimbledon and the US Open . . .' teased the boy, enjoying himself at Madson's expense.

'Not Pete Sampras.' Madson sighed, the boys all fell about laughing.

As they laughed and went back to their food and

chatter, Madson noticed the door of the café open and a couple of thuggish heavies march up to the counter and have heated words with the Irish proprietor, who wiped his hands down his apron nervously.

The voices rose threateningly and the proprietor looked scared. But before Madson could think of doing anything, the two men had headed out, leaving the proprietor looking shaken. A waitress went over to see if he was all right, and from their conversation Madson began to work out something of what had been going on.

It was morning by the time Madson got back to the flat. Sarah was standing at the stove looking brighter.

'I'm making breakfast,' she announced. A night's sleep had evidently put her in a better mood.

'Look, I'm sorry about yesterday . . .' she said, as she sat down beside him to eat. 'I know you're just trying to help me. I'll get the new edition of *Loot* today and I'll keep checking for flats,' she said, in a mood to make the best of things.

'Good,' Madson responded, digging hungrily into his breakfast. 'And what's all this?' he said as he noticed a pile of letters tied with red ribbon lying on the table.

'Rob kept all the letters you wrote him from prison. I thought –' Sarah hesitated. She was trying to give him back something of Rob, as he had tried to help her through her grief by talking. 'I don't know if he told you but he used to read them over and over. Especially one you wrote just before Christmas one year.'

Madson was hugely touched. He put down his fork and picked up the bundle of letters. 'Thank you,' he said. He opened one of the letters and began to read it. Tears pricked the back of his eyes. It brought back all too clearly the loneliness of his time in prison, the effort he had made to communicate with his son, the difficulty of building a relationship in the circumstances. He had never known his own father, an engineer who had been killed in an accident when he was very young. With Rob it had felt like the blind leading the blind, but now it was over.

'I wasn't a great dad,' he confessed to Sarah. 'I got better when I went inside. Did he talk about me much?'

Sarah shook her head regretfully, and he noticed that she had put on a bit of lipstick for the first time since Rob's death.

'He talked about the rows,' she said truthfully.

'It wasn't all like that. We were a family once,' he said positively, though he struggled to remember when they had been.

'Rob saw you hit her,' Sarah stated flatly.

'I know. And it's not something I'm proud of. But I didn't kill her. He knew that, didn't he?' Madson looked directly into her eyes, willing her to believe him, to reassure him that Rob had known he could never have done such a thing.

'I don't know, John. Honestly. Rob never talked about it.'

DC Poole, in his regulation Sierra, watched from a discreet distance along the street as Madson strode purposefully across the ground-floor walkway on his way out of the flats. He ran a large hand through his nearly shoulder-length dark hair and waited to see Madson emerge into the street. Madson climbed into the Rover and drove off.

Poole pulled out to follow him through the morning traffic.

Outside an antique furniture shop on the Portobello

Road Madson met up with Berry and Donald. Berry quickly outlined his plan to Madson.

'Can I help?' Madson suggested.

'You're straight out of nick. You're not going straight back.'

'Neither are you.'

'I won't,' Berry reassured him. 'Luck of the Irish.'

'You're not Irish,' Madson pointed out.

'No, but I go boozing with them,' he said conclusively, and pointed Madson up the road towards the market, handing him an extensive shopping list written by Cheryl. 'One good turn deserves another.'

Berry and Donald swept through the doors of the Bella Café, and marched up to the counter at the front, causing a look of concern to spread across the tired face of the proprietor. Berry leant menacingly on the counter. 'Our friend last night – we hear you give him hassle about the cash,' he paused, and then whispered confidingly, 'the special insurance policy. Not on, son . . .'

'Who are you?' the café proprietor blustered.

'Oh, you know who we are,' said Berry confidently. 'We're here to tell you the next time you get lippy with our friend, the special insurance goes up, maybe so high you can't afford it.' He blinked. Then in a low growl he threatened, 'Then you've got problems.'

The café proprietor was desperate. 'I've already got problems. I can't pay. I can't!'

'So pack your bags, piss off,' Berry suggested in as nasty a voice as he could muster.

The café proprietor opened the till with a loud ting. It was virtually empty. 'Look!' he said, waving a hand in the air for emphasis. 'You can tell Mr Dartnell I haven't got it.'

Berry put a warning finger up to his lips. 'Sssh!' he whispered unpleasantly.

The café proprietor was clearly frightened, but he shrugged hopelessly. 'Every time he puts up the price. I can't pay it.' He shrugged again.

'You want me to say that, exactly that?' Berry repeated, as if this were a ghastly threat. Donald nodded silently, his teeth bared. Berry gave Donald a knowing nod, and they turned on their heels as one and headed for the door.

They picked up Madson from the corner of the market on Westbourne Park Road, where he was waiting with an assortment of fruit and veg in mint-green carrier bags. Berry was already dialling on his mobile phone.

'Well?' Madson asked, as Donald loaded the bags into the boot.

'Whether he's paying it or not, the Irish gent is getting protection from the Dartnell organization,' Berry summed up briefly from his position in the front passenger seat while he waited for the phone to be answered.

'So who are they?' Madson asked, as he climbed into the back seat.

'You have been away a long time,' Berry said, surprised that he had managed to miss the notorious Dartnell. 'George Dartnell,' he filled Madson in. 'Every whore, pimp, copper, knows him. Shy sort of geezer. Doesn't like publicity. Has a finger in the vice game all over town.' Madson was not fazed. 'How do I get to him?' he wanted to know.

'You don't,' Berry replied crisply. 'But I know a man who can,' he added quickly as his phone was at last answered, 'Gerry, Gordon here,' he said into the little mobile, fending off Madson's questions with a raised hand. 'The favour you don't owe me,' he joked. '. . . yes you do, son . . . No, you're not saying that. I'm saying that,' he paused for effect, 'and I'm collecting . . .'

Berry clicked off the phone as Donald sped through Ladbroke Grove with cheerful abandon, honking at a car which had double-parked on Oxford Gardens. Berry turned to grin at Madson in the back. 'Got him,' he said.

Unknown to them, D C Poole was hot on their tail. He followed discreetly in an unmarked police car. A Pentax swung low round his neck; at any suitable juncture he fired off shots of Madson and his companions, following Rourke's instructions to the letter.

Poole was still following Madson, now alone in his Rover, when he navigated the junction by the Hampstead Pond, slid through the narrowed road beside the pub, and drove out into the generous sweep of Bishop's Avenue. Madson gaped at the enormous properties on the avenue – London's answer to Beverly Hills, he thought. He drove slowly now, searching for a particular house. He paused, and turned into a long drive which swung round and up to the front of a large house. From the number of builders' and decorators' vans parked outside, it was apparent that substantial work was being done on it.

Madson braked and got out. A couple of burly minders came out to greet him – he was expected. Poole meanwhile left his car on the main avenue and moved under cover of the many leafy trees until he could see the front of the house. He clicked some pictures of Madson with the heavies, and then waited in the undergrowth.

Madson was right about the house – once inside, it was clear that it was being completely stripped and refurbished. Builders scurried around in grey overalls. An immaculately suited man of about forty, who

Madson supposed to be Dartnell, stood in the vast entrance hall arguing with the unfortunate architect, who was clearly being given a hard time.

'I said wood,' boomed Dartnell. 'A wood finish. Didn't I say that?' He looked round with a glare, ignoring Madson.

The architect responded bravely. 'You can see the spec. sheet, Mr Dartnell. That's what we agreed.'

'I want wood,' insisted Dartnell. 'What are you going to do about it?'

'We'll have to strip it out and start again. I can do it next Tuesday,' the architect responded.

'Don't give me next Tuesday,' roared Dartnell unreasonably. 'The bloody world could end Monday!' Madson could see that this man was not going to be much fun to deal with. 'Tomorrow. No excuses or you're out!' Dartnell gave the architect a final glare, and looked round to focus his attention on Madson.

'Madson, right?' he queried, turning on his expensive Italian heels and marching out of the room. Madson followed.

Dartnell slammed the door behind them, and the sound reverberated through the house as the two men stood facing each other on bare floor boards in an enormous empty room. Dartnell gave Madson a piercing look. 'You're looking for a rent-boy.' Madson pulled out the Polaroid and showed it to him. Dartnell gave it a quick glance. 'Didn't know you played both sides of the street,' he said flatly. This time it was Madson's turn to be surprised. Dartnell clearly knew about his prison years.

'Not just any rent-boy. Pete. A northern lad.'

'Fancy John Madson finding true love in the Scrubs.' Dartnell was having some fun at Madson's expense.

'I'm doing a favour for a friend,' Madson answered rapidly.

'Name?' barked Dartnell.

'We're not that friendly,' Madson answered, and then eyed Dartnell with some concern. The man had a notoriously short fuse. Was he about to be kicked out, or were the heavies about to enter and give him a good kicking? It was impossible to tell. So he remained silent.

Dartnell smiled a manic smile. 'You ever seen round one of these places?'

Madson was shown round a number of large rooms, some with galleries, others with huge windows looking over extensive gardens and broad window-seats. Eventually they reached a tiled veranda looking out over a marble indoor swimming-pool. They sat down at a table, and smiling, Dartnell casually produced a pack of cards. 'You don't remember me, do you?' he said, enjoying the fact that he was catching Madson out.

'Should I?'

'Early eighties. Just before you went down. We played poker at the Playboy Club. You drew three full houses, four in a row, almost statistically impossible. You don't remember?' He began to cut and shuffle the cards ominously. Madson had hoped to simply get his information and go; this was an unexpected development.

'I remember the cards.' All of a sudden he did remember them, and he felt the itch of the reformed card shark begin to attack his senses. He felt trapped, like a former alcoholic suddenly propping up a bar. 'I don't do that any more. It's over.'

He stood up to leave.

'Jesus, you're touchy. Don't drink so much coffee.' He paused, then slipped in a bet. 'We play for thirty minutes. You win, you get your kid. OK?'

Madson was drawn back. 'And if I lose?'

'You owe me five grand.'

'I haven't got five grand,' he said.

'I'll take it out of your wages.' So that was what he was after. It was ironic that just at the moment when he was trying to get work on the right side of the law, he should be offered employment in the criminal underworld. 'I can always use a guy like you,' continued Dartnell. 'Company car. Private medical insurance. You seen the NHS waiting-list?'

Madson didn't respond.

'You want the information, don't you?' he hissed.

'I do,' Madson admitted reluctantly.

'Then sit down.' Madson still stood uncertainly; he had not played poker for eight years. 'No play, no say. Come on, Madson. What are you frightened of? You're a pro.'

Was a pro, reflected Madson. Was he going to play this crazy thug, and win? Or was he going to fail Sir Ranald and kiss goodbye to a legal career for good? He sat down, picked up the cards, fanned them out and surveyed his hand. Suddenly it was as if he had never been away.

Still waiting in the bushes D C Poole stretched his stiffening legs, flexed his fingers and yawned. He thought longingly about the Big Mac he intended getting from McDonald's for his lunch. He adjusted his camera, ready for anyone who emerged into the daylight.

At long last he was rewarded by the sight of Madson and a dark man in a slick suit talking animatedly and shaking hands on the doorstep. He fired off a dozen shots before Madson got into his car and drove away up the driveway.

*

As Madson sat in the Rover in the usual traffic jam on Hampstead High Street he felt a mixture of emotions, both pleasure at winning the poker game so seductively easily, and confusion at being sucked back into that world so rapidly and unexpectedly. He was determined to discard his past, not be destroyed by it.

His mobile burbled into life just as the traffic began to move again; he flicked the switch on the phone.

It was Dartnell who spoke: 'This kid. He's called Peter Nolan. 14 Ruskin Street, W9.'

CHAPTER SIX

'Peter Nolan, yes?' Madson had been waiting in his car on Ruskin Street, and got out as he saw the dark-haired youth, his sad face by now familiar from Haldane's snapshot, walk towards number 14 carrying a sports bag. He grabbed the boy as he made as if to run away.

'I've got no money,' he yelped, struggling against Madson's grasp. 'I've got nothing.'

'Pete?'

'Yes.'

'I think you may be able to help us with our inquiries.' Madson said sternly.

'Shit! Cops?'

Madson let go of him and smiled. 'Not exactly.'

Pete was only slightly mollified when Madson explained his mission from Haldane. Reluctantly he invited Madson in.

The bedsit was not far removed from a squat; food in one box, clothes in another, a bare light bulb hanging from a cobwebby cord in the centre of the ceiling. A kettle sat on the rough wooden floorboards. Pete bent down and switched it on to make tea.

'I've got no milk, no sugar,' he warned casually, without apology.

'How old are you?' asked Madson, ignoring the matter of condiments.

'Twenty-two.'

Clearly Pete was not twenty-two. Rob had been twenty-two and in comparison he had been a grown man. This lad was considerably younger. He looked up at Pete with scepticism bordering on sympathy.

'OK, I'm seventeen.'

Madson nodded; this was more like the truth. He waited for Pete to continue.

Pete looked down at his grubby trainers. 'I was a footballer. YTS at Leyton Orient,' he explained proudly.

'You've gone up in the world since.' The words were out before he realized it; immediately he wished he could take them back. There were many kids in desperate situations these days.

'Huh?' Pete looked up at him in confusion.

'What happened?' Madson began again. Pete poured boiling water into two chipped mugs containing used tea bags and deliberated whether to tell the whole story. Could this man be trusted?

Pete handed Madson a mug of tea, and they both sat down on the floorboards, leaning their backs against the wall while they drank.

'I didn't grow,' said Pete dejectedly. 'They said I wasn't big enough. Or fast enough.'

But Madson knew a thing or two about football. 'That's no substitute for skill.' He said reasonably, 'If you're good enough you're big enough.'

'Where've you been, man?' Pete was incredulous. 'It's not like that any more.'

Madson sighed; he had indeed been out of it for some time.

'Why didn't you go home?' he suggested. Then, gently, realizing that something must be amiss to bring him so far away from home on his own: 'You got family there?'

'Oh sure. Me dad's not been sober since me mam died,' he said bitterly.

'When was that?'

'1987.'

'Bad year, 1987,' reflected Madson, almost to himself. The year of Elizabeth's untimely death, and his own conviction.

'They split us all up,' continued Pete, eager now to tell him the whole story. 'There was seven of us. I was the youngest. I got the treatment. From the brothers. At least I get paid for it now.' He looked up nervously, but Madson felt only sadness for him, not disgust.

'I'm sorry,' he said inadequately.

'Why should you care?'

'I'm sorry Orient let you go,' Madson replied, trying to lighten the atmosphere. 'You look like you could have been a nippy Billy Bremner sort of player.'

'Who's he?' queried Pete.

'Tell me about the judge,' said Madson, deciding they had better get down to business. 'What happened?'

'He hurt me. He's a sick bastard,' Pete said in a hard, pained voice, full of hatred. He sat for some minutes, smouldering in silence.

Madson waited patiently, drinking his barely tolerable mug of tea, the horrible tea bag still bobbing about.

At last Pete, tears streaming down his face, began to fill in some of the grisly details of Haldane's sexual predilections, the dressing up, the caning, the humiliation. His back had ached from the blows he had received from Haldane, and he had not been able to sit down at first. Now he was merely bruised and the cuts were healing.

Madson had to remind himself that he had been employed by Sir Ranald to sort out this mess for the judge. With this in mind, he spoke carefully to Pete.

'If you go to the papers they won't believe you. It's your word against his. He's a High Court judge. You know how the world works.'

He looked uncomfortably at the tear-stained face. Pete, pulling himself together, got up in silence, and went over to his jacket, which hung over the single chair in the corner of the room. From an inner pocket he pulled out an audio cassette. He looked over at Madson and smiled oddly. 'I got proof though, haven't I?'

Despite the uncertain bravado of the blackmailer, Madson was sorry for the boy, and as he got up to leave he began to work out a plan that would benefit him.

In a darkroom lit only by a dim red light, DC Poole stirred the photographic paper around in the development fluid, concentrating intensely. As he watched, the two faces of Madson and Dartnell began to appear.

Madson stood, rather uncomfortably, in the library at Judge Haldane's house. Haldane sat behind his stately desk, on the telephone to Sir Ranald. As he waited, Madson looked round at the shelves full of legal tomes, and shivered slightly as he recalled Pete's graphic description of his nights there.

'You've got a little treasure here, Ranny . . .' Haldane was busy singing Madson's praises. 'I know you did and I'm grateful as always, dear boy,' he continued. 'Least I can do is a recommendation for leniency.' He laughed. 'No, I wouldn't dream. Tell him yourself. Oh and love to the beauteous Kate. Goodbye.' He hung up, and without looking round at Madson, left him standing awkwardly while he gathered together ten bundles of notes from a locked drawer and placed them on his desk. Finally he turned to address Madson.

'Are you sure this boy won't come back again?'

'He's a kid, not a professional blackmailer,' Madson stated flatly. 'He's just a kid.'

'You're very trusting for a criminal. There you are. Ten bundles. Fifty £20 notes in each. Count it if you like.'

Madson looked at him with dislike, and placed the bundles of cash carefully in a zip-up bag he had brought for the purpose. He did not take the time to count it.

'If you can't trust a High Court judge . . .' he began with a shrug.

'Our relationship is at an end, Mr Madson,' Haldane cut in harshly. 'I wish you well in your future career. You will forget you ever came here or met me. I trust I will not see you in front of me in the dock.'

Madson picked up the bag and departed, glad to see the back of him.

As Madson put the Rover into gear and pulled out into the street, a black Mercedes, parked a hundred yards further back and concealed behind a milk float, took note and began to indicate it was moving off. Unaware that he was being followed, Madson turned left at the end of the street and headed for Ruskin Street.

A dozen drying photographs of Madson and George Dartnell were strewn across a Formica table in a disused interview room at the Organized Crime Squad. Poole stood pondering their purpose as D C Lear burst in looking for him.

'Jesus!' exclaimed Lear, stopping in his tracks at the sight of the photographs and blowing cigarette smoke directly over a large red 'No Smoking' sign on the wall. 'You know who this is, don't you?'

'Rich geezer,' responded Poole coldly. 'Hampstead way.'

'When's Rourke back?' smirked Lear, realizing the full implications of this scoop.

'He's not back till tomorrow. Why?' Poole asked, a touch of suspicion creeping in to his voice. He did not want to let Lear get the better of him again, but none the less he was curious.

'You just gave him the best birthday that bastard ever knew!' Lear bounded off without enlightening him further.

Madson pulled the wads of money from his zip-up bag while Pete watched in astonishment; he had never seen this much money before. The joy on his face was that of a child let loose in a sweet shop, dazzled by the mounds of pink sugar cane, sherbet and chocolates. Sternly Madson advised him about putting it into a building society. But Pete's eyes had grown huge, and he was hardly listening. He looked up at Madson. 'I'm gonna buy some wheels and a suit, ten suits, and then I'm gonna get pissed!'

'That's a much better idea.' Madson sighed, and turned to go. It was no use trying to reform the young.

Then Pete looked up from the frenzied counting of his money, realizing that thanks were in order. 'Listen. I didn't think you'd do it. But thank you.'

Madson nodded. Then he ventured, 'Trust me enough to give me the tape? He's paid you. I got you what you asked for.' He hesitated. Then he scribbled his mobile number on a piece of paper pulled from his pocket. 'Anything happens, ring me on this number. OK?'

Pete looked at Madson's sober expression. He unzipped the inner pocket on his leather jacket, and held out the tape to Madson, taking the phone number in exchange.

'Where's the duplicate?' asked Madson, catching him off guard. Pete raised an eyebrow, as if surprised. Madson smiled. He was glad this particular mission was over; now he could go and cook himself some dinner.

The kitchen looked small but friendly when Madson got back. He quickly got out pans, chopping board and vegetables, and began to prepare a favourite recipe he had learned at cookery classes in prison. He put some water on the stove to boil, adding a pinch of salt, and began to chop onions, tomatoes and peppers finely on a wooden board. As he worked he reflected sadly that he had heard an MP on the radio only that morning saying that education cuts in prison would not be noticed by the inmates. But they were not going to have the chance to learn to cook as he had. Spending more hours banged up in a cell could only result in resentment and riots, he thought.

As the sauce began to simmer, the door opened and Sarah came in, her eyes ringed with tired lines.

'You're just in time,' Madson greeted her cheerfully. 'Ten minutes and it will be perfect.' He ignored her lack of communication, and asked, 'Find anything?'

Having had a dismal day, finding neither work nor accommodation, Sarah felt a failure, and did not want to talk about it. 'No. And I'm not hungry. I just want a drink,' she said, opening the fridge and pulling out a beer. Sometimes she wished she could just be alone.

'I'll make you some tea,' Madson suggested brightly, thinking the beer might not be such a good idea.

'Stop it.' She turned on him as she took her first swig, directly from the can. 'I told you, I don't need this.'

With that, she turned her back on him and switched on the transistor radio, tuning it to loud pop music.

'Do we have to . . .' he turned from his cooking, waving a wooden spoon wildly in the air to indicate the radio.

At that moment his mobile burbled into life, and he pulled it from his jacket pocket.

'Hello? Pete! What? I'll be right there.' He clicked off the phone, and put it back into his pocket thoughtfully. Pete was calling from St Mary's casualty department. Something had gone wrong.

He turned to Sarah as he headed for the door: 'I'm going out. Just keep stirring for five minutes.'

'I'm not hungry,' came the defiant response.

'I don't care what you do with it. Throw it in the bin if you want. Open another beer, score some dope, get stoned, why not?' He swept out angrily.

The casualty department was predictably chaotic. People waiting in sorry lines at the reception desk, others sitting impatiently on hard metal chairs. Bypassing the system, Madson walked quickly along a row of cubicles separated by drab green curtains. At last, at the far end of one row he found Pete. Madson stepped back in horror as he opened the curtain and found him. Pete had been badly kicked and beaten, he was appalled at the swollen, bloody mess they had made of the lad's face.

Pete looked him straight in the eye. 'I thought you said I could trust you.'

'I . . .' Madson faltered under the desperate gaze. 'I had nothing to do with this. I want you to believe me. It's important.'

The boy regarded him in silence.

'Where's the money?' Madson queried.

'Where do you think?'

'They took it?' Madson was incredulous. Had he been followed? Haldane was clearly even more of a bastard than he had suspected.

'My name is Peter Nolan. I am seventeen years old.' The young voice was loud and clear on the tape recorder in Sarah's kitchen. Madson rewound the tape quickly and inserted a blank cassette in the other side, and then pressed the play and record buttons at the same time. He went over to the stove to check the damage to his culinary efforts as he listened to the recording.

'. . . I come . . . from nowhere. Barnsley I suppose. On Tuesday, October 3rd, 1995, I went to the house of Judge Haldane in Belgravia. He made me dress up as a schoolboy. I taped what he did to me. He's a dirty, vicious old man.'

The sound quality on the tape changed, and Madson could hear the muffled, but unmistakable sound of Haldane's voice.

'You are an evil and wicked boy and I have no choice but to cane you. You will receive six strokes. Bend over.' It would have been ludicrous, thought Madson, if he had not known just how real the incident had been. He listened with increasing disgust to the voice drone on and to Pete's screams. He looked again at the burnt remnants of the cheerful dinner he had been cooking, and scraped the lot into the bin. He decided to go back to Belgravia and confront Haldane.

The confrontation in Haldane's library proved fruitless. Haldane refused to accept any responsibility. He had paid £10,000 and he knew nothing of any attempt to get it back. Madson did not believe him. Haldane's parting words had been, 'I don't need lessons on civic virtue from a criminal like you. Now get out of my house before I have you thrown out!'

It was nearly nine o'clock by the time Madson showed up with his twin tapes on Gordon and Cheryl's doorstep. Berry greeted him warmly and showed him into the cluttered lounge. Berry as always was happy to help Madson with anything he needed, but this particular mission surprised him. 'You want me to take this down to Wapping?' he said incredulously. Madson was busy sticking down the buff-coloured envelope containing the audio cassette, and addressing it to Miles Bradshaw at the *Sun*.

'Why am I doing this anyway?' Berry asked suspiciously, the warm scent of his dinner wafting enticingly from the kitchen.

'He'll print the story,' explained Madson, 'but I don't want him to know it's from me.'

'Who is this geezer?' He read the envelope out loud: 'Miles Bradshaw?'

'Crime reporter.'

'You've met him?

'We had differing views on my case.' However, he knew that Bradshaw was the sort of journalist who would love this particular sex story, and for all he cared he could elaborate on it as much as he liked. Cheryl put her head round the door, her blond pony-tail bobbing about, her hands full of cutlery as she began to set the table in the kitchen.

'You'll stay for dinner, John?'

'What is it, love?' inquired Berry, wondering whether he could defer his trip to Wapping until later.

'Steak and kidney,' Cheryl called through cheerfully.

Berry groaned a theatrical groan, which brought Cheryl laughing back into the living-room. 'Plenty left when you get back,' she smiled.

'Oh great! I'm stuck in traffic in Wapping and you're here guzzling steak and kidney.'

'With mashed potato and cabbage,' she teased.

'I appreciate the sacrifice, Gordon.' Madson cut in seriously, with a smile.

'Is it too late for me to change my mind?' he begged.

'Go on,' said Cheryl fetching his coat. 'I'll keep it warm for you.'

'You'd better,' Gordon responded suggestively, kissing her fleetingly on the lips before departing into the night with the package.

Cheryl blushed. 'It'll be ready in twenty minutes,' she said as she went back into the kitchen to finish the cooking.

Madson sat down on the sofa, feeling the tension in his back evaporate at the thought of a job well done. His mind turned to the more relaxing subject of a woman. Magda. He was a trifle surprised at himself; after all, he had been away a long time. But now he thought longingly of her curvaceous figure, delicate china-doll face and pink lips. Throwing caution to the wind, though she was the contact through whom he was hoping to get a job, he pulled out his mobile phone and dialled her home number.

'Hello? Oh hi. Where are you?' Magda greeted him warmly. The strains of Mozart wafted gently through her flat.

'I was just thinking,' said Madson casually into his mobile, 'I'm not too far from you. I was wondering if you'd like a drink or something . . . ?' Though he was spinning an old line, he was, he realized, not in fact that far away; Magda had what must be a St John's Wood or Maida Vale telephone number – only minutes from Notting Hill.

Magda took a sip of her wine, and smiled to herself. 'I'd love one. In fact, I'm drinking it.'

'Well I can buy you another,' Madson said. 'Or if you want to be egalitarian about it you could buy me one,' he joked.

She snuggled down on the sofa, enjoying her wine and this pleasant flirting, but she pondered, should she invite him round? After all there was Geoffrey to consider – would he be hurt? Geoffrey was busy in the kitchen putting together the salad, and a lasagne was keeping warm in the oven. He was an old friend, and she considered him as such, but deep down she knew he wanted more and it would be tricky to invite another man. Her mother liked Geoffrey, who had a safe job in the City. Fortunately, thought Magda, her mother remained safely in Poland, and she could pursue her career, and her taste for 'unsuitable' men as her mother persisted in calling them. Feeling rather pleased with herself at this particular moment, she decided to risk it.

'I'd love to but I'm with someone,' she explained. 'He's cooking dinner. Do you want to come over and have a bite with us?'

Suddenly he felt foolish. For no concrete reason he had presumed she would be alone.

'Thanks, I've already eaten,' he said quickly. 'Look, I'll see you in the morning. And I'll buy you lunch.' He snapped the phone off.

'Madson?' Magda hung up her receiver slowly. Surprised by the haste of his departure, she found she was strangely disappointed.

Sarah stumbled yawning into the bathroom in the morning dressed only in her bra and pants; she had drunk one too many beers the night before and was nursing a slight hangover.

'Jesus! There's a lock on this door!' she said in embarrassment as she found Madson already inside, semi-dressed and shaving.

'I don't like locks,' he said mildly, as she fled in search of her dressing-gown. After the years in prison, he preferred to leave doors ajar. He followed her out into the hall, his face still half-covered in shaving foam.

'I'm sorry. I didn't mean to embarrass you,' he called. He had hoped to start off on a better footing today. 'And I'm sorry about last night,' he said conciliatingly as she appeared again, now dressed in a cream cotton robe decorated with black Chinese letters.

'Me too,' she agreed. 'I let your dinner burn, didn't I?' She looked down apologetically.

'It's OK. I had steak and kidney pie.' He dismissed the subject of last night's failings with a smile.

'There's a friend of mine, Dominic, his dad's a record producer,' she began shyly, but eager to impart some good news at last. 'He rang last night when you were out. Some friends of theirs, they've gone back to the States. There's an empty flat. It's got two bedrooms. We can have it for six months. It sounds great but I've learned not to get my hopes up.'

'It sounds good.' Madson was indeed pleased, this would save them a lot more worry and legwork. 'It's our lucky day!' He grinned at Sarah, feeling slightly silly standing there half-shaved and in his vest.

'How do you know?' she countered, smiling back.

'The sun's out,' he said flippantly, his mind playing on the prospect of Haldane's ruin as he turned and hurried back into the bathroom to finish his ablutions.

In Belgravia, there was a surge of activity later that morning, as a growing crowd of reporters and photographers gathered outside Judge Haldane's house, and TV news crews jostled for space on the front steps with agency cameramen. All were poised for action, like coils waiting to be sprung. The tension was tangible.

A copy of that day's *Sun* lay trampled and dirty, casually kicked into the gutter. The headline was 'Top Judge in Rent Boy Sex Scandal'. At that moment the judge's car swung into view and drew up outside his house. As he got out and fought his way grimly through the scrum, the journalists hurled questions at him. 'What did the Lord Chancellor say, judge?' 'Do you intend to resign, judge?' 'Did you know sex with a young boy is a crime?' The voices merged and swam around Haldane, as he struggled to his front door, furious and humiliated.

Madson waited calmly in reception at Hearnley & Partners. He was beginning to feel familiar and at ease there. He had arrived within half an hour of Sir Ranald's telephone call, dressed sombrely in a suit. He did not really expect a cordial reception, but he had acted according to his conscience. Sir Ranald must at least intend to hear what he had to say.

Magda suddenly emerged from her office, and spotted him in reception.

'Hi!' She greeted him warmly. 'You should have come over last night. It was only a friend. Do you want a coffee?' She looked about unsuccessfully for a secretary to help her.

'Maybe later. I'm waiting for Sir Ranald.'

'Oh?' Clearly she had not listened to the news that morning.

'He rung me at home half an hour ago.' She looked at him in surprise.

Five minutes later Madson was shown into Sir Ranald's office. There was an ominous silence as he stood uncomfortably by the door. Eventually Sir Ranald looked up and gestured for Madson to sit down. Slowly he screwed the top back on to his pen.

'Mr Madson,' he began, 'yesterday at four o'clock I received a phone call from Mr Justice Haldane complimenting you on a very professional piece of work. This morning at eight o'clock I received another phone call at home of a rather different tenor. Quite spoiled my breakfast.'

Madson was well aware that this was the sort of interview where he was not expected to contribute very much. However he felt he must say something now. 'I'm sorry,' he said into the pause.

'Indeed.' Sir Ranald waited a moment and then continued. 'Mr Madson, I thought I made it perfectly clear that Jonathan Haldane needed particularly diplomatic handling.' He emphasized the 'diplomatic'.

'Yes,' Madson agreed, diplomatically, looking about him at the vast panelled office, discreet but 'good' paintings hung tastefully on the picture rail. This was the place where he wanted to be, the firm he longed to join, and yet he wondered about Sir Ranald.

'Yet,' Sir Ranald continued, 'you took it upon yourself to release certain confidential items to the press last night.'

'I was having dinner with friends last night,' Madson assured him politely. 'I don't know how the press got hold of the story.'

'I'm impressed with your initiative, Mr Madson,' Hearnley said suddenly, to Madson's surprise and relief. 'Very commendable.'

'Thank you.'

Sir Ranald stared at Madson with a beady-eyed intensity, perhaps checking that the man was not sending him up. Madson returned the gaze unblinkingly, awaiting the final verdict. Troubled, Sir Ranald got up and wandered over to the window, from where he could look out at a view stretching along the Thames. 'I'm sure you appreciate,' he said carefully, 'that on certain occasions discretion is the better part of valour.'

Madson, though disappointed, was realistic. He stood up to leave.

Hearing the scrape of the chair Sir Ranald turned quickly from the window to face him. 'Where on earth are you going?' he said, not apparently having intended the interview to end.

'I'm sorry,' Madson said, in confusion. 'I thought you'd decided I wouldn't fit in here.'

'Oh, sit down, sit down! You're obviously a useful chap. We could do with a useful chap in this firm. If you would like a job with us as an outdoor clerk I'll take you on. There will be a probationary period of three months.'

Madson was stunned. He sat down.

'I retain some doubts . . .' Sir Ranald added, frowning. He raised an eyebrow. 'I am given to understand you have some trenchant views on the British legal system.'

'Yes . . .' Madson said. He sensed that this would not be the right moment to air his views; in his mind's eye he could see the job offer being swiftly snatched back.

Sir Ranald smiled. 'I would be interested in hearing them . . . sometime. Meanwhile . . .' He stood up and held out his hand. 'I think you owe Miss Ostrowska a small debt of gratitude. She has been quite an advocate for you.'

Madson shook his hand. 'Yes. I know. Thank you.'

'Welcome to Hearnley & Partners.' Sir Ranald gave a watery smile as Madson departed.

*

Along the manicured footpaths, Madson walked in silence beside Magda. He had not yet told her his news. His head buzzed with a confusion of euphoria and panic. He had talked his way into a top firm of solicitors, had his foot on the bottom rung of the ladder.

'Oh come on, Madson,' Magda broke into his thoughts. 'Tell me. Is it a job? What?'

'It's going to have to be a wine bar rather than a restaurant,' he teased, jostling her playfully along the path.

'Why?' She frowned slightly, not getting it.

'You know what they pay outdoor clerks?'

Magda hugged him, delighted. 'You did it!'

'I think *we* did it,' he said gratefully. 'Thanks, Magda.'

They hurried up the path, and through the Temple courtyards towards a suitably cheap venue. Magda chatted as they walked: 'When do you start? Did he give you an office? God knows where you're going to work! It'll be a broom cupboard somewhere knowing that lot . . .'

As they reached Chancery Lane they spotted a newspaper seller hawking the first edition of the *Evening Standard*. The white billboard read, 'Sex Scandal Judge Resigns', in bold black letters. Magda turned to look quizzically at Madson, and he smiled back at her.

A blue Ford Sierra followed undetected behind them, pulling up quietly in sight of the wine bar. The large blond head of DI Rourke could be seen at the wheel. On his face was a smirk, in his hand a collection of clear photographs of Madson in the company of the notorious George Dartnell.

CHAPTER SEVEN

The dozen guests ranged around the generous walnut dining table in Richard and Elaine Dews's dining-room had reached the coffee and port stage. Uniformed maids hired in for the evening bustled about clearing plates and replenishing the drinks. Richard handed round cigars to the men, several judges and MPs, and sat back, lighting up his own cigar and puffing contentedly. Madson had found the invitation slightly daunting; when Elaine suggested he come with Magda he found himself taking the time to think first before accepting. Where once he might have seen himself as an equal guest, though admittedly in a rather unorthodox profession, now he was too close to his prison days to see himself as anything but the underdog amongst the top brass, a convict in the company of the law. His life was moving and changing so rapidly he had barely had a chance to blink since his release. He sipped at his port, rolling it around his mouth to savour it. But despite the delicious wines and cordon bleu cuisine, Madson felt stressed, tense under the pressure to perform.

Glancing across the table at Magda, he observed with appreciation her elegantly swept-up hair, and noticed with affection the few strands beginning to escape on to her cheek. His eyes followed the line from her neck down to the swell of her breast as she leant forward, her black dress falling slightly away revealing perhaps more than she might have intended. She was engaged in animated conversation with a judge whose nose and cheeks glowed from overindulgence, her brow creased by a little frown of concern.

'Take the young offender,' she was saying. 'He's sentenced. They lock the door on him.' She leaned towards the judge earnestly, her wine glass glowing ruby red in the candlelight. 'That's the end. Why he did it is never discussed.'

'Come, come,' chided the judge, 'you're talking about these people as if *they* were the victims. I've sat on the Bench for thirty years. I'm telling you, not one crime is without its victims.'

'Your honour,' Magda replied, her voice still angelic, though it wobbled slightly with drink, 'if the system goes on this way, we'll have a nation of victims.' She sat back sharply for emphasis.

'Nonsense, my dear,' the judge responded with a practised sweep of his hand; this was the sort of issue that he had often been called upon to discuss. 'Every year crime is increasing. Some people attribute this to some sort of social phenomena. But that's nonsense – if an old woman is mugged for money to buy drugs, there is one victim, not two.'

Elaine came to Magda's rescue, smoothly carrying out her duty as hostess. 'I don't think Magda is saying that,' she said pleasantly.

'I believe she is,' the judge retorted.

Madson leaned across the table, raising his voice slightly to make himself heard over the general contented hubbub of noise. 'Nothing is solved by locking problems up in prisons!' They all looked over at him with interest. 'Keeping people there, letting them out, locking them up again. What's the point?'

The judge was aware, as they all were, that Madson had experienced the prison system from the inside, and indeed that he had only recently walked free. But he felt obliged to press his point. 'I may be a judge but I'm also the man in the street,' he reasoned. 'And we all want our cities, towns and villages to be safe. People who won't obey the law must be excluded from society. We have a system that goes back a thousand years.' He looked round at his audience with piercing eyes, and drank deeply from his glass of port. 'And it is just,' he threw in emphatically. Then he continued more mildly. 'The innocent are free to walk the land; the guilty are locked away from them. How can you argue with that?'

Elaine felt obliged to question his logic. 'I know a lot of judges,' she said. 'They nearly all went to public school and Oxbridge, to the Inns of Court and then on to the Bench. That's not the man in the street.'

'I know who Gazza is,' the judge retorted with puzzling logic. 'I don't accuse women who have been raped of provoking their attackers.'

'This isn't personal, your honour,' Magda felt bound to reassure him.

The judge turned to her confidingly. 'I don't enjoy sending people to prison but if the jury finds them guilty, prison is the best place for them.'

Elaine cut in, 'If there were more judges like you that might be an argument.'

'Now who's personalizing it?' he smiled. He was fond of Elaine and had kept company with Richard for many years at the club. 'The point is,' he continued, 'for all its imperfections, the system works.'

Clearly Madson could see that it did not work. He had spent eight years in prison for a crime he did not commit. This had not been justice. He looked sceptically at the judge. The judge returned his gaze sympathetically. He knew Madson's story and regretted it. But Madson could not believe that this man, his role enshrined in the system, cared.

The diners began to filter through to the living-room where more coffee was being served. Some guests carried their drinks in with them. Madson stood beside the fireplace sipping coffee and making small talk with a couple of other guests who were more interested in discussing the Ashes cricket tour than in matters legal. Hailing originally from Yorkshire, Madson had once had quite a bit to say about the subject, but recently the movements of Michael Atherton and Graeme Hick had passed him by as he focused on the more pressing matter of his law degree and his appeal. Elaine came across the room to him bearing a fresh pot of coffee. He accepted a refill with a rueful grin. 'I'm sorry. Some of these people make me angry.'

'Poor old Judge Barrett. He's actually quite a reformer.'

'He'd like to reform the Third Reich,' Madson snapped, not pleased to be told what to think.

Elaine was cross. 'I have to talk to Dame Elizabeth,' she said vaguely, moving off, coffee-pot in hand, to attend to another of her guests.

Having watched this exchange, Magda approached Madson with a friendly query. 'You're enjoying this?'

Madson was tired, and he was beginning to feel that the strain of the evening was getting to him.

'Do you want a brandy?' she suggested noting the tiredness in his eyes.

'No. Thank you.' He turned and headed upstairs in search of the bathroom.

Madson dried his hands on one of the lavishly heaped towels and glanced at his face in the large framed mirror over the sink. He seemed to have aged; the strain of recent events had been too great. He stepped away from the mirror towards the door, and as he opened it he almost collided with Magda, who was just coming in.

The two of them looked at each other. Magda did not move aside to let him pass. She reached out and put her hand on his shoulder, gently pushing him back into the bathroom, and then moving slowly into his arms. He kissed her, at first inquiring, uncertain, and then more urgently. Eight years of solitude began to fall away and an unaccustomed hunger overwhelmed him. He reached behind her and locked the door, there was no stopping him now. His lips tasted hers; his hands were in her hair, drawing her head back; passionately he kissed her neck. Magda was overcome by the intensity of his need; she began to pull at his shirt but already his hands were lifting her skirt as he pushed her up against the mirror. She could feel his cock pushing against her, pressing between her thighs. In an instant he was inside her; he let out a groan, a guttural sound like a wounded animal, releasing all the emotions of his years in prison.

They slid spent to the carpet. He let out a sob, and she clutched his head to her. The door handle rattle. They ignore it, lost momentarily in the aftermath of their passion. Less than three minutes had passed. All the years of pain released by this moment. An image of his dead wife flashed through his mind, the judge passing sentence, the cold prison cell, his son.

In the gloom of the badly lit suburban street, with its neat lawns and parked cars, a man was running frantically, a slightly podgy man in jeans and a black bomber jacket. He skidded round a corner and into a street heavy with traffic, and dodged in and out of the cars as he crossed to the far side of the road. When he came to the steep main road, panting heavily, he began to walk more slowly, trying to thumb a lift. A big container lorry pulled in and he climbed in beside the driver.

Some time later the lorry stopped and the man jumped down, thanking the driver with a waved salute. The lorry headed off into the night, and the man began to jog down the deserted lane in search of a telephone box. When he found it, an old-fashioned red telephone box, the man entered and felt under the pay-phone unit with his gloved hand. He tore out two taped-up packages and examined the contents; one contained cash, the other a Smith and Wesson .38. With an expert eye he checked the chambers; then, picking up the telephone receiver, he punched out a number.

In the living-room of Mrs Holland's Willesden semi, the grey-haired Mrs Holland was sitting in her green Dralon-covered armchair, her feet propped on a leather pouffe as she watched the end of 'Nine and a Half Weeks', for the third time. The phone rang and she answered it distractedly. 'Three nine three seven. Hello?'

'Is Caroline there?' A gruff, but all-too-familiar voice came down the line.

'No,' she answered shortly, suspecting the worst, but hoping she was mistaken.

'And how are you, Angela?' he sneered. 'Forgotten the voice?' he said casually into the silence, enjoying her shock.

'Is that Barry?' How could he be phoning, she wondered.

'Brilliant!' he said, in a voice full of disdain. 'I'll tell you where I am. I'm in a phone box in Reading. Listen to this.' Before Mrs Holland had a chance to be any more surprised, there was a bang and a reverberating crash. Then the rough voice came back on. 'I'm out. I've got a gun and I'm coming to London to kill your slag daughter.' The phone was replaced.

Mrs Holland sank down in petrified silence. Then,

taking a deep breath and gathering her wits together, she dialled her daughter's number.

Caroline Rowe answered the phone from the depths of the beige duvet in her lover's bedroom. Paul was already snoring, but Caroline had not felt like sleep and was browsing through a copy of *Cosmopolitan* she had picked up at the tube station. She pulled the warm duvet up around her naked shoulders as she heard her mother's voice. Then suddenly sat bolt upright. 'What . . . ? Escaped? You called the police?' she screeched in panic. 'You do it. Do it now . . . !' She leapt out of bed, sending the covers flying and waking Paul. 'Get up. Get dressed,' she shrilled hysterically. 'Barry's out!'

At 7 a.m. Sarah was already up and engaged in painting the living-room fire surround in the new flat. Her energy and zest for life had been somewhat restored by the move, and she had decided to make the most of the place for the six months that they had it. Madson came in buttoning up his shirt, already mostly dressed for his first day at Hearnley & Partners.

'You're up early,' he said.

'You were back late?' she answered quizzically, pretending to be a stern parent. 'I heard you come back.'

'Interesting night,' he replied without giving away any details.

'First day at school?' she suggested, noting the tidy suit and the early hour. 'Yes,' he confessed, realizing how odd he felt about it. Before his years in prison he had always shied away from regular hours, preferring the gung-ho world of the night-club gambler.

'I've invited Dominic for dinner,' Sarah added quickly as he turned, about to go and make himself a cup of coffee in the kitchen. 'Can you join us?'

He looked round at her with a frown, unsure who she was talking about.

'His dad's the one who got us this flat, remember?'

'Oh right,' he said vaguely; in his mind he had not reached dinner yet. 'Sure, that's fine.'

He walked round to the kitchen, and then changed his mind about the coffee, deciding he did not after all have enough time. He pulled on his jacket and headed out into the morning drizzle.

At the reception desk at Hearnley & Partners Madson found a startling orange pot plant awaiting his arrival. He looked at the card as the receptionist handed it over: 'Good luck, John – from Gordon and Cheryl,' it read. He smiled and picked up the plant, tucking it under his arm as he walked across to Magda's office.

Madson rapped on Magda's door briefly, and strode in. No point being bashful about last night's episode he thought to himself.

'Oh, you shouldn't have . . .' she said looking round from the window where she had been gazing dreamily out at the busy street.

He was confused by this, and then looked with silent embarrassment at the plant in his arms. Clearly she thought he had brought it for her. He opened his mouth to explain, but words failed him; it seemed too silly. Instead he began, 'About last night . . .'

'You don't have to say anything.' She looked at him reassuringly.

'Yes I do,' he retorted, feeling a need to explain his actions.

Magda looked at him, and then said with great gentleness, 'It's OK.' Then she caught sight of the card with the plant and read it out loud. She laughed at her mistake.

She had a lot of paperwork to get through that morning and an appointment with a new client at eleven. 'OK,' she said, leading him to the door. 'Ranald wants to see you, and there's a consultant here, Cara, who's going to show you the outdoor clerk stuff, and then you'll meet the other partners.' She swept out, leaving him to follow her up to Sir Ranald Hearnley's office.

Hearnley waved them briskly into his vast panelled office. He came straight to the point.

'My partners and I have decided how you will function here. When you're doing what we will call your "investigations", you'll enter in a daily diary that you're working on a particular matter, and give an estimate of how long you think it will take.'

'Yes.' Madson nodded gravely, a picture of Berry and Donald and their investigations coming unbidden into his mind.

'As you know,' Sir Ranald continued, 'we've not employed a full-time outdoor clerk before.' He paused, as if searching for an explanation. 'We've always used law agencies. But our consultant, Cara Wilton, seems to know all about it. She'll show you the ropes.'

'Thank you,' Madson said, and they turned to go.

Sir Ranald looked up again at Magda. 'When you have time,' he called, 'can we have a chat on the union funds business.' He returned to the clutter of case files on his desk.

It smelt horribly of stale urine in the gentlemen's toilet on the second floor of the Organized Crime Squad's dilapidated headquarters. Rourke crinkled his nose in distaste as he entered the white-tiled suite, unzipped his trousers and pissed into the urinal. As he stood there it dawned on him that there was probably a connection between a certain criminal and the warehouse drugs case he was investigating. It had been preoccupying him for some time, and now he suddenly felt sure that he had the missing piece of the puzzle. He smiled smugly to himself.

As Rourke was washing his hands, Poole came in and availed himself of the facilities. Standing at the urinal, he called over his shoulder to Rourke, 'Guv, your ex just rang.'

'Let me guess,' Rourke suggested sarcastically. 'Maintenance payments or mortgage?' He sighed, his mood plummeting. He had been married to the woman for the best part of twenty years, but they had hated each other for at least ten of them. Sadie Rourke had been a pretty, curly-haired nurse when he met her, and they had soon fallen in love and married. She had given up her job to have children, which they had failed to do, and there had been bitter recriminations. He had done more and more overtime, to avoid the accusing home atmosphere, and it had not only been disastrous for their marriage but had caused physical battles as well. This had led to a bitter, shameful break-up and subsequent divorce. Now she did battle in the only way she knew, through his wallet.

'Oh yes,' Poole added, 'Superintendent Burridge rang as well.'

'So?' said Rourke, impatient to hear the verdict.

'Eleven fifteen with him and the top brass at Chief Superintendent Walton's office. Both of us.'

Rourke left the room silently, a worried frown on his forehead. This was not what he had planned.

Cara Wilton was a trim twenty-six-year-old; she wore her hair in a stylish bob and her skirts were just a trifle too short. As she spoke on the telephone in her small office, Madson noticed that her lips were painted an ebullient red, to match the equally brightly painted fingernails which held the receiver. Magda caught him looking, and he blushed.

Cara was saying, 'Right, we'll need another twenty-eight days. No one's dragging their feet. We want this to go to trial as soon as possible.' She looked up with a smile.

Magda made the introductions, and returned to her own office. She had a busy morning ahead of her.

As Cara led Madson down the corridor they met one of the partners, the jocular Nigel Alwyn, who was one of the more senior partners.

'Good show,' he said, shaking Madson's hand warmly. 'Never understood why we didn't have an out-door clerk. Ranald has spoken about you. You've got a law degree, yes?'

'Yes, sir,' Madson nodded gravely.

'Useful around here. No one seems to know anything about it.' He paused to laugh uproariously, then stopped when he saw the blank look on their faces. 'That was a joke,' he explained mopping the tears from his eyes with a large handkerchief. He headed amiably back to his office.

'Copyright, libel,' Cara informed Madson, nodding at Alwyn's retreating back. 'He's the best.'

'Next,' she said moving on down the corridor and tapping briskly on a door, 'Jock Grigson.'

Grigson was of a similar vintage to his colleague Nigel Alwyn, and equally approachable.

'Ranny told me all about you,' he said, looking at Madson. 'You've got quite an interesting CV, haven't you? Look forward to a long chat with you at some point.' He grimaced at the pile of papers on his desk and the flashing light on his telephone. 'You'll have to excuse me,' he said finally, with a smile. And Madson, hovering uncertainly near the door with Cara, felt relieved that here was someone who truly welcomed his presence at Hearnley & Partners; he had braced himself for a less positive response.

George Lodge kept them waiting when Cara led Madson into his office; he was dictating to his secretary. 'The writ was delivered on the 27th, to be returned on the 24th. We have been given no reason for the litigant's failure to appear in court.' He was thin-lipped and humourless, and looked about forty; his hair was already thinning on top. Madson feared that he could expect the sort of reaction from this man that had worried him from the outset. Lodge continued his letter without looking up. 'I must inform you that your company will have to carry all costs if he does not turn up at the new hearing, on the 7th. Yours, etc.,' he concluded, dismissing the secretary with a turn of his head.

Cara took the initiative. 'Mr John Madson,' she said formally, 'Mr Lodge. John is starting today as our out-door clerk.'

'I'll have papers for you to deliver to Southwark Crown Court. Come for them at 2 p.m,' he said briskly.

'John will also have other duties,' Cara said, tactfully.

'So I hear,' Lodge replied shortly. 'Sir Ranald said something about them. I doubt I'll be using his so-called expertise.' Lodge turned dismissively to Cara. 'Ring me later, Cara. We have to discuss this Costigan business.' The telephone rang and Lodge answered it; Cara chaperoned Madson out.

Outside Caroline Rowe's two-up, two-down council house on the edge of a large estate, the street was buzzing with uniformed activity. A black Transit van was parked squarely opposite her front door, and a marked police car drove down the road and drew up, causing neighbouring net curtains to twitch. DI Mostyn emerged from the police car and stretched his limbs, looking about him expectantly.

Two uniformed policemen came over to greet him. 'Any sign?' queried Mostyn.

'No, sir,' the taller of the policemen replied smartly.

'Any calls to her?' he asked. Rowe could be in France by now. The policeman shook his head.

Mostyn entered the house. He found Caroline Rowe in the living-room, speaking on the telephone and in a state of considerable distress. 'Mr Lodge?' she said shrilly into the receiver. Mostyn waited for her to finish. 'My name is Caroline Rowe. I've just been talking to Sir Ranald. He asked me to tell you about my husband Barry . . .' For many years Caroline's mother had worked as a cleaner at Hearnley & Partners, and had often told her stories about the solicitors there and the work they did.

Mostyn cleared his throat, deciding that it was time she explained the whole story to the police; perhaps she had missed some vital detail that would lead them to Rowe.

Having introduced Madson to the other partners, Cara led Madson up a second and considerably narrower flight of stairs to the very top of the building, to see what was to be his own office. She smiled at him brightly, and mentioned tactfully that he probably wouldn't be spending much time there anyway. There was no other office space available for the moment.

Madson was in fact slightly taken aback when he saw the windowless cubby-hole of a room, dominated by a monstrous copying machine. Still he reflected, there was a desk and a chair, and he had grown used to living in a restricted space. He almost laughed as the thought struck him – it was just like the 'home' he had endured over the last eight years. He put the bright plant down on one corner of the desk, which gave the room a more friendly aspect. Cara waved her arms about, indicating the room. 'We'll get some furniture in,' she indicated confidently; 'pigeon-holes for the post, shelves and so on.' She paused, and added, 'And you'll be supplied with a cellular phone.'

'Right,' he agreed, taking his coat off and settling in, as she briefly described the usual duties of an outdoor clerk. The job seemed to consist of such things as sorting and stamping the mail, organizing the ledgers on the various cases being dealt with, and keeping a basic diary of his own movements and times in and out of the office.

He had just sat down when Sir Ranald appeared, breathless, in the doorway. Madson gave a start of surprise.

'Ah, Madson. Good. Glad you're here. I've just had a call from Caroline Rowe. Her mother used to be one of the cleaners here for years,' he blustered. Madson thought he detected a hint of embarrassment. 'Lovely girl. Watched her grow up, you know. Husband's a bad lot, I'm afraid; record of violence as long as your arm. Two years into a nine-year sentence for GBH. He's escaped from jail. It appears he's coming to London to shoot her – Caroline. I've asked Mr Lodge to look after her. Could you go along with him?'

Hearnley left as swiftly as he had come. Well, well, thought Madson, wondering briefly about Sir Ranald's affection for the former cleaning lady. Anyway, he considered, as he took his coat off its hook and put it on, it looked as if the day would prove to be livelier than he had expected.

Madson stared out of the taxi window en route to the Ealing housing estate. The Uxbridge Road looked grey and unpromising, rows of newsagents' and shops with vegetables piled in boxes outside and handwritten notices in the windows. Lodge had been extremely grudging about Madson's presence on this mission; he obviously would rather have handled the matter on his own and had advised Madson in no uncertain terms to keep his mouth shut when they met the police dealing with the case. Now he sat glaring on the back seat, as far away from Madson as could be achieved in a black cab.

The taxi pulled up outside the house and they got out. George Lodge instructed the cab driver to wait for them, and they headed up the short path to the front door. The police outside watched them suspiciously; Mostyn greeted them with a hostile, 'Yes? What's your business here?'

'Who are you?' Lodge responded belligerently.

Mostyn reached into his breast pocket for his ID with a slight frown.

Lodge waved him briskly aside. 'Hearnley & Partners, lawyers representing Caroline Rowe. I'm here to see her.' He marched in determinedly, Madson following in his wake. Mostyn directed one of the uniformed men to accompany them.

It was with considerable relief that Caroline let them in to the house. She led them into the living-room for a more private conversation, Lodge insisting that the policeman remain in the hall.

Caroline outlined her situation quickly, explaining

about her difficult husband. 'Last time I visited Barry, in prison,' she explained, 'he said I'd been fooling around with other blokes. But I haven't. He's bloody paranoid. And now the police are here' – she indicated the back and front of the house, waving her arms in frustration – 'and they won't tell me anything.' She ran her fingers through her thin blond hair, causing it to stand on end.

'All right, Mrs Rowe,' Lodge said in a stern but placating tone. 'We'll sort this out.'

Out in the backyard, which consisted mainly of a rotating washing-line and a few pots of sad geraniums standing on a seventies concrete terrace, Madson looked over the low wooden fence, and a plain-clothed policeman in the adjoining garden returned his stare. He looked around, over the other fences in the row, and into the alley beyond, but could see no other signs of life. He went back into the house to rejoin Lodge and Caroline. Lodge was just asking whether Caroline had been ordered to stay at home. 'Inspector Mostyn told me to stay in for me own good,' she responded unhappily.

Madson was looking around the simply furnished, uncluttered room; there was a modern three-piece suite in dusky pink and a vast up-to-date television and video in matt black. A few photographs were arranged on the mantelpiece. He picked up a framed photograph and turned to Caroline. 'This a photo of your husband?'

She nodded. 'Yes. That's him.'

Madson gestured to Lodge to come out with him into the hallway. 'I don't like this,' Madson confided, once they were out of earshot. 'The place isn't secure. These look like local noddies, unarmed. We should get her out of here, as fast as possible.'

Lodge looked at him sternly. 'I told you, I'll make the decisions.'

But nevertheless Lodge took Madson's advice, though without giving him any credit for it. He instructed Caroline to pack a small bag, and swiftly they escorted her from the house to their waiting taxi.

Mostyn was furious. 'What are you doing?' he bellowed at Lodge.

'Mrs Rowe is not charged with anything. I'm not satisfied with her security here,' he said pompously, handing Mostyn his card. 'She'll make herself available as and when you want her, if you telephone the number on this card.'

'Tell me where you're taking her,' insisted Mostyn as they climbed into the cab.

Lodge rolled down the window and leaned out as the driver started the engine. 'We're going to look for a hotel. When we've found one we'll let you know.'

DI Mostyn watched impotently as they roared off down the street.

CHAPTER EIGHT

Nothing happened. Rourke kicked the coffee machine in frustration, and suddenly hot brown liquid began to pour out over his shoes. He jumped back. His only fifty-pence piece wasted, he looked down with annoyance at the messy stain on his left shoe. Then sat down to wait, on one of the four metal chairs positioned in a line outside the OCS conference room. He fiddled with his watch irritably; he hated summonses which came out of the blue.

Six top brass from their division came walking down the corridor, towards the conference room; clearly there was a problem. Rourke looked up at them; Superintendent Burridge, his immediate boss, was one of their number, the only one he knew. Burridge nodded at him as they went past him into the room. The door closed sharply behind them.

Photographs of Madson with Dartnell were passed round the conference table. AC Walton of the Flying Squad handed them to Burridge for his inspection. 'Fortunately, Mr Burridge, these snaps were spotted in the photo lab, last week,' he said severely. 'They were taken on the instructions of one of your team, DI Rourke. Explain.' He waited, tapping his fingers on the polished table.

Burridge improvised. 'I believe,' he said slowly, 'that Rourke was carrying out a surveillance on a known criminal, George Dartnell, and his meetings with another known criminal, John Madson, reference our interest in Madson and his possible involvement in Soho.'

AC Walton gave him a hard look, and raised an eyebrow. 'This Madson,' he began sceptically, 'won his appeal against a life sentence at the High Court three weeks ago. Rourke was involved in his original trial' – he paused to let this sink in – 'and in fact faced a disciplinary hearing as a result of the evidence he produced at that trial.' Walton raised his voice sarcastically. 'Let me put a scenario to you. Madson's released. Now Rourke decides to sort him out, perhaps involve him in some business with this Dartnell.'

Burridge jumped in rapidly in Rourke's defence; he could not let it be believed that one of his officers had got himself into such a mess. 'I don't think that's the case at all, sir.'

Outside the conference room Rourke strained to hear what they were saying. He heard his own name being mentioned a couple of times, and he began to fidget nervously, glowering down at his shoes.

Walton meanwhile continued to give Burridge a hard time. 'Listen to me,' he said. 'Let's stop pissing about. Early this morning Darrant here' – he indicated the police officer at the far end of the table – 'interviewed one of your Jacks, the one who took these photos. He told us most of what we wanted to know. But it still leaves me with a few questions.'

Burridge supplied most of the information, but on one point thought he had better check the facts with Rourke. He stepped out into the corridor where Rourke was sitting. He was too angry with Rourke for deliberately compromising himself and the department to offer any helpful explanation. 'Your DC Poole took surveillance snaps of Dartnell and Madson,' he barked indignantly. 'On how many occasions? Once or several?'

'Once,' Rourke confirmed. 'About ten days ago. Let me explain.' But Burridge went back into the meeting.

Walton explained the situation to Burridge in no uncertain terms. 'Dartnell is one of our key target criminals. Whatever his sodding agenda is, if your DI Rourke goes within spitting distance of Dartnell again, we'll have him out, and for good. Convey that to him,' he finished flatly. The high-ranking officers all got up smartly and left the room.

Rourke was relieved to see Burridge coming out, after the others. 'What's going on?' he asked nervously. Burridge did not beat about the bush. 'Dartnell's a top target. They had Poole in. Poole must have told them you were trying to roll up Madson in some involvement with Dartnell.' He looked at Rourke in annoyance. 'They want your guts,' he finished. He was in fact very angry that one of his officers could be so stupid.

'Will this be taken any further?'

'I honestly don't know,' Burridge replied.

'Poole!' Rourke fumed. 'I can't work with him again.'

Burridge sighed. 'I'll move him,' he said.

Rourke began to calm down. Realizing that he had put Burridge in a difficult position, he asked, 'What about you, sir?'

'You shouldn't be asking, Dennis.' He looked at Rourke, and shook his head despairingly, but with a slight smile. They had known each other for a long time, both as colleagues and as friends. They had dealt with many cases together, and downed a great deal of whisky and many pints of bitter; they had kept each other company over the difficult years of Rourke's divorce and Burridge's wife's illness.

The two men stood silent. Finally Burridge offered Rourke some advice: 'You want to stick one on Madson. There are other ways. Subtler.'

At the travel agency near Folkestone Harbour, a well-built man came in asking for ferry tickets to Boulogne, going on by train to Paris. The young agent noticed that the man was rather dirty and dishevelled. He began to fill in a form, and while he was about it Barry asked in a friendly tone, 'While you're doing all that, can I use the phone, mate? Short call,' he added. The agent nodded distractedly and Barry crossed the room to an empty desk, picked up the receiver and dialled.

'It's me,' he said. 'Everything okay?'

'No,' snapped Ronald Rowe, Barry's cousin, from behind the bar of a north London pub. He was heavily built, over fifty, and wheezed slightly as he spoke.

'What's going on?'

'You've got a problem. You'd better get back here.' Ronald was not at all sure what was going on, but he was not going to say so. He had made the arrangements for Barry, and had expected it all to go smoothly. Unfortunately, for no apparent reason, Caroline Rowe had disappeared from the scene.

Barry replaced the phone. He sighed; it was clear that he would have to go back. Damn, he thought to himself; then he turned to the agent. 'Sorry,' he said, 'changed my mind.' He fled out into the street, and was gone before the travel agent could even look up.

Outside a small, rather seedy hotel in a square in Bayswater, Madson asked the taxi driver to stop, and he and

Caroline Rowe got out. Lodge rolled down the window, calling out to them, 'I've got to get back to the office. Let me know when you've set things up properly.' The taxi drove off up the road towards the junction with Westbourne Terrace and turned right. Almost immediately, a blue Ford turned into the square and drove slowly in their direction. Madson and Caroline had just reached the stone steps of the hotel when they spotted the car, with Mostyn in the passenger seat, bearing down on them. The police car pulled in at the kerb. A uniformed policeman emerged from the back seat, got out of the car and took up his station by the front entrance to the hotel. Then the police car pulled away, leaving him there.

Madson and Caroline walked up the stairs, which were covered with heavily worn red carpeting. Madson unlocked the door of room 23, and they walked in. In one corner there was a mini kitchenette; otherwise the room contained a bed with a nylon bedspread and a single chair. The bathroom, they had been informed, was communal. Caroline's face was a picture of disapproval.

Warning Caroline to phone no one but him, Madson handed her a card with his mobile number.

'Why can't I phone?' Caroline whined.

'You're upset, you might tell someone where you are, someone who your husband might contact,' Madson explained reasonably. He looked at her with compassion, and added more positively, 'We'll assume Barry will be picked up shortly. I'll ask reception to send up some tea, OK?'

Caroline looked doubtfully about the unappealing room; what on earth was she going to do here?

'It'll be fine,' Madson assured her, assuming that she

was thinking of Barry and his gun. 'He'll be picked up. You'll be out of here in a few hours.'

He hovered momentarily by the door, and then left with a shrug – she was safe for the time being. Glancing at his watch, he realized that he was going to be late for lunch with Berry. He hurried down the stairs, and out on to the street to find himself a cab to take him to Notting Hill.

In a workmen's café on Ledbury Road Gordon Berry and Madson sat eating shepherd's pie and drinking steaming mugs of milky tea, surrounded by men from the local building sites. Berry was pleased to see him; he had thought that Madson might not be so friendly now that he had started a job with a firm of solicitors. It had been Cheryl's idea to send him a plant, to show that they approved of his leap on to the other side of the fence.

Berry pulled a set of keys from his pocket with a smirk of pleasure. 'I brought you a Merc.' He winked. 'Get it back to me by the weekend.'

Madson desperately needed Gordon's help, in a matter which was not entirely legitimate. Berry had once robbed a bank, or at least had boasted of it, and Madson wanted to get hold of the papers from his original trial. Presumably they would be still filed away in a back room at Hanley, Gardner, Green, Solicitors. Berry eyed him incredulously as he explained about the need to break and enter – one moment his old pal was whiter than white, the next he wanted to rob a bank.

'I'm not going to rob a bank. I just want your advice. Advice . . .' he emphasized.

Because of the heavy traffic in the Edgware Road progress was slow. Madson drove, and Berry sat beside him in his snappy suit and dark glasses, both sombre and dignified, like a pair of gangsters or American film directors. After the junction at St John's Wood the traffic began to move more freely; soon they were speeding through Kilburn, and on to Cricklewood Broadway.

They parked in a side street, and then walked up the Broadway, stopping on the corner between McDonald's and a makeshift market. Madson looked at the sign on the building on the opposite corner: 'Hanley, Gardner, Green, Solicitors and Commissioners of Oaths'.

Madson at last began to tell Berry what he was up to. 'Eight years ago those people, who were supposed to defend me, did some deal, I don't know what, with Inspector Rourke. At some point I have to get into that building.'

'The door's open,' Berry said reasonably.

'No. Somewhere in that building's my file. And somewhere in that file is the explanation of why I went down. They won't hand it over if I just ask them for it.'

'Shufti?' Berry suggested.

They strolled casually across the road, politely helping a girl get her pram up on to the kerb.

Casting a professional eye up at the windows of the large thirties office building, they walked past it and round the corner. 'Not brilliant,' Berry commented, squinting up at the side of the building. 'All windows, Bolton and Paul steel latticing.' Madson looked doubtful. 'You know,' Berry continued; 'latticing drawn across when the office closes, then deadlocked. A bugger. Might have a go in office hours?' he suggested.

'Not on, Gordon. I may need a few hours inside.'

Gordon continued his examination of the building. He noticed an odd corner jutting out at the back. 'One small ray of hope . . .' he began, walking further along the side road and looking thoughtfully up. Madson followed his gaze. 'Up there,' Gordon indicated. 'Flat roof. Toilet window. Won't be steel latticing on a toilet window – even in Cricklewood,' he added with a grin. They stared for a moment up at the tiny frosted window and the drainpipe running down to the ground. Gordon looked pleased with himself, but Madson was sceptical.

'Come on Gordon,' he said disbelievingly. 'That opening is twelve inches by maybe fifteen. No one can get in there.'

He paused, but Gordon was not put off. 'Let me think about it,' he said, beginning to work out a plan.

Madson decided to leave it at that. He had brought Berry here to seek his advice; now that Berry had taken stock of the situation he would come up with something.

Dressed in a white towelling bathrobe Caroline walked self-consciously past the policeman who stood on guard in the passageway, clutching her damp flannel and soap bag. There was no privacy, she thought. Then she tripped over a jagged hole in the worn carpet just outside her room, letting out an undignified whimper.

Back in her room, she reached across the bed to retrieve Madson's card, picked up the phone and dialled the mobile number.

'I'm frightened!' she screeched when he answered. 'I can't stay here. I go to have a shower down the hall, and the cop that was outside the hotel . . . he was standing there. What's he here for?'

Madson sighed; he would have to go back and get her. He had hoped she would stay there quietly until Barry had been found and taken safely back to prison. 'Take it easy,' he said, the phone wedged under his chin as he indicated and swerved to the right off the main road. 'I'm on my way . . .' A dark blue Toyota estate with a boat on the roofrack hooted as he turned up

Blomfield Road. 'I'm coming,' he muttered into the phone, switching it off.

'Trouble?' suggested Berry, amused. But Madson had regained his composure. 'All in a day's work for an outdoor clerk,' he said.

When Madson reached the Bayswater hotel, he found Caroline sitting in her room watching a television she had wheedled out of the receptionist. She was dressed in her blouse and blue jeans, and appeared to have calmed down. 'So, what's the problem?' he asked.

'I know he's going to find me. I don't trust this place. I'm not staying here.' She looked him in the eye, and then added challengingly, 'I'm checking out. I'm going home.'

'No,' Madson said firmly, his mind racing through the possibilities. The police? Would Berry and Cheryl look after her? Then it occurred to him: Sarah. Caroline did not look much older than her, and they might get on. Talk to each other.

'Give me a minute,' said Madson, placating her. 'You have to stay away from home for a bit longer.' He picked up his cellphone and rang Sarah.

Outside the council house in Ealing, Barry Rowe crouched behind a neighbour's fence surveying the scene. He had hurried back on the train from Folkestone, after the cryptic conversation with his cousin, thinking that he had better find Caroline. The house looked abandoned and empty, though he could not be sure. On the other hand there were quite a few policemen about; and children would soon be coming home from school. He retreated into the undergrowth and crawled back the way he had come.

*

The foreign receptionist looked up at Madson as he pulled out some money to cover Caroline's hotel bill. 'Mrs Rowe made three phone calls, one long-distance.' She pointed out the additional charge on the handwritten bill, and Madson pulled another note from his wallet. He was startled for a moment; he had told her not to make any calls.

'Can I have the details?' he asked hopefully.

'We don't keep records, except how many units,' she answered disappointingly.

'I see.' Madson pursed his lips and paid the bill. He did not see. Why would she deliberately endanger herself?

When Madson arrived at the flat with Caroline, a tall, thin man in his mid-twenties was helping Sarah. Dominic, Madson assumed, taking an immediate dislike to him. Had he been a friend of Rob's or Sarah's?

'Come in,' Sarah said with a welcoming smile. She introduced Dominic to Madson; he did not look as welcoming as she had done. He looked like a born-again hippie, in worn-out jeans and scuffed sandals.

'I'm really sorry about Rob,' Dominic began nervously.

Madson was sceptical. 'Hang on a minute,' he said. 'I have to show Caroline the room.' He swept out of the living-room, with Caroline and Sarah following.

'I've made up the bed,' Sarah said reassuringly to Caroline. She had been quite moved when Madson had phoned her and told her the story. 'I hope you don't mind sharing with me.' Sarah pointed to the mattress she had made up as a bed on the floor. She herself was left with the divan base and a blanket for the night.

Caroline smiled hesitantly. 'All right . . .' she said, in a voice which was not quite all right.

'Sure?' said Madson kindly.

'Yes, I suppose so.'

'Right then, girls,' said Madson with a smile, 'I'll try to be back for dinner. I've got to drop some papers off at Southwark . . .' He left them to sort things out, reasonably confident that Caroline would cheer up in the company of people of her own age.

Before going back to his office at Hearnley & Partners Madson took a diversion past Sainsbury's in Ladbroke Grove, and turned in through the tall iron gates of Kensal Green cemetery. He felt the need for a short walk. And not only that, he felt suddenly lonely. Sarah seemed to have found a new friend, he thought bitterly, and he was left alone to bear his grief. He strolled down a path, picking a red rose from a bush that some other mourner must have planted and thought about the day. He focused on the grim facade of Hanley, Gardner, Green. That, he felt sure, was where his answers lay. Where he had once felt like a ship blown off course, he now could feel the wind taking him in the right direction, towards discovery and revelation. He was both desperate for information, and frightened of what he might turn up.

He sat down on a patch of grass beside the grey stone crypt of some long dead family, and pulled off the silky petals of the rose one by one. He thought of his dead wife, and then of Magda, and he smiled. Perhaps he was not alone after all. She would be expecting to see him at the office. He had a job, and he had friends. Berry was probably ready with a plan for breaking into the solicitor's. Pulling himself to his feet and brushing off the dirt from his trousers, he turned to go back to his Mercedes.

On the corner of Cricklewood Broadway Berry and Jenny, a young girl in jeans, her hair in a pony-tail, munched hamburgers thoughtfully on the pavement out-side McDonald's. As dusk fell they made their way across the road and round the back of the building. Berry waited, casually looking at his watch as Jenny shinned expertly up the drainpipe.

CHAPTER NINE

In his office at the Organized Crime Squad Rourke was pacing angrily backwards and forwards across the room as if he were a caged lion. There was a knock at the door and DC Poole entered, like a large mouse scuttling into a trap.

'Nice chat?' Rourke growled, as Poole sat down on a hard wooden chair beside Rourke's desk.

'OK,' Poole said warily.

There was a long pause while Rourke struggled to control his anger; Poole was one of his men, and had wounded him deeply. 'That's not what I hear,' he said at last.

Poole muttered a noncommittal response; he knew only too well what was coming.

Rourke began pacing the room again, and said slowly, 'They said you –' he turned his head to make sure Poole was listening, 'and I'm quoting – told them all they needed to know.'

'It was like the Gestapo,' Poole squeaked.

'Did I say I wanted to hear an explanation?' Rourke bellowed, making him even more nervous.

Poole looked at his shoes. 'No, sir,' he stammered.

'I never want to see you again. You're transferred to Mr Wolfram. I've warned him about you! Get out!'

Still looking at his shoes, Poole got up and left. He was stunned by the unfairness of it all.

*

In the warm kitchen of their new flat Sarah had cooked a simple supper of spaghetti bolognese. Rob had loved it, in the days when he had still had an appetite. She sighed; that life seemed a long way in the past.

She dished up, and took the four laden plates of food to the table in the living-room, where Madson, Dominic and Caroline were already seated.

'So what's your line of work, Dominic?' Madson inquired, helping himself to some green salad.

There was a pause while Dominic finished his mouthful of spaghetti. 'My dad's a record producer.'

This Madson already knew. 'Yes,' he said, 'I've heard about your dad. I'm asking about you.'

Adopting a vague, Bob Dylan manner, Dominic at last responded. 'I've worked all over the music scene, man. I've done tour management...' He munched another mouthful of bolognaise thoughtfully. Deliberately slowly, Madson thought with irritation.

'He's also a performer...' Sarah leaned across the table coming to his rescue, 'drums. Right, Dominic?' She smiled at Dominic.

'Really. What kind of music?' Caroline asked with interest. She was enjoying the meal, and the company, the change from her usual boring routine, was making her feel slightly intoxicated.

'Yeah. Well...' drawled Dominic. 'Heavy Metal really. I've done backing tracks for some of the big boys...'

The party continued to eat in silence. Sarah looked with irritation at Madson. She wondered why he was being so difficult. Why did he have to interrogate Dominic? It really was unnecessary. Dominic was also irritated by the questioning, and began to dislike Madson. Only Caroline was relaxed and keen to chat.

She turned to Dominic enthusiastically. 'It must be fascinating . . . I mean, on tour . . .'

'Oh, it's great fun at first.' He addressed himself to Caroline. 'You know, hotels and all that. But living out of suitcases gets boring after a while.'

'Is that where you met Rob?' Madson cut in.

'We met at a club. He said he'd written some songs and was looking to lay down tracks. I got him the studio.'

'So you weren't into drugs with Rob?' This was what Madson really wanted to know, and it had not taken him very much time to work round to the question. Sarah looked at him startled.

'No,' Dominic replied. He had turned white.

Sarah was furious. She had anticipated a pleasant, friendly dinner, and now it was all being ruined. 'Don't bully him, John,' she said crossly.

'I'm not bullying anyone,' he said flatly, and looked down at his plate, but he had already finished.

'Look,' said Dominic in an attempt to calm the situation, 'I think this would be a good time to get over to the Blast in Willesden. I told Andy we'd be there tonight.' He stood up and began to clear some of the dishes.

'We?' Madson remained seated. Dominic looked him straight in the eye. 'Me and Sarah.'

Madson looked coldly at Dominic. 'Sarah's going to be with Caroline, here . . .'

'Right . . .' Dominic was slightly perplexed, but thought it best to retreat. 'Well, another time. It was a terrific meal, Sarah.' He put the dishes he was carrying down, and looked awkwardly towards the door.

Madson's mobile phone sprung to life with a loud 'bring, bring', conveniently breaking into the charged atmosphere. Madson pulled it out of his pocket.

'Yes?' he said, still with slight irritation. 'Gordon,' he added more calmly. 'Now? On my way.' He switched off the phone and got up from the table with relief. 'I have to go.' He looked round at Dominic who was still standing rooted to the spot. 'Dominic, I'm going Willesden way. I'll drop you off at that club.'

Sarah was annoyed at his presumption. 'Who says Dominic wants to go with you?' she said petulantly.

'What do you say, Dominic?' insisted Madson.

'Sure,' said Dominic, deciding not to become embroiled in this row, 'that'd be fine.'

Dominic picked up his jacket, and the two of them began to take their leave. Madson looked across at Caroline, almost as an afterthought. 'Anything you need, ask Sarah. I shouldn't be long.'

'Night, you two . . .' Dominic muttered inadequately.

'Phone me tomorrow,' Sarah replied.

Dominic nodded as they headed out of the door.

It was quite late by the time Madson greeted Berry in the bar of a pub on the Kilburn High Road which had clearly seen better days. A few serious drinkers nursed their shorts perched on velvet bar stools; some kids were playing the fruit machines. Berry laid out a rough drawing of a basement storage area on the cracked wooden table beside their drinks, and explained: 'There's a Yale lock on the stairs. My associate did that in with a credit card, inserted.' He spoke cryptically, without revealing any details about the 'associate'. 'Then my associate went downstairs, and that's where the files are kept.' Intrigued, Madson looked down at the drawing, studying it carefully. It showed a central corridor with little cubicles labelled 'A to C', 'D to F', right through to 'W to Z'.

'Gordon,' Madson asked, 'how did your associate get into the building?'

'Up the downpipe to the bog window,' Berry said rapidly, looking pleased with himself.

'Not possible,' Madson remonstrated. 'That window was about a foot by fifteen inches.'

'It was possible 'cos it happened,' Berry insisted pleasantly, taking a swig of his drink and smacking his lips with satisfaction.

'Your associate was a trained monkey?' Madson suggested, faintly irritated.

'No.'

'Who, then?'

'Rather not,' Berry finished casually.

'I want you to tell me. I mean it . . .' Madson insisted. What had Berry got him mixed up in now, he wondered.

Berry explained finally. 'In our business we sometimes have to get a small person to break a window, crawl in.'

'What small person?' asked Madson with alarm. 'Come on, Gordon. I want to know.'

In answer Gordon pointed over at the kids playing the fruit machines in the corner near the toilets. 'That small person.'

Madson looked across the room and saw that he was pointing at a slight girl in an outsized biker's jacket and a denim miniskirt. 'She can't be more than twelve. Thirteen?' he said, shocked.

'Course she is,' said Berry confidently. 'She's fifteen, at least fifteen. Lighten up, JP. You've been away a long time. It's all the younger generation now.'

'What's her name?'

'Jenny.'

Berry and Madson got up from their table and strolled over to the far corner.

*

'Jenny,' Berry said.

'Jenny?' Madson tried again more loudly, but she was busy feeding in a string of ten-pence pieces to the voracious machine. Then lights began to flash and images of planes and guns appeared.

'So?' inquired Jenny, her eyes firmly glued to the machine.

'You gave Gordon some information for me.'

'Yeah, I did, Grandad,' she said, glancing at him for a split second.

His eyebrows shot up – 'Grandad'! Surely he was not that old? Feeling tired, Madson got out his wallet, and handed her a wodge of notes, five twenties. 'You climbed the drainpipe, opened the toilet window, opened a Yale lock, all on your own?' He was incredulous.

'No,' she responded sarcastically, pressing the buttons on the side of the machine rapidly to shoot down some Migs, 'Arnie Schwarzenegger come with me.'

'What about the alarms?' Madson asked, looking at the flashing machine with disgust.

'No alarms.'

'You do a lot of this work, do you?' Madson asked casually, leaning on the corner of a neighbouring machine, and trying to get her attention.

'What are you? A TV documentary?'

He was not doing very well with the younger generation that night Madson reflected sadly. He hoped he was not turning into a 'grandad'. 'You got parents?' he persisted, realizing he was digging his own grave. 'You live at home?'

Jenny turned her face to him, for the first time taking her gaze off the screen for a micro-second. She gave him a jaded look. ' "This is Your Life", right?' She turned back to her game.

'It was wrong to do it. Don't break into cars for Berry, or do burglary.'

'Here, hold on!' Berry was aggrieved; after all Madson had specifically asked him to do a job for him. He had no right, thought Berry, to be making such an about-turn.

'Because in the end,' Madson continued, 'they get you, and they keep you. They keep on locking you up until you've got no life left.' Having said his piece, Madson lapsed into a gloomy silence. He had not intended to tell the girl off, but he had seen too many young people in prison who had gradually drifted into crime, and had ruined their lives.

Jenny gave him a long cool stare. 'You're boring,' she said, before feeding more coins into the slot of her monstrous machine.

'Come on,' Berry said, leading him back to their table. They finished their drinks in silence. Berry reached under the table and picked up a plastic carrier bag. 'One more item,' he said playfully. 'While she was about it, she nicked your file . . .' Madson's mouth fell open in astonishment. He picked up the bag and pulled out a brown box file. He looked across the room to thank Jenny, but she had gone.

In the bar at the OCS which remained open as a club late into the night, Rourke chain-smoked a full packet of Dunhill and coughed into his neat whisky. The lights were dim, and he was deep in thought, hardly noticing as Burridge slipped into the bench on the other side of the table from him.

'DC Poole dealt with?' whispered Burridge.

Rourke jumped. 'Yeah,' he growled.

Burridge nodded, taking a deep swig of his single malt. 'I've been thinking about your Madson problem. You know the son died of drugs.'

'Yes,' Rourke responded with an awakening interest.

'Which leaves a daughter-in-law,' Burridge continued,

'Sarah Madson. She was once rolled up with her husband, arrested, fined, carrying a minute amount.'

Rourke looked thoughtfully into the bottom of his glass, hatching the beginnings of a plot. 'Madson's living with her. If I got her for possession on the premises and Madson with her, I get him.'

'If there are drugs on the premises,' warned Burridge, taking the final swig of his drink, and hoping that Rourke would take the cue to order another round.

'Could be arranged,' said Rourke looking up at the barman and indicating that both their glasses needed refilling. Rourke spent many evenings there drinking at the club, and George knew him well.

'You can do better than that,' murmured Burridge unpleasantly. 'Well,' he added with a gleeful slur in his voice, 'planting drugs is step one. But if you're really serious about this, there are plenty of other ways to go.' In his whisky-filled daze Rourke was rather impressed by this, and yet . . . he wondered whether Burridge might have a hidden agenda.

Caroline made large mugs of cocoa for herself and Sarah, and they sat companionably on the mattress in Sarah's bedroom, both quite enjoying the atmosphere of a girls' dormitory. It was a long time since either girl had sat with a girl friend to talk about themselves, and both had been through a difficult time recently. Caroline confessed to not getting out much; even from prison Barry always kept tabs on her. 'He's got friends,' she explained woefully; 'they come over without phoning first.' Sarah was sympathetic, she knew what it was like to be lonely, with Rob's long illness and death behind her. They sipped their cocoas. 'You can have the bed if you want. I'm happy sleeping on the mattress on the floor,' Sarah suggested.

'I'll be fine on the mattress,' said Caroline, embarrassed. They finished their drinks and began to joke about the hotel room where Caroline had nearly stayed. 'Well, it would have needed the right man,' Caroline laughed.

'There's never a good one around when you need one, is there?' added Sarah. They fell about giggling like schoolgirls.

It was good to hear Sarah laugh, thought Madson, breaking off temporarily from his study of the solicitor's file. With a yawn he took off his glasses and put them down on the bedside table; he was too tired to concentrate any longer. He reached out and switched off the little bedside light, and fell into an exhausted sleep on top of his bed, still fully dressed.

The moon shone through the window in the girls' room. Sarah and Caroline lay half awake in their makeshift beds.

'Sarah?' whispered Caroline.

'Mmm?' Sarah was nearly dropping off.

'You still awake?'

'Yes, why?'

'I was just wondering ... does John always talk to you like that?'

'Like what?' Sarah was unsure what she meant, and struggled in her sleepy state to make sense of it.

'Like the way he dealt with Dominic?' suggested Caroline.

'Sometimes ...' Sarah was noncommittal.

But Caroline wanted to talk. 'My whole life,' she explained, 'seems like that, you know, taking orders from men. A month after our marriage Barry started. Shouting and threatening me, and then after he'd drunk too much he started hitting me. He terrifies me.'

Sarah was now more fully awake, she sat up. 'Why don't you divorce him? Nobody could blame you.'

There was a short pause. Both girls lay back on their pillows, thinking, in the dim light.

'I love him,' Caroline confessed, in a small voice.

Madson woke up with a start; he sat up rubbing his eyes, and snapped on the light. What was it, he thought; something had just come to him. He picked up the buff-coloured file, which had fallen to the floor, and began to examine the contents again. Putting on his glasses, he frowned at the pages, turning them backwards and forwards until he realized what was wrong: there were some pages missing. Feeling sure he had made a significant discovery, he put the file down on the floor. Wriggling out of his trousers, he got under the covers and switched off the light. He closed his eyes contentedly.

Early in the morning Madson walked into the kitchen to discover Caroline in Sarah's dressing-gown simultaneously making toast and talking on the telephone. He hovered discreetly at the door and caught the last few words of her conversation.

'Yes,' she was saying. 'Yes ... OK. Yes, I'll be there, midday. Right ...' She looked up and saw Madson by the door, and quickly replaced the receiver.

'I know you told me not to,' she stammered. 'But I had to phone me mum. I know she'd be dead worried.'

'OK,' Madson said tiredly.

'Mind if I use the bathroom?' She excused herself, darting out of the door.

Madson looked after her retreating back thoughtfully,

and poured himself a cup of coffee. He crossed over to the phone, picked up the receiver and pressed the 'redial' button.

'The Warrington. Hello?' said the husky voice of Ronald Rowe.

'Sorry, wrong number,' Madson muttered into the receiver, swiftly replacing it as Sarah came into the room. He wondered about Caroline as he drank his coffee.

'Do you want anything? There's eggs and bacon,' suggested Sarah as she made her own breakfast.

Madson shook his head. 'No, I'm off in a moment. Two of you comfortable last night?' he inquired.

'Yes,' Sarah answered; she had enjoyed the girlie chat with Caroline. 'She told me all about her husband. Five years of hell. Beatings, humiliations. She had to sneak off once and get an abortion because she didn't want a child by him.'

Madson was worried, he had brought the girl into their flat, and now he was unsure about her. 'Sarah,' he warned. 'Just be careful with her, don't buy everything she tells you.'

Sarah looked at him in confusion, which turned to anger. 'You know, you're paranoid about people. Just like you were with Dominic last night! She's had a night-mare five-year marriage. Of course she's all over the place, not trusting anyone, including you. What do you expect?'

But Madson was concerned; he did not want to have an argument about this. He looked at her seriously. 'I'm just saying be careful with her, Sarah.' She looked slightly worried, though still angry, but he patted her on the arm reassuringly. 'See you later,' he said, as he hurried out to his car.

*

The photocopy machine was working overtime, its light flashing like a pinball machine. Now, thought Madson, as he copied the entire contents of the stolen box file, he was really making progress. Now he could begin to put together the pieces of the puzzle. He looked round the small, windowless office, Cheryl's cheerful pot plant the only touch of décor, and laughed quietly to himself.

There was a terrible groan, then a clunk, and the machine ground to a halt. Madson in mid-chuckle looked round with annoyance; it was nearly time for him to leave if he was to be at the Warrington by the middle of the day. He glared at the machine. He tried shaking it a bit but nothing happened; then he gave it a kick. It immediately roared into action and finished the job. Madson rapidly sorted the post into the labelled pigeon holes, gathered up his papers and headed for the door.

From a position fifty yards up the street, Madson watched in the wing mirror of his Merc. as Caroline climbed out of a taxi, and went into the Warrington pub. He waited patiently, watching the door. Minutes later she emerged and hailed another cab. Madson pulled out to follow the cab. It wasn't long before it turned into a wide suburban street. On either side of the street was a row of two-storey, semi-detached houses, each with its own short driveway and a garage.

Caroline's taxi pulled up outside number 101, and she got out hastily, paying the driver through the window. Madson pulled in some way down the street, and watched her stop for a moment to survey the front of the house. It looked like all the others, except that the front door was a dirty green, where most appeared to be blue, and the up-and-over garage door was open. She walked up to the front door, rang the bell and waited. No one came, and she rang the bell again. Then she walked over and peered through a ground-floor window. She went back to the door and tried the bell again.

Meanwhile a red Fiesta drove slowly up the street, reached number 101, and turning into the driveway, drove straight into the garage.

A man came out of the garage and round to the front of the house. Caroline's mouth fell open in astonishment; Barry was supposed to be in Paris. She rushed to greet him and tried to throw her arms round him, but he pushed her off. 'Inside,' he said sharply, getting out some keys and unlocking the door. He almost pushed her in.

Inside there was a single open-plan room on the ground floor, with an open staircase and French windows overlooking a small back lawn. Caroline stood in the middle of the room. 'Barry!' she screamed angrily. 'What the hell?'

'Sit down,' he ordered. 'Open your mouth – you'll get my fist in it,' he threatened, looking very much like he meant it.

'Christ, Barry . . .' she stumbled backwards to an armchair and sat down, frightened.

Madson sat in his car, hesitant. He recognized Barry from the photograph he had seen on the mantelpiece at Caroline's house. But now he looked dishevelled and tired, and Madson could not tell whether he had a gun or not. Madson felt pissed off; Caroline had conned both him and Sarah, but she could well be in danger. Reluctantly he started the engine, and drove the Merc. into the driveway of the house, blocking the garage. He got out of the car and went over to the front windows, but he could not see anything through the lace curtains. Then he noticed a pathway to the left of the house leading to the back garden. He looked around to see if anyone was watching, but the street was deserted.

From his view through the windows at the back of the house he could see that Barry and Caroline were having a nasty row. 'We had it worked out, you stupid bitch,' he was saying, taking hold of the front of her shirt and giving her a shake. 'I break out, the Old Bill think I'm coming to kill you, I get to France, wait for you there. You come when the heat's off . . .'

'That's what I was going to . . .' She broke off terrified.

'And you screw the whole thing up because you can't keep your hands off that wimp Paul Ronson.' He stared at her, white with fury.

'You've got it wrong,' she pleaded desperately.

'No I haven't, you slag. Ron knew at the pub. God knows how many others!' He was beside himself.

Caroline got up from her chair, alarmed by this outburst, and took a few steps back. 'No, no! That's over. It's been over years . . .'

Barry was too upset and enraged to know or care what he was doing; he smashed his arm across her face, sending her with a nasty thud to the floor. 'You slut,' he repeated. She lay in a crumpled heap on the floor, still begging forgiveness.

'I was lonely, just lonely,' she whimpered.

Enraged, Barry shouted at her to shut up; he picked her up and hurled her hard against the wall.

Madson decided to intervene, but before he could do anything Barry had grabbed Caroline and was hustling her towards the front door. Caroline struggled and screamed.

'We'll see your Paul,' Barry shouted as he shoved her out of the door, 'and I'll sort you both out!'

'Barry, don't! Please!' she screamed, as Madson appeared at the front of the house.

'Leave her alone, Barry,' he warned sternly.

'Who are you? Another bastard fuck?' Barry shouted, and stepped forward to attack Madson.

But Madson was too quick for him, and punched straight at the heart, winding Rowe immediately, though he struggled to get up. Madson grabbed him by the scruff of his neck, punched him a second time and then, half-dragging him, hurled him straight into the garage, bringing down the metal door with a resounding crash.

Quickly he jumped into his Merc. and drove it tight up to the garage door, rendering escape impossible. Fists thundered hopelessly on the inside of the door.

Caroline sat weeping on the doorstep. Madson took out his mobile phone. 'You stay there,' he said to her, without much sympathy. What a mess. Reluctantly he dialled 999; with his recent history it was the last thing he wanted to do. 'Police,' he spoke clearly into the phone.

Rourke walked into his office at the Organized Crime Squad smiling inanely. Lear looked up from the side desk where he was sitting catching up on some paperwork. 'You look cheerful, guv,' he said, surprised to see him at all that evening, let alone in a good mood. 'Your missus fell under a bus did she?' he teased.

But Rourke was too smug to care. 'Even better, son,' he murmured with an evil glint in his eye.

The black Mercedes made slow progress through the evening traffic on Kilburn High Road. The traffic lights all seemed to remain persistently on red. And masses of buses clogged the lanes. At last he came to a halt outside a pub and after locking up went quickly in through the doors carrying a package.

He soon spotted Jenny in the far corner, playing the

ghastly electronic machine. She had attained a fairly high score, and her eyes remained fixed on the screen for fear of losing it. He waited near by, watching her while she pushed the buttons, expertly upping her status with the flashing lights and the zany coloured images. Finally, she acknowledged his presence.

''Lo, Grandad – you again,' she said.

Madson reached his hand into his jacket and carefully extracted a hundred pounds in cash. He offered the box file and the cash to the girl. 'Have a nice time,' he said. 'Put it back.'

CHAPTER TEN

It was early morning, and Madson stood naked, staring out of the window of a country-house hotel in the depths of the Kent countryside. In his mind he was still puzzling over the papers in the stolen file, which were now strewn across the top of a white dressing-table. He hardly noticed the intricate lawns and statues of the garden, the few late roses growing against the walls.

Behind him Magda snuggled up under the William Morris bedcover, which matched the swagged curtains at the window. Madson turned from the window, not as yet having found a solution to his problem, and went over to the bed, getting in beside Magda and giving her a gentle kiss on her forehead. He put his arms round her, closed his eyes and drifted off into a light sleep.

Sarah lay sleeping peacefully in Dominic's arms, under her white duvet in the new flat in Ladbroke Grove. Only their tousled dark hair was visible on the pillows; the yellow alarm clock on the bedside table was ticking loudly.

Suddenly they were wakened by the terrible tearing sound of splintering wood. The front door had been broken down and policemen were rushing into the flat, searching it, taking it apart, throwing aside pots and pans, tables and chairs. Unnoticed, Rourke slipped a tiny plastic bag of white powder down the side of an armchair. Sarah and Dominic began to pull on their clothes in panic, wondering what on earth was going on. As they did so the police burst into their bedroom.

The policemen crashed into Madson's bedroom, but it was empty, the bed unslept in. Rough hands pulled the bed apart and emptied out the drawers on the floor.

Rourke and Lear entered Sarah's room.

'Who are you?' Sarah screamed, tripping over her words in her panic. 'What do you want?'

'Where is he? Where's Madson?' Rourke shouted back at her. He was beginning to panic himself. This was not what he had planned: he had come for Madson, not his daughter-in-law. Madson's car was outside, he had seen it with his own eyes, given it a slap as he went past. The man had to be here. He looked about wildly.

Dominic, now properly dressed, had pulled himself together sufficiently to say, in a belligerent tone, 'Look, you can't just come barging in here. Who the hell do you think you are?'

Rourke realized that they had no idea who he was. He pulled out his ID and search warrant. 'Detective Inspector Rourke, Organized Crime Squad. We have reason to believe there are illegal drugs on these premises,' he explained. 'Where is John Madson?'

'He's away for the weekend.' Sarah was crisp. 'What drugs?'

'Let's find out, shall we?' Rourke concluded, with a nasty curl to his lips. They could still make something of this raid, despite Madson's absence.

Curled together blissfully in the warmth of each other's flesh, Madson began to kiss Magda gently on her face, her blond hair, her warm lips. Magda murmured with pleasure, still half-asleep. Then Madson's mobile phone burbled loudly into action, shattering the quiet moment. He reached out and pulled it from his jacket pocket. 'Hello?' he muttered.

Magda opened one eye. 'Did you have to bring that thing?' she said with annoyance.

Ignoring her, he sat up in bed, a look of concern on his face. 'Sarah? What? I can't understand you,' he said. 'Who did? When? . . . Sarah?'

'I don't know where it came from, honestly,' Sarah sobbed into the phone; her eyes were fixed in total incomprehension on the little bag of powder in the policeman's hand. Dominic stood beside her, his face as white as the heroin. 'I've never touched heroin,' she continued, the tears beginning to flow. 'What? I'll ask. Where are you taking us?' She looked across the room at the heavy figure of Rourke.

'Hindle Road nick,' he said with relish, imagining Madson's response.

'Hindle Road nick,' Sarah repeated.

'Us?' Madson queried. 'What do you mean us? Who's he taking? Sarah?' he asked, as Rourke took the telephone from her.

Hurling the telephone across the bed in frustration, Madson heaved himself out of bed and began to pull on his trousers.

By now fully awake, Magda looked at him in astonishment. 'Do you mind telling me what the hell's going on?'

Madson looked down at her tousled head; in fact he was not sure exactly what was going on, but it smacked of Rourke, and bad blood. The very thought of Sarah becoming involved made his heart leap with agitation and fury. 'I have to go,' he said at last, inadequately.

'What? This is our first weekend away together.' But she already knew that the cause was lost, something major had gone wrong.

'Yes,' he replied sorrowfully, as he got the rest of his things together.

She quickly began to pull on her clothes. In silence they gathered up their belongings and checked out of the hotel. Not an auspicious start to a love affair, Magda thought, as they headed out into the driveway to her sports car. Magda climbed into the driver's seat and started the engine as Madson stowed their bags in the tiny boot.

'Can we talk now?' Magda asked nervously, her hair blowing in the wind as they sped up the motorway towards London. She wondered if he was still angry, or just preoccupied. She made a stab at humour: 'It was swept for bugs only last week,' she said, indicating the car. 'Let's try the easy ones first,' she continued. 'Where are we going?'

'Hindle Road nick,' he said flatly. But at least he had spoken to her. 'Just where you want to be on a Sunday morning,' she said, with an attempt at a smile. She reached out as she drove, and put a hand on his, hoping to convey sympathy. He could not even give her the consolation of a grateful look. He knew Magda meant well, but he found himself unable to confide in her. It occurred to him that perhaps he had been locked up for too long, perhaps it was too late, and he no longer had the capacity for sharing his emotions. It came to him bleakly that he did not know how to relate to this woman.

Having collected her five-year-old daughter Michelle from the childminder's, Samantha Conners, Cheryl Berry's younger sister, let herself into the little flat, really no more than a glorified bedsitting room, that the two of them called home. Still in her nurse's uniform from the night shift, Samantha opened the wardrobe to get out a change of clothes. Dolls, books, and a pink Lego model of a princess's castle cluttered the floor.

'Incy wincy spider . . .' sang Sam, engaging Michelle's attention.

'. . . climbed up the water spout!' Michelle joined in with gusto, doing all the actions with her fingers, the rain coming down and the spider being washed out, the sun shining and the spider climbing up again. The little girl laughed with pleasure, and rolled happily on the floor, while her mother finished changing.

Then came a hammering at the door, and a man let himself into the flat.

A tall, well-dressed man in his forties, with lank blond hair pulled back severely into a pony-tail, stood smiling at them. He tossed the door keys irritatingly backwards and forwards from hand to hand.

'What are you doing here?' Sam asked.

'I might ask you the same question,' he said, with a malicious smile on his smooth face. 'I thought we had an arrangement.'

'I thought so too,' she said quickly.

'You broke it,' he retorted.

Sam looked down at her little daughter, who had picked up her Cindy doll and was combing her hair; she was beginning to look nervous. It was clearly no good having this conversation now. Sam banked on Ray behaving decently for once. 'I'm taking Michelle to the park,' she said in a high, strained voice. 'We can discuss it tonight.'

Ray McGreevy remained silent. He stood for a few minutes, still tossing the keys from hand to hand, as if undecided. Sam stood uncertainly, holding Michelle's hand, ready to go out but too frightened of him to move. Eventually he turned and left.

*

'Hello, John.' Sarah greeted Madson with relief in an interview room at Hindle Road Police Station. Magda swiftly arranged for Sarah and Dominic to finish and sign their statements and bail forms so that they could go home. Dominic looked apprehensively at Madson, keeping quiet and as far in the background as he could manage. But Madson had realized that Dominic must have been in bed with Sarah if he was with her at that time in the morning. This was not the time or the place for discussion or accusations, however, and Madson was hardly in a position to make accusations. Magda had been admirable: she had checked the details on the forms and was dealing efficiently with the desk sergeant.

Sarah cried on Madson's shoulder as she finished signing her bail form. She felt terrible about calling Madson back from his weekend in the country, but she had not yet taken in the enormity of her predicament – there would be a jail sentence for possession of that amount of heroin – nor could she understand how the stuff had appeared from nowhere. She caught hold of Madson's arm to steady herself. He looked at her with concern. 'I didn't do anything,' she said in small scared voice, which was muffled in his sleeve. 'I've never touched heroin. I don't know where it came from.'

Madson pulled her close to him and edged her towards the door, turning to bid farewell to the desk sergeant. 'Give my best to Mr Rourke, will you?' he said. It was clear to Madson that this was his doing, and he was furious that Rourke was attacking his family. It would not be the last he heard from him.

Magda, with a shiver, hurried them towards the car; she had looked into Madson's eyes and seen a cold hatred. But all she said was, 'We don't want a parking ticket, do we?'

*

The atmosphere in Magda's car was tense as they drove back along the Marylebone Road. They were all separated by their own thoughts; no one wanted to look anyone else in the eye.

Sarah, sitting with Dominic in the back, was too nervous of Madson to comfort herself by holding Dominic's hand. She could see that Madson was deeply hurt by her involvement with Dominic. Yet Rob had been ill for a long time. She only craved comfort and love, but it seemed impossible to explain this to Madson. He was a man who appeared to need very little, and he had been out of touch with the throbbing world for eight years. She wished she had not fallen short of his expectations. But she felt overwhelmed by all her troubles.

'Where can we drop you off, Dominic?' Madson cut in to the silence.

Sarah took Dominic's hand. 'I need to pick up my stuff from Sarah's . . . er, your place,' he replied.

'What's going to happen to us?' Sarah asked Magda, changing the subject.

'It's me they want,' Madson muttered bitterly.

Magda turned to look at him for a moment. 'It's them who've been charged with possession, Madson. You want to think about them.' They all looked away for a time.

'There was no heroin in the flat,' Dominic declared flatly into the silence.

'It's true, John,' Sarah added. 'I don't do heroin.'

'Rob died of it,' Madson retorted, from between pursed lips.

'Can you think of a better reason?' said Sarah, quietly.

Madson thought about this for a few moments, and began to calm down, accepting the logic of her argument. 'OK,' he said. 'We serve a writ for wrongful arrest.'

He looked round at Magda for support. But she was looking at him in alarm. Serving a writ on a police officer would be opening a very nasty can of worms. He leaned across and gently guided her hand on the steering-wheel to straighten the car. He would get that bastard Rourke yet.

In jeans and a cotton sweater Sam pushed Michelle higher and higher on the swings, her straight blond hair flying out in the wind until she whooped with delight. Then Michelle jumped on to the brightly coloured roundabout, leaping on and off, pushing it round, giggling all the while. Hand in hand they skipped happily out of the playground; for a moment Samantha had forgotten the misery of being a single mother with little money, and a landlord who had not yet been paid. 'Old MacDonald had a farm . . .' they sang, doing silly animal noises and laughing all the more.

As they turned into their street in Notting Hill, Sam stopped still in disbelief. 'What's going on?' she shouted, running across the road, Michelle in tow. Two workmen were throwing all their possessions on to the pavement: clothes, toys, a mattress, all crashed unceremoniously out of the front door. Sam was horrified; she rushed around grabbing things, trying to put them into bags. People appeared at their windows to watch, but no one came to help.

Michelle bent down amongst her toys. 'Mummy, what's my toys doing here?' Sam gave her a hug. She looked defiantly at the men. 'You can't do this!'

'No?' said one of the men, appearing again in the doorway. 'Watch yourself!' he shouted, as he hurled the rest of Sam's clothes into the street.

'No! Stop it!' Sam cried, with mounting hysteria. A lady with a pram came over to try and comfort her; others stood by watching curiously, embarrassed.

'Mummy!' Michelle grabbed on to her mother, terrified.

Dominic was trying to find his things, but the flat had been turned upside down by the morning's stampede of police officers. The others sat dolefully round the table drinking mugs of coffee. Magda had been considering Madson's suggestion. 'In a situation like this,' she said thoughtfully, 'you wouldn't serve a writ on an individual officer like Rourke.'

'But he was the one who did it,' Sarah said logically.

'That doesn't matter,' Magda insisted, taking a sip of her coffee.

'Then who?' asked Madson.

'The Commissioner of Police for the Metropolis.'

'You're joking!' Madson was impressed.

'That's the law,' she smiled.

A pick-up van turned the corner and came to a halt outside Sam's flat. She and Michelle were sitting waiting on the steps, and greeted Berry's arrival with considerable relief. She had called her sister in floods of tears, from the pay phone on the corner, and Berry had immediately offered to rush round and collect her. He was furious; it was incomprehensible to him that anyone could throw a young girl with a child out on to the street. He loaded Samantha and Michelle's belongings on to his van, his teeth clenched in anger. They waited on the steps, Michelle on Sam's lap, until he had finished.

'Right,' he called to them, tying a strap over the top of the load so that nothing would fall out. 'That's everything. Let's go.' As they were making their way to the van, a gleaming BMW swept up to the kerb and stopped. The window descended electronically and Ray

McGreevy leant out, jeering. He did not see Berry, who was at the other side of the pick-up tying the rope. Berry erupted on to the pavement beside him, spitting with fury. 'You piece of piss,' he spat at McGreevy. 'You take my sister-in-law back into that rat hole you call a bedsit or I'll kick the living shit out of you!'

Sam rushed to intercede. 'No, Gordon, don't!'

'Stay out of it, Sam,' Berry warned her, preparing to launch a fist at McGreevy.

'Why don't you go to the law?' he sneered.

'You know she can't do that,' Berry shouted back indignantly.

'And neither can you,' McGreevy warned, the window rising back up as he prepared to go. 'But I can.'

Cheryl welcomed her sister into the house with open arms, and gave her a stiff whisky. She packed Michelle off to play with Dan and Jeff, and instructed Berry to go and bring in Sam's stuff, though where it was all going to go she was not sure. Michelle could sleep on a mattress in the boys' room for the time being, and Sam would have to camp on the sofa.

Gordon was still furious. Sam was exhausted from the emotions of the day and from working the night shift.

'Look, I know how you feel,' she begged her brother-in-law, 'but I don't want to go over it all again now. OK?'

But Berry was determined to have his say. 'What did you ever see in him?'

'You heard her, Gordon. Leave her alone.' Cheryl came to Sam's rescue, handing Gordon a drink. He took the scotch, and began to calm down.

'If it wasn't for Michelle . . .' he muttered darkly.

'Michelle's fine,' snapped Cheryl, not liking this. She

did not want her husband getting into a brawl which could get him arrested.

But Berry was hard to deflect. 'Arseholes like him only understand one thing.'

'No!' Cheryl shouted at him, 'you're not going back inside for a bastard like him.'

'I could, you know,' continued Berry, 'do him over so he wouldn't know it was me.'

'The only way he wouldn't know it was you would be if you killed him!' Cheryl's voice began to wobble.

Berry turned to Sam. 'I don't know why you ever fancied him. He's a scumbag.'

Sam began to cry. 'He was kind to me once,' she whimpered. 'He was. He helped me with things. With the social security and everything, it was hard on my own.'

Berry began to feel embarrassed. Cheryl glared at him. Then she had an idea. 'There's John,' she suggested.

'JP,' Berry whispered to himself, looking thoughtful. In his anger the idea had not occurred to him.

Cheryl persisted: 'Isn't there a law protecting people like Sam?' she asked vaguely.

'If there is,' Berry retorted, 'McGreevy'll have found a loophole.'

But Sam was frightened; she did not want to get herself in a worse mess. 'I don't trust the law,' she confessed. 'Any of them.'

Cheryl was cross with her. 'So we just let men like McGreevy do what they want?' she snapped.

Berry looked at his wife. 'If we go to the Old Bill it'll all come out, Sam will lose all her benefits, the free child-minding place, she'll be worse off than before.'

Sam blew her nose. 'I don't know what to do. I can't stay here for ever. We've already taken over the living-room.'

Cheryl put her arm round her. 'You can stay here as long as you want to,' she said, with reassuring warmth. Though, truthfully, she too could see that they could not stay for ever.

The flat was practically back in order. They had all pulled their weight to tidy up, so that all evidence of the police raid was gone. Madson was now attacking the washing-up in the kitchen, aware of the intense whispered conversation going on at the front door.

Dominic was reluctant to go and leave Sarah. Sarah, however, thought it would be best to talk to Madson on her own.

'You want to come round later?' Dominic suggested; he particularly wanted her company that night after the ordeal of the day.

'I don't know,' Sarah hedged. 'Depends how it goes.' She kissed him and watched him go.

'See you later,' he called.

Shutting the door thoughtfully, Sarah walked back slowly to the kitchen. Madson was methodically washing all the dishes, and she picked up a tea towel to help him. They worked in silence for several minutes, Madson frantically scouring a pan.

'John, for God's sake, talk to me! . . .' She broke off. 'And that's a non-stick pan you're ruining.' He looked at her, at a loss as to how to put it. Sarah tried to make it easier for him. 'Is it the drugs or is it Dominic?'

'How do you mean?' he responded unhelpfully.

'That's upsetting you.'

'Am I upset?'

He was determined to have a row, thought Sarah. 'I told you about the heroin,' she pleaded. 'I told you the truth.'

'OK,' Madson snapped at last. 'Let's talk about Dominic.' She knew he felt betrayed about Dominic, but Rob had been a terrible junkie, from very early in their marriage. In the end she had turned to Dominic for help and support, and it had been Dominic who had stopped her from taking to drugs too. It was hard to explain all this to Madson, hard to explain the extent to which his son had failed her. But she now told him the whole story: she and Dominic had been lovers for nearly a year now. She had clung to the healthy, strong man while his friend, her husband, deteriorated slowly over the months.

The receptionist at Hearnley & Partners had hardly turned on the lights when Madson arrived at the office bright and early the next morning. Madson picked up an enormous heap of mail, waved a good morning to the receptionist and went upstairs to his cubby-hole to sort it all out. By the time that Magda popped her head round the door he was engrossed in his work.

'I've just printed out the writ,' she said. 'Want to see?' She handed it to Madson to inspect.

'In the High Courts of Justice, Queen's Bench Division,' he read out loud from the front page, with much pleasure.

'Satisfied?' asked Magda.

'Not yet,' he replied fiercely. 'But it helps to be on the inside pissing out.'

CHAPTER ELEVEN

A dark-haired man in his forties, wearing a Savile Row suit, lolled back in an armchair in Magda's office radiating confidence, and with an obvious air of conceit.

'Any idea of when the SFO would be looking to go to trial?' he asked casually.

Magda looked up from the heap of paperwork regarding his case on her desk. 'From what I've seen of the correspondence it won't be this year.'

Magda's client, Henry Richardson, responded with an irritating air of bonhomie. 'I was hoping to spend the autumn in the Bahamas. Robert and Caroline Newton, do you know them?' If he had been hoping to impress her, Magda thought, he was certainly going the wrong way about it. He was expecting her to put up a defence against the charge of fraud, and all he could do was talk about holidays in the Bahamas.

'You must be careful about any display of wealth at this time,' Magda said.

'That's why I'm going to stay with them,' Richardson explained chirpily, deliberately missing her point.

Magda sighed. 'You have been granted legal aid as a technical bankrupt. How is it going to look in court if you've spent the past three months in the Bahamas?'

He searched her face for a scrap of sympathy – after all he was employing her, he thought to himself.

'And how are you going to get to the Bahamas?' Magda persisted, seeing that he was apparently taking in what she said. 'First class?'

'Certainly not!' Richardson looked shocked. 'Robert has his own Learjet.'

There was a knock at the door, and Madson came in. She had asked him to come in to meet this client after he had finished delivering the writ at the court. There was a missing witness to find, and she thought Madson might come up with some useful insights on the man. 'John,' she said, 'I want you to meet Henry Richardson.'

Madson nodded towards Richardson. 'The Serious Fraud Office,' he said gravely; he had seen the paperwork. He sat down, and opened his notebook.

Henry Richardson began to fill him in on the details. 'I was telling Miss Ostrowska here that there was a young man I took on at the bank just before the . . . er,' he hesitated for a moment, 'the roof fell in. Name of Martin Horton. He'd been highly recommended by Graham Ewing at Barnes, Ewing & Paul. Bright young man. Made a fortune in futures trading.'

'Why did they let him go?'

'Hmm?' Richardson looked at Madson without comprehension.

'If he'd made a fortune for the stockbrokers, it's odd they would have let him go.'

But Richardson waved his doubts aside. 'There were personal matters,' he said airily. 'An unfortunate liaison with Graham Ewing's daughter. I'm sure you don't need all the details.'

The man looked genuine enough, thought Madson, though he had taken an immediate dislike to him. Perhaps it was only because he looked so pleased with himself.

Superintendent Walton sat calmly in his large office in the barrack-like building that housed the Organized

Crime Squad. He was a meticulous man, and he was carefully reading through the pile of letters his secretary had left on his desk.

There was a knock at the door, and he looked up over the top of his glasses as his secretary entered with a fresh pile of mail. 'Thank you,' he said formally, as she put it on his desk and left him to go through it. He continued to check through the original correspondence, and then noticed with a start that there was an embossed writ in the new heap of mail. He picked it up from the pile and opened it out. At first he frowned over it, slightly puzzled. Then it became clear to him, and he picked up his telephone in fury. He had thought he had explained himself in no uncertain terms regarding Detective Inspector Rourke. 'I want to see Superintendent Burridge,' he barked into the phone. 'As soon as possible!'

Rushing out from the middle of a day shift at the hospital, Sam missed two buses, and then had to wait twenty minutes for the next one. By the time she had reached the street where she used to live, she was late and out of breath from running. She had arranged to meet Ray McGreevy, to sort out the problem with her flat. She felt sure that she would only have to explain, and pay off some of the money, and he would relent, without the need for all the fuss that her sister and brother-in-law were making. At any rate she was convinced that it was worth a try. He had been kind in the past.

She pulled out her key and tried to turn it in the lock of her former flat, but it would not fit. Then she rang the doorbell, and Ray came to open it.

'You look red in the face,' he said.

'I've been running,' she explained, still short of breath. 'I've only got an hour for lunch.'

'What do you want?' he said.

'I told you on the phone,' she said nervously. 'I just want to talk to you.'

He turned and locked the door behind them and went into the grim bedsitting room, turning to face her with a manic grin. 'Come here,' he smirked, grabbing her and pushing her harshly down on to the bed, gripping her painfully so that she cried out in surprise.

'No, Ray,' she screamed, as he ripped open her coat.

'Shut up, bitch,' he shouted at her, causing her to cry out again. He pulled up her skirt and ripped off her tights and pants. She could feel his hard, erect penis, pushing at her. She screamed and struggled to get free. But he only hit her harder, pulling open his trousers, and biting her lip so hard that it bled. He shoved himself brutally into her, pushing her face down hard with one hand to stop the screaming. His breathing grew rasping and heavy, and he came; then he heaved himself off her, and pushed her to the floor with distaste, like a discarded piece of rubbish. She lay there in a heap, shaken and weeping. He stood up and did up his flies.

'You'd better get back to work. Don't they dock you if you're late?' he sneered at her. 'And the answer to your question is "No, you can't." I've got a family of Pakis moving in tomorrow. For three times what you were paying. I only let you have it for that because I liked you.' And he let himself out, leaving her to pick herself up.

In Madson's cubby-hole the heavy Xerox machine ground to a sudden halt – for only the millionth time, thought Madson ruefully. Cautiously he opened the top and side panels and peered inside.

'Wondered what you did here,' said the cheerful voice of Berry as he bounded in through the door. 'You're a bleeding repairman,' he continued. 'You don't need a law degree for that!'

'I think you need a degree in civil engineering,' Madson said seriously, straightening up.

'What's up?' queried Berry.

'No idea,' sighed Madson. 'It's always doing this.'

Berry began to roll up his sleeves. 'Let me,' he offered.

'You know about these things?' Madson was dubious.

'They're like women. Just need a kick up the arse,' Berry said with a grin, slamming closed all the open panels, before Madson could stop him.

'It doesn't respond to violence,' said Madson; 'neither do women!' But he was too late, the machine had roared back into action before he was halfway through his sentence.

Berry had come to talk to Madson about Sam, in the hope that he might be able to sort something out for her, but Madson was in a hurry to get to the Legal Document Exchange in Chancery Lane. Picking up his coat, and his batch of documents, Madson suggested that Berry should accompany him, and explain as they walked.

'He can't do it,' Madson said, when Berry told him about Samantha being thrown out on to the street.

'He just did.'

Madson was adamant that she must be protected, she would have rights as a sitting tenant. Berry reluctantly explained that she had only ever paid cash in hand, had no rent book, and that sometimes she had slept with the landlord instead of paying rent. But Berry was sorry for her; he admired her pluckiness in carrying on her work as a nurse and bringing up the little girl all on her own. Madson, however, thought that the situation was clear: she should go to the police.

Unfortunately, Berry revealed, there was more to it than this. Sam had been receiving benefits from the social services for some time, and had not informed them that she was back at work. Though she did not earn very much, she was no longer entitled to free child-care facilities, school lunches and such. Samantha was now terrified that if she rocked the boat they would make her pay all the money back or, worse, they would prosecute her.

'Does he know about all this, this McGreevy?' Madson asked Gordon.

'Does he know? It was his idea. She's terrified he'll turn her in. That's why she can't go to the cops.'

'So where do I come in?' Madson asked.

Berry was losing patience. He could see that Madson was not sure what to do either. 'I'm going to kick the shit out of this bastard!' he concluded.

'Look,' suggested Madson. 'Do you want us to start legal proceedings?'

Berry calmed down, and pointed out Samantha's debts and general lack of funds. 'Cheryl thought we could get help, something, what's it called?' he said tentatively.

'You mean legal aid?' Madson filled in the term for him.

'That's it.'

Madson was thoughtful. 'This McGreevy. He'll still let everyone know about the Social Security fraud.' He frowned.

But Berry was looking pleased. 'If she got legal aid it might not matter. She could start again.'

'Worth a shot,' Madson concluded, holding the swing door open for Gordon to go into the DX with him. 'You'd be amazed at the sort of people they give legal aid to. Met one this morning. City banker living in the Bahamas.'

'Shame,' mused Berry, not really taking in what Madson was saying. 'I was looking forward to giving that McGreevy a good kicking!' An elderly clerk who walked past them at that moment eyed Gordon with disapproval.

Rourke was well aware that there was trouble afoot. He had received an order to go and see Chief Superintendent Walton in his office.

Having knocked on the door and entered, Rourke stood stiffly in front of the desk until his superior officer had finished signing his correspondence. Walton looked up at Rourke when he was ready and said sternly, 'Sit down, Mr Rourke.' Walton then pulled the writ from his desk drawer and waved it at Rourke, who did a swift double take; he had not anticipated this. For a moment he was speechless.

Walton looked at him with piercing eyes. 'It alleges wrongful arrest by Detective Inspector Rourke of the Organized Crime Squad,' he informed him gravely.

'Who's the plaintiff?' Rourke inquired, regaining his voice.

'You mean' – Walton was sarcastic – 'there are so many, you don't know which one it's likely to be?' He looked at Rourke with a certain amount of scepticism.

Rourke looked down at his feet. 'I presume it's Madson,' he murmured. Walton nodded slowly, and waited for him to continue. 'I didn't arrest Madson, sir,' he said. 'I arrested his daughter-in-law and her boyfriend.'

'Only because he wasn't there when you went blundering in at 6.30 in the morning.' Again he waited for Rourke to defend himself. It was necessary to hear the whole story from the point of view of the officer concerned.

'Standard procedure, sir,' claimed Rourke calmly.

Walton began to question him further, keen to get at least this part of the whole unpleasant business out of the way. 'The writ claims you planted one ounce of heroin on the defendant. Is it true?' He looked expressionlessly at Rourke, awaiting his answer.

'No, sir.' Rourke was again calm. 'I hope we're going to contest the action, sir?' He raised a questioning eyebrow.

'We have no choice,' said Walton sternly. 'Not to do so would be to admit liability. I told you before: do not tangle with this Madson.' His voice rose in anger.

'No, sir,' Rourke repeated.

'You'll have to provide our solicitors with the file. Bear in mind their solicitors might wish to see the correspondence. I understand that's something you're good at.' Walton looked at him very severely indeed. Rourke squirmed. He had no idea how much Walton actually knew about the history of the Madson affair, and he resented being given such a dressing down by his superior officer.

Walton continued relentlessly. 'You're becoming an embarrassment to the Force, Mr Rourke. You might be advised to check the status of your pension rights in the event of early retirement.'

Rourke's jaw dropped. Surely Walton did not have the authority to go that far. But the interview was clearly over. Walton returned to dealing with his correspondence, and Rourke rose to his feet and left the room.

Having finished his business at the Document Exchange Madson suggested to Berry that he return with him to seek Magda's advice regarding his sister-in-law; he felt sure that Magda would know the appropriate course of action to take.

However, both Madson and Berry got quite a shock when Magda explained that on her nurse's salary Samantha would probably not be eligible to receive legal aid.

'You're telling me,' Madson spluttered incredulously, 'that that prat whatsisname, Henry Richardson, can get legal aid and Sam can't?'

Magda looked sympathetic. 'She'll probably get assisted legal aid. A contribution.'

'How much is that then?' asked Berry with a certain amount of scepticism.

'It'll be assessed on a *pro rata* basis. The point is she earns above the minimum.'

'And Henry Richardson?' Madson inquired.

'He's technically bankrupt,' she explained with a sigh, knowing they would hate her for saying so, 'so he gets the lot.'

'That's fair?' Berry protested.

'No, of course it's not fair, but it's the law.'

Madson thought it might be best to try another tack. 'Look,' he said. 'Gordon's a friend; you know how much he's helped me.'

'I know,' Magda agreed. 'That's why I'm giving him free legal advice instead of charging him £200 an hour.'

Gordon could not take in what he heard. He could not believe they could be so callous. 'I've got to go,' he muttered, as he walked out in a rage, almost running through the corridor and lobby in his haste to get out into the fresh air. Madson tried to follow him, calling out, 'Gordon, wait, we'll work something out.'

'I'm going out there to really help,' Gordon flung back at him bitterly, striding out of the door.

*

Lear looked up, worried, as Rourke returned to his desk in the second-floor office at the Organized Crime Squad. 'How did it go?' he prompted.

'They promoted me,' Rourke said flatly, sitting himself down and determinedly changing the subject. 'You got a number for Taffy Davies?'

Lear was surprised. 'He only got out of Parkhurst two weeks ago.'

'That's why I want him.'

Reluctantly Lear began to thumb through his little black book, searching for the right number, but he was not keen to be involved. 'This wise, guv?' he asked nervously.

'More Dennis than Ernie,' Rourke said, losing his cool and grabbing the book from Lear. Lear began to wonder whether his boss had gone stark raving mad.

Madson went back into Magda's office feeling that he had failed. 'He's gone,' he said to her, while she sat tapping a letter into her computer.

Concentrating, she did not look up. 'I heard,' was all she said.

But Madson was looking for an argument. It was not good enough to simply tell someone you could not help because they could not afford you. 'I'm sorry, but I think he's right,' Madson persisted.

Magda looked up, having finished her letter, and attempted to explain. 'Yes, he's right. But get real, Madson. This is a top London law firm. We're not the Citizens Advice Bureau. And we don't take on charity cases.'

'I wasn't asking for charity,' Madson said angrily. 'I was talking about common justice.'

Visiting the offices of Barnes, Ewing & Paul later in the day, in the course of his investigation into the Richardson fraud case, Madson found to his consternation that nobody there had ever heard of Martin Horton. He found this particularly odd as Henry Richardson had been very specific about the firm that his former employee had come from. Their recommendation had apparently been significant. Madson puzzled over this, wondering whether it could possibly be due to the unpleasant business with the Ewing daughter.

Then he returned to his office, picked up the telephone and started to dial all the numbers listed under 'Horton, Martin' in the directory.

This proved curiously unsuccessful. It then occurred to him that it might be worth checking the Electoral Register, and he began to pack up his papers, ready to go down to the council offices in Victoria.

Berry's car screeched on to the kerb in front of his house. He banged the car door behind him and strode up to the front door in a filthy temper.

He was hardly in through the door before he began a blazing row with Cheryl. Samantha jumped to her sister's defence. Then she mentioned that she had tried to get her flat back in her own way, by appealing to McGreevy. She told them only something of what had happened. Angrily Berry picked up the phone and rang McGreevy.

'Get off, woman,' he shouted, shaking Cheryl off as she tried in vain to prevent him from making the call. He got through to McGreevy. 'I warned you before, you touch her,' he yelled, 'and I'll kill you. I warned you, didn't I!'

McGreevy in his minimalist bachelor apartment in Hampstead, depressed the cut-out button and then dialled a friend to round up some assistance.

*

Berry meanwhile had grabbed hold of a baseball bat and was trying it for size. Cheryl hung on to him desperately, and Berry tried to wrench himself free without harming her.

'You said you never would,' she screamed, as she tussled with him for control of the baseball bat. 'You said it, when you came out!'

'It's all my fault,' Sam whimpered, 'I should never have come here.'

'It's got sod all to do with both of you,' Berry shouted, having finally shrugged himself out of Cheryl's grasp.

'What did he say, John, didn't he tell you this is stupid?'

'He's too busy earning £200 an hour.' Berry spat the words out in fury.

Jeff and Dan Berry appeared suddenly in the room, frightened by the raised voices, and Michelle came in behind them, hanging on to Dan's sweatshirt from behind. 'Dad, what's happening?' Jeff asked in a small voice.

Berry pulled himself together and took a deep breath. 'It's all right kids. Go back upstairs. I'm just talking to your mum.' Cheryl was beginning to be frightened by her husband, and she did not want a scene in front of the children.

'I've started looking for somewhere,' Sam turned to Berry with a rather strained brightness. 'We've already started, haven't we, Michelle?' Michelle did not know what to say; tears welled in her eyes.

'She has, you know,' Cheryl said desperately. 'We went through the paper together. We ringed the ones we liked.' But Berry was not interested; he made for the door.

'I wouldn't go back there anyway,' Sam called after him, 'not even if I got a rent book.'

But it was too late – Gordon was far beyond reason. 'Not the point!' he flung over his shoulder in reply as he reached his car, threw himself in to the driver's seat and roared off into the night. In her mind's eye Cheryl could already see the prison doors clanging behind him.

'I'm sorry,' whispered Sam, as they went back into the living-room. 'I never meant anything like this.'

Cheryl ignored her sister's apologies; she picked up the telephone and dialled Madson's mobile number.

Berry pulled up quietly outside McGreevy's flat. He picked up the baseball bat, marched up the stairs to the front door and rang the bell. When Ray McGreevy came to the door, Berry pushed his way in and began jabbing the baseball bat at him.

'I warned you,' Berry growled. 'I warned you what would happen if you went near my sister-in-law.'

'Fancy her yourself do you?' McGreevy sneered, inflaming Berry even more.

McGreevy backed towards the scrubbed white kitchen, and three muscular goons leapt out, grabbing at Berry, and ripping the bat out of his hands. Mercilessly they turned the bat on him, beating him savagely over and over again.

CHAPTER TWELVE

Berry's living-room looked like a hospital casualty department. Gordon lay moaning on the sofa, stripped to the waist, with a mass of bruises and cuts about his chest. His face was an agony of swollen weals, his chin immobile with pain. 'It's my fault,' Sam wailed as she and Cheryl attempted to clean up the damage with damp wads of cotton wool.

'Will you stop saying that,' moaned Berry.

His wife looked at him sceptically; she was just glad that he had managed to get home. 'You want to be bloody grateful,' she said ungenerously.

'How's that then?' Berry asked.

'If you'd done what you were going to do you'd have been back inside,' Cheryl explained seriously.

Donald, who had just turned up, chipped in, 'I told you not to go there without me.'

'I thought you were on my side.'

Madson interceded. 'We all are. But mindless violence doesn't solve anything.'

'But strategic violence does,' Berry joked, unrepentant.

Madson was not amused. 'Well,' he said sternly, 'your attempt to beat up McGreevy comes under the first category. There are other ways of getting what you want, besides using a baseball bat,' Madson continued, intending to imply that he had begun to work out a plan.

'Not as quick,' replied Berry, not getting the point.

'Ultimately more effective.'

The alleyway between the road and the small block of flats was dimly lit. Locking his car, Madson made his way thoughtfully down the alley towards his flat. Suddenly two thugs sprang out at him at the end of the alley. The thickset one swung an iron bar at him and Madson ducked to avoid it. Then the other one, who was tall, with lank hair and a strong, stale smell, came at him with a knife. Desperately Madson fended him off, grasping his hand and knocking the knife away just as the first one aimed his bar again, this time hitting him between the shoulder-blades and sending him sprawling to the ground. Then the thugs kicked him about a bit, clearly enjoying themselves.

A figure at the entrance to the alleyway lit up a cigarette in the darkness, puffing out a mouthful of smoke into the cool night air. Rourke watched Madson on the ground; then he turned nonchalantly away and sauntered casually back up the street to his car.

At last Madson crawled gingerly up to the flat; no bones seemed to be broken, though his pride was distinctly tender. The flat was empty. Sarah was out. He pulled himself up on to a chair in the kitchen and picked up the phone. Swallowing his pride, he found Dominic's number and dialled it. 'Dominic,' he stuttered uncharacteristically into the receiver. 'It's John Madson. Is Sarah there?' he asked. 'Look, before you defend her, she's not under attack OK? Oh . . .'

At that moment Sarah walked in to the kitchen clasping a carton of milk, and looked at him open-mouthed.

'It's OK,' Madson said carefully into the phone. 'She's just walked in.' He hung up the receiver.

'Jesus!' Sarah exclaimed, 'I only went out for five

minutes, we had no milk in for breakfast . . .' Her voice trailed off. Realizing that he had been in some kind of fight, she went to him and putting her arm around him led him gently to the sofa.

Not only was he in considerable pain, but Madson felt distinctly annoyed to be in exactly the same position that Berry had been in earlier in the evening; he had done nothing, as far as he knew, to provoke this attack. He had checked his wallet immediately the thugs had run off, and it remained in his pocket, so the motivation was not robbery. He must have been deliberately singled out for a beating, but why?

'I'm very impressed,' Sarah announced.

'Wait a couple of days,' said Madson ruefully. 'It'll look a lot worse!'

'I meant with you,' she explained, 'not with the bruises.' Madson had never asked her for help before, and she was glad to feel needed. As she gradually mopped him up she wondered at his relative complacence. 'How did you deal with violence in prison?' she asked curiously.

'I walked away from it whenever possible,' Madson replied quietly.

Sarah carefully unbuttoned his shirt and helped him out of one sleeve so that she could survey the damage to his torso.

'The basic principle,' Madson revealed, wincing slightly with pain as he struggled out of his shirt, his shoulders stiff from the beating, 'is that you turn your opponent's force on himself.'

Sarah frowned, wondering how this was possible.

'It works,' Madson assured her, 'especially when you've got someone coming at you in anger.'

Sarah looked at him, still partly unconvinced. 'Didn't work tonight, did it?'

'Those guys tonight weren't angry,' Madson snapped. 'It was a warning.'

'Who from?'

Light dawned. Madson suddenly knew what it was all about; it had taken Sarah's question to nudge him into the revelation. 'Our common friend,' he said slowly. 'Detective Inspector Rourke.'

'Now there is one angry man,' agreed Sarah.

Madson looked at her triumphantly. 'Sarah! You're a genius!'

'I am?'

He sprang up and almost flung his arms round her, though a sudden flash of pain stopped him.

The next morning Madson staggered into work looking as smart as he could, though there was not much he could do to disguise the damage to his face. The bruising around his left eye spoke volumes. He sat at his desk, noting down his predicted movements for the day in the journal and thinking that he loathed Rourke more than ever.

Magda popped her head round the door. 'How are you getting on with the elusive Martin Horton?' she called across the Xerox machine to him.

'I think I've got some news.' Madson turned to face her, and for the first time she caught sight of his eye.

'Oh!' she exclaimed, her jaw dropping in horror. 'What happened?'

Madson did not want to explain about Rourke to Magda at this stage, so he made light of his injuries. 'Oh, this! I walked into a door,' he joked.

'Sure?' she asked with concern. She frowned, uncertain what to do.

Madson began to pack up the things on his desk. 'I'll

be back after I've been to the Master in Chambers. And done the final check on Horton.'

Magda watched him as he cleared up his things. 'You sure you don't need anyone to go with you,' she half-joked, half-wondering if he did need help. But Madson only smiled. With his black eye, she thought, he looked decidedly boyish.

The telephone rang in the office of the Organized Crime Squad. Lear answered it, and then transferred the call to Rourke. Dominic was pleading into the phone, 'My dad's been out of work for two years and my mum's very ill. They rely on me.'

Rourke was not very impressed by this. 'I'm crying,' he retorted unsympathetically.

'It's only possession,' Dominic continued. 'You don't care about possession. It's dealers you want, right?' There was a pause. 'You're not interested in me,' Dominic repeated emphatically.

Rourke put his cards on the table. 'I'm interested in Madson,' he said.

'I hate him,' Dominic spat into the telephone. 'He's made Sarah's life a misery since he got out. He wants us to break up!'

Rourke could not believe his luck: he had this lad in the palm of his hand. 'If he was back inside he wouldn't be able to, would he?' he suggested.

Dominic was only too eager to help. 'Will you drop all charges against me and Sarah if I give you the name of Madson's supplier?'

'Madson's dealing?' Rourke asked coolly; inside he was leaping for joy – here was a chance made in heaven.

'Not in a big way,' Dominic hedged slightly.

'But he is dealing?' He needed confirmation and details.

'The charges,' Dominic reiterated. 'You agree to drop them?'

'Tell me,' demanded Rourke.

'You can get that writ overturned if you get Madson,' Dominic added, spinning out the conversation.

'Right,' Rourke snapped, looking over at Lear and giving him the thumbs up. Lear grinned; he had been lolling back in his swivel chair throughout the exchange, resting his feet on the desk and taking in the gist.

'I want it official,' Dominic continued. 'No changing your mind later.'

'Tell me,' Rourke persisted, getting impatient with him.

'His name's McGreevy,' Dominic imparted slyly, giving Ray McGreevy's north London address, as Madson had instructed him to do.

Rourke wrote it down, and banged the phone down with a triumphant glance at Lear. 'Got him!' he said.

Dominic put down the phone in Madson and Sarah's kitchen. 'Got him,' he commented, with a conspiratorial grin.

A couple of police cars homed in on Ray McGreevy's Hampstead apartment, screeching to a halt outside the door. Rourke, Lear and several uniformed officers leapt out and pushed their way into the galleried studio room where McGreevy was sitting listening to Stockhausen on his CD player.

McGreevy was perplexed. Surely it must be some kind of mistake – he did not deal in drugs. But the police were determined. In the space of half an hour they tore his flat apart; they even tried to pull up the sanded floorboards. Ray insisted that he was a respectable businessman, but Rourke would not accept it. 'Now that is ridiculous,' he said callously. 'You're a slum landlord with the morals of a snake!' But the police could find nothing save a stack of pornographic videos. McGreevy insisted they were for his personal use, but it seemed worth taking them away to investigate further.

'Do you know John Madson?' Rourke asked at last.

'Who?' Ray had never heard of him.

'Don't mess with me,' Rourke snarled. Though he tried for some time, using all the dirty tactics he could think of, he could get nothing out of McGreevy, who kept insisting that he did not deal in drugs and had never heard of Madson. But he was a criminal as far as Rourke was concerned, and he had it on good authority that the man was dealing. He might not get him now, but he was going to get him eventually. He glared at him threateningly.

'Look,' said McGreevy, trying to sound reasonable, 'you want this Madson geezer. I've never heard of him. You've made a mistake.'

Rourke took hold of his collar and looked him directly in the eye. 'I don't think so,' he said. 'You sneeze and there'll be one of my men with a hankie up your nostril. Understand?'

McGreevy nodded slowly.

Rourke released him and the police left the apartment as suddenly as they had come. Trembling, McGreevy pulled himself on to a bar stool, white as a sheet.

Berry watched from his car on the other side of the street, and smiled with satisfaction as he saw the police cars pull away. One way or another McGreevy was going to be taken care of. He turned on the engine and accelerated smoothly away, to report back to Madson and his family at home. Hungry after the excitement, he hoped Cheryl would have the dinner on the table.

*

After dinner Berry and Madson sat at the table drinking coffee and feeling pleased with themselves. 'It's not over till it's over,' Madson reminded them carefully, as the girls tripped over themselves thanking him.

With a grin Berry went over to a briefcase he had left propped against a chair. He unlocked it and took out a parcel wrapped in brown paper which he opened on the table in front of them. The bundle contained several small plastic packets, each containing an ounce of white powder. 'How're Michelle's bowel movements?' he asked jokily.

Sam looked at him in confusion. 'What?' she asked.

'A bit of this in her cereal . . .' He paused for effect. 'It would do wonders.'

Sam was horrified. 'That's coke!' she exclaimed.

Berry laughed, happy to have made his point. 'Mannitol,' he enlightened them. 'It's what they cut coke with.'

'What?' asked Sam again. 'Baby laxative?'

It was early morning, and the sun was just breaking through the clouds. Ray McGreevy strode into his kitchen in a white towelling bathrobe, yawning and skimming a copy of the *Mirror*.

Tossing the paper on to the kitchen table, he stretched his arms and then turned to get a pint of milk from the fridge. With sudden realization he froze, and turned slowly back to the table in horror. There, illuminated by the shafts of light from the window was a plastic bag of white powder. He staggered slightly and blinked; his mind jumped back to the visit from Rourke. He had no wish to go through that again. Then the telephone on the kitchen wall began to ring and he grabbed it in trepidation. 'Yes?' he asked.

*

Just along the road, Berry, Madson and Sam sat tense in Berry's car.

'You found it then?' Berry said into his mobile.

'Who's this?' McGreevy was puzzled. He was sure it was not the policeman.

'There's another bag,' Berry warned, neglecting to identify himself.

McGreevy turned his head from side to side in panic. 'What? Where?'

'Somewhere in the house,' he said vaguely, infuriating McGreevy.

'Where?' he shouted desperately into the phone. Berry was silent, enjoying this part of the plan thoroughly. 'You bastard!' McGreevy yelled, so loud that they could all hear him clearly. 'I'll kill you!'

'No you won't,' Berry retorted. 'You're going down for ten big ones, 'cause as soon as I hang up I'm gonna dial your friend DI Rourke.' With that, he switched off the mobile and turned to grin at the others in the back seat.

'Let's go,' Madson beckoned Sam. Then he looked sharply at Berry; he did not want him to get so carried away that he forgot the arrangement. 'Five minutes, OK?' he said.

'OK,' Berry agreed. 'Be careful.'

Madson and Sam got out of the car, he confident in a neat suit, looking every inch the lawyer, she more nervous in her blue nurse's coat. By the time they reached the door Ray McGreevy had turned his place over even more thoroughly than the police had done, desperate to find the other bag of powder. He had swept every item off every flat surface and pulled out every drawer. The floor was covered in debris. They rang the doorbell; several crashes and bangs emanated from inside.

Madson banged on the door firmly with his fist, and at last McGreevy staggered to the door and opened it. He stood there, uncertain what was going on.

'Mr Ray McGreevy?' Madson asked formally, handing him a business card. 'John Madson, Hearnley & Partners. I believe you know this young woman.'

McGreevy ignored Sam, and glared at Madson. 'Madson!' he said incredulously. 'You're the one the cops want.'

Madson stepped inside, with Sam in tow. 'It won't take five minutes,' he assured McGreevy, stepping over the mess in the hall. McGreevy could only splutter in reply. Standing beside the kitchen table, Madson pulled out a folder and enlightened him. 'I believe you had a phone call from an acquaintance of mine a few minutes ago. I'm instructed to inform you that, once we have concluded our business satisfactorily, I shall be able to tell you the whereabouts of one ounce of cocaine.' Madson looked at him mildly, playing his part with aplomb. Sam was terrified; she almost held her breath; she wished she had not come. Their previous encounter came back shockingly into her mind, and she was shaking. But McGreevy was not paying her any attention, his mind was only on Madson and the cocaine. 'You bastard,' he said slowly and deliberately.

Madson made McGreevy sign an agreement, legally binding under the Landlord and Tenant Act 1985; Sam was to get her flat back. Police sirens were wailing ominously in the distance as Madson handed McGreevy his copy of the agreement. He swept out, dragging Sam behind him. At the door, he turned to face McGreevy. 'Have you used the dishwasher this morning?' he asked, in the same professional, even tone he had used throughout the encounter. McGreevy did not take the time to reply, but dashed back to the kitchen to search the dishwasher.

Sam and Madson reached Berry's car just before the police arrived. He accelerated away swiftly. They did not intend to be caught out at this stage. McGreevy was left searching his dishwasher desperately, as the police began to hammer at his door. At last he opened the compartment where the dishwasher salt was normally placed, and discovered the bag of powder. He pulled the bag open and washed the stuff down the sink.

In the calm of Magda's office, Henry Richardson was sitting in a comfortable leather chair, waiting to hear how Magda felt his defence was developing. He stretched his legs in anticipation, and glanced at the arrangement of hothouse flowers at the other side of the room. It reminded him of Barbados, and he thought of the months of pleasure he was looking forward to. In his mind he could see the blue sea, and the pretty girls in skimpy bathing suits parading on the golden sand. He came back to reality with a sudden start when he heard Magda exclaim, 'Martin Horton doesn't exist?' Madson was laying out a copy of the computer printout from the Inland Revenue on the desk in front of Magda and Richardson.

'This is ridiculous,' Richardson said, without taking the trouble to look at Madson's evidence. 'He worked at Barnes, Ewing & Paul.'

'It's quite true that someone called Martin Horton worked for them . . .' Madson began.

'There you are then.' Richardson nodded his head at Magda.

Madson laid out further papers for their inspection. Magda got up and looked at them carefully. She turned to Madson for an explanation. He pointed to the papers.

'The tax records for the man calling himself Martin Horton give an address which doesn't match the address on the Electoral Register.'

'For God's sake,' Richardson exploded, 'the man moved.'

Then Madson showed that the National Insurance number used by Martin Horton was the same as that of a certain Christopher Richardson. Magda and Madson looked at Richardson for an answer.

There was an awkward pause. 'My cousin,' Richardson enlightened them. 'He's a very bright boy,' he added helpfully.

'Bright enough to help you embezzle over two million pounds?' queried Madson. Magda looked startled; she had not realized the full extent of the fraud.

'I suppose you'd like me to find another lawyer?'

Magda pulled herself together; it was her job to advise him. For a moment she considered what was best. 'I think it's time to come clean with the SFO. The best we can do now is save the taxpayer the cost of an unnecessary trial.'

Henry looked at her seriously. 'I need to find my cousin,' he said feebly. Madson glanced down at his notebook. 'The Excelsior Hotel, Barbados.'

For Madson it was enough to know that the legal aid system would not protect Richardson from his financial obligations. He had completed his investigations.

When Richardson had left, he told Magda that he had managed to resolve things for the evicted tenant, though he refrained from telling her how this had been achieved.

'Without legal aid?'

'Without legal aid,' he confirmed.

'I told you the system works if you know how to operate it,' she said, a touch smugly.

Madson was annoyed: these were real people they were dealing with, it was not a game. 'That's your system is it?' he berated her. 'Justice for those who can afford it or know how to bend the rules?'

Magda knew that he had worked hard, and that he cared deeply. 'Madson, let's not fight again,' she said softly. 'You and I, we're supposed to be on the same side, aren't we?'

'I don't know, Magda.' Madson shook his head. 'I really don't.'

CHAPTER THIRTEEN

The grim concrete council estate off west London's busy Carlton Vale looked even more neglected and sad in the dull November light. Some youths were kicking a football around the parking lot; a man washed his rusting Triumph, scrubbing it until it gleamed.

The man stood back to admire his work, and picked up his bucket ready to go back inside. Watching him, one of the boys deliberately kicked the muddy football directly at the car. It bounced off the bonnet leaving a dirty mess. The man looked shocked, and the boys jeered, and then ran off up the road; the man by this time was waving his fist and shouting at them, but he did not give chase – they might be carrying a knife. The lace-trimmed net curtains of an adjacent ground-floor flat twitched, and a grey head appeared at the window.

High up in a neat fifth-floor flat a whte woman and her black teenage son were eating their Sunday meal of roast chicken in silence. Roy Holt was a pleasant-looking, studious seventeen-year-old, but he was currently serving a sentence in a young offenders' institution. He was allowed out for weekend home visits, but the leave was strictly supervised, and he had to return at specific times. His mother Margaret had been widowed soon after her marriage and had worked as a cleaner for years, rising before dawn to reach city offices. More recently she had been working long shifts as an auxiliary nurse at the local hospital, which was more rewarding, but it was badly paid. There were deep lines of strain on her face, and she looked older than her forty odd years.

Margaret stood up and began to clear the dishes; she turned and addressed her son. 'What time do you have to be back?'

'Four,' he replied succinctly, still chewing his last mouthful of food.

'I'll get ready then,' she said sadly.

'You don't have to,' he said, shrugging his shoulders.

'I want to,' she insisted. 'Will you wash up?'

Roy nodded at her from the table, and she went off to her bedroom to get ready.

Roy quickly finished eating. Standing up he went quietly over to the sideboard, slid open the door and helped himself to a handful of coloured boiled sweets which he put into his pocket. He washed the dishes perfunctorily, and then left them by the sink to drain. He did not have much time. Hating the institution – he was there for an offence which he had not committed – he had made the decision not to go back. He went into his room, where he turned on his ghetto blaster loudly, threw a few T-shirts and things into a sports bag and extracted a note he had written in advance from under his pillow. He pulled on an extra sweatshirt, picked up the bag and the note, and, leaving the music playing, crept out into the living-room. He propped the note prominently against a vase of flowers and skipped out, shutting the door gently behind him.

It was not long before Margaret called to him to turn off the music. When she got no response, she went to his room and turned off the ghetto blaster herself. Then she looked about the room and saw that his bag was gone. She went back out into the living-room with trepidation, and found the note almost immediately.

Opening the note, she sank down into a chair in tears; she had tried her best to make him understand that they must fight this the proper way, through the law. It would not help to run away. She took a deep shuddering breath, wiped away her tear with a tissue and blew her nose. She picked up the telephone and rang the institution. 'This is Margaret Holt speaking. I'm phoning to report that my son's gone missing from weekend leave. I don't know where he's gone.'

When Sarah got back to the flat later that day, she was bubbling excitedly with news, but had trouble finding Madson. At last she found him underneath the kitchen sink. She giggled.

'Be careful,' a muffled voice came from under the sink.

'What's all this?' she asked with amusement. But he was not so amused, claiming that someone had been pouring cooking grease and tea-leaves down the sink. But Sarah wanted to impart the good news, that she had got a job.

'What job?' Madson asked, popping his head out.

'Well, more like an interview,' she admitted.

'What's the interview for?' he inquired.

'Graphic design.' She smiled; it was what she had trained for, and the sort of work she had done in the past. Madson smiled back at her, pleased that she was happy. 'You'll be all right, kid,' he said, before ducking back under the sink to finish dealing with the U-bend.

The next day Madson was sitting in his cubby-hole sorting out the mail into the appropriate files. His small office overflowed with a profusion of files, papers, books and used coffee cups. Surveying the mess with a sigh, he decided to put a clean-up on his list of tasks for the day. Magda rushed in and thrust an enormous bundle of papers at him.

'Poyser v. Metropolitan Chemicals. Copy them and get them round to John Hewitt's chambers before eleven. OK?' she asked, hardly pausing for a reply in her hurry.

'I am,' Madson said, taking the papers. 'Are you?'

'Partners' meeting. I'm late,' she muttered, as she flew off down the stairs.

Magda was the last to arrive in the boardroom. Nine partners, all men, were sitting round the table. She sat in the last chair. At the head of the table Sir Ranald looked carefully down his list. '*Pro bono* work?' he suggested as the next item for discussion, glancing expectantly down the table.

George Lodge jumped in immediately; it was something he felt strongly about. 'I thought we'd been through this before,' he said petulantly.

'All in good time, George,' Sir Ranald said diplomatically. 'Magda?' he queried, seeing that she looked ready to speak. 'I know we've talked about this before but we had an example recently of how the legal aid farce is harming our reputation . . .'

'I think,' said Magda, 'that we're in danger of becoming a little blinkered. We need to justify the increasing cost of our fees . . .'

'Oh, Ranny,' Lodge intervened impatiently, 'we've heard all this before.'

Magda was irritated by this and decided to say so.

'You know I have always stressed how important it is for this practice to be seen to be doing more than just turning over a fat profit.'

Sir Ranald listened to her point seriously, and then

commented mildly, 'We haven't done that for a few years now.'

Madson began to photocopy Magda's papers. He sorted them carefully into separate bundles, and then inserted one bundle into the machine. Almost immediately the machine ground to a halt. A sign on the instruction panel read, 'Replace toner.' Madson glared at it in frustration.

He reluctantly removed his jacket and rolled up his sleeves.

At that moment Berry stuck his head round the door. 'Every time I come here you're fixing that machine. Don't tell me you're a lawyer!' he laughed.

Madson looked up from the machine and glared good-naturedly at his friend. 'Every time you come here it needs fixing. Stay away.'

Eventually, however, Madson stood up. 'I've done it,' he announced.

'Good,' Berry retorted, 'but I've got bad news for you.'

'What?' asked Madson, over the renewed whirr of the machine.

'I need the car back.'

'Fine,' Madson responded, without enthusiasm.

'Sorry, JP, but you knew the deal. Come on,' said Berry, 'I'll drop you off.'

The meeting had finished and the partners were beginning to file out. Lodge, still in a belligerent mood, was accusing Sir Ranald of being a sucker for a pretty girl.

'Oh, I don't know,' replied Sir Ranald evenly.

Magda caught the gist. 'I haven't been a girl for quite a few years now,' she remarked.

Lodge ignored her. 'Basically,' he continued, 'we're

subsidizing her love of fighting these hopeless criminal cases.'

Ranald was too experienced, and too much of a gentleman to be drawn into an argument. 'I think it was all given a pretty thorough hearing,' he said conclusively.

'I don't want to be an embarrassment to you,' Magda temporized.

'Oh no, my dear, you could never be that,' he said, taking her arm as they walked out of the room. This only served to infuriate Lodge.

'Good heavens,' – Sir Ranald looked at his watch in surprise – 'is that the time? I'm having lunch with Lord Justice McDowell. Shall we talk about this later?'

A black and white police car drew up outside the flats where the Holts lived. The parking lot was as usual peopled by youths hanging about, playing football, drinking, chatting to pass the time of day. A couple of men with rasta locks struggled with jump leads beneath the bonnet of an old Cavalier in an effort to get it going; two policemen emerged from their car and walked over to speak to them. The other bystanders mostly stopped chatting and looked over at the policemen. The curtains of the ground-floor flat twitched with interest, and a stone ricocheted off the side of the police car, apparently from nowhere.

Roy Holt stood in a bus queue near Westbourne Park Underground station, nervously glancing about. He turned up his collar, and tried to shrink into it as he saw a police Panda car cruise past on the other side of the road. He looked at his watch, and then up the road, and was relieved to see a large red bus appearing. As the bus drew up, the Panda car also stopped, perhaps only twenty yards along the road, Roy estimated. Should he get on the bus nonchalantly or should he run for it, he wondered. But the bus queue was moving irritatingly slowly, and he was loath to draw attention to himself by pushing. A policeman got out of the car and began to walk towards the bus queue. Roy took one desperate look and decided to run for it. He sped across the road, heading for the canal, with the policeman, who had signalled to the other officer in the car to turn and follow, in hot pursuit.

Roy was no Linford Christie, and the policeman caught up with him near the concrete skateboard gully. Roy soon found himself forced to the ground, and the policeman handcuffed him.

Dominic left Sarah outside the Islington Graphic Design Agency. 'Chin up,' he said, giving her a quick peck on the cheek. He watched her go in.

Sarah waited, while Andrew, the young man who managed the agency studied her portfolio. Without taking his eyes off the drawings Andrew opened a drawer with one hand and pulled out an inhaler, taking a deep puff. 'God, it's crap,' he said, pushing the inhaler back into the drawer. Sarah was so taken aback that she tried to gather up her portfolio.

'Hey,' said Andrew, holding on to the drawings. 'What are you doing?'

Sarah was almost in tears. 'I thought you said it was all crap!'

'I meant the air,' said Andrew, pointing to his inhaler. 'I'm asthmatic.'

Sarah laughed with relief. 'I thought you meant my work . . .'

'No, your stuff's OK.'

'Really?' Sarah smiled hopefully.

'Are you interested in freelance work?'

'Sure,' Sarah said eagerly.

'I might have something for you,' he continued. 'It's not what you'd call glamorous and I can't go beyond £12 an hour.'

'It's a start,' Sarah said breathlessly.

'You've got an Apple Mac at home?' he queried.

Sarah only paused fractionally before lapsing into a lie. 'Yes,' she said, thinking that she would get hold of one somehow.

Andrew pulled out a file and showed her a wad of paper with text and pictures on it. 'Pritchard & Banks. Big engineering firm. They do this quarterly newsletter for their two thousand staff. Eight sheets of A4, text and pictures.' He looked up at her to make sure she was taking this in. 'I need it at the printers by Friday, so deadline Thursday at five. Should do it in three days. I'll round it up; call it a hundred quid a day. OK?'

'OK,' Sarah agreed, absolutely thrilled.

Gliding up to the steel electronic security gates of the young offenders' institution, Elaine looked distinctly out of place in her Audi. She stopped by the booth and, taking her ID card from her handbag, showed it to the guard, who opened the gates for her.

She strode purposefully down the corridor consulting her list as she went. She had several visits to make. She passed the health visitor's office and emerged into a glass-fronted reception area.

'I'll start with Roy Holt,' she said.

The guard smiled at her and shook his head. 'Sorry, Elaine. He's been a naughty boy. He's on the block.'

Elaine was very concerned. She knew how vulnerable Roy Holt was; he had been in a nervous state ever since he had arrived. She headed for the punishment block. The corridors in this part of the building were windowless, and bright fluorescent lights lit up as you moved along them. The cell doors were low and had two extra steel bars across them. Several guards stood at the entrance.

'What do you want?' A uniformed guard who did not know Elaine glared at her.

'I've come to see Roy Holt. I'm his visitor,' Elaine replied, just as severely. Her northern accent tended to come to the fore under stress.

'Well,' said the guard, 'you'll have to go and visit someone else.'

'What?' Elaine was shocked; she was normally allowed access.

'He tried to escape,' the guard said with finality. 'You'll have to visit someone else.'

Elaine stood her ground. 'I understand,' she said calmly. 'I just want to see him.'

The guard began to get annoyed. 'Not today,' he said firmly.

'Do I have to ring the governor?' Elaine threatened.

The guard looked at her scornfully. 'Ring who you want, love,' he replied. 'Nobody gets in to see that scumbag unless I say so.'

'Right,' Elaine snapped, turning on her heel.

The matter of the writ was a pain in the neck, thought DI Rourke impatiently, looking at his watch. He was sitting in a police interview room opposite Armstrong, the police solicitor who had been allocated the task of preparing their defence.

'The problem is,' Armstrong was saying, 'that this writ has been issued by the girl and her boyfriend, not Madson.'

Rourke was confused; surely that was all to the good. 'Why should I want to plant an ounce of smack on them?' he inquired reasonably.

Armstrong sighed and explained again. He felt sure Rourke was hardly listening to him at all. 'A judge might be inclined to look less favourably on a writ brought by an ex-convict than on one brought by two young people. And there is also the question of the history.'

'Sorry,' remarked Rourke, to Armstrong's irritation.

'Your relationship with Mr Madson goes back over eight years,' he said.

'Is that relevant?' Rourke wanted to know.

'It might be.' Armstrong could only discuss possibilities, he could never be sure. 'It could easily be made to look like a personal vendetta,' he suggested, taking the role of devil's advocate.

'I've been led to expect complete back-up by this department,' Rourke barked angrily back at him.

Armstrong filled him in quickly on some background. 'The writ is not issued against the Organized Crime Squad. The case is being dealt with by the Commissioner of Police for the Metropolis. You're in foreign territory here, Mr Rourke.'

'You're saying,' Rourke leaned forward conspiratorially, 'that the Met wants this case to come to court?' He was well aware that this would not be the case. He was not going to let this grey solicitor with his balding head and glasses frighten him.

Armstrong hesitated. 'DC Lear is separately named on the writ. We may be able to delay proceedings again while we apply to have both hearings heard simultaneously.'

'How long before we have to go to court?' growled Rourke.

Armstrong smiled briefly. 'Oh,' he said, 'we could probably keep this thing going for weeks' – he looked at Rourke – 'if they choose to back you.'

CHAPTER FOURTEEN

It took Elaine nearly an hour to arrange to see Roy Holt. Finally she swept back to the punishment block, where she was met once again by a certain amount of opposition. The sour-faced guard insisted on telephoning the governor himself. 'Yes, sir. I understand. Five minutes. I'll make sure she doesn't stay any longer. Yes, sir.'

He led Elaine through the gate to Roy's cell. He slid back a shutter in the cell door, and stood back.

'Can you open the door please?' Elaine requested.

'No,' the guard barked. 'You've got five minutes. Doyle! Heslop!' he shouted over to a couple of other guards. He then walked off, and Doyle and Heslop stood beside her as she peered through.

Roy was sitting on the floor in the far corner of his cell, his arms wrapped round his knees. He was perfectly still, his eyes closed.

'Roy,' Elaine called to him, 'it's me. Elaine. Are you all right?' Roy did not look up. She only had the five minutes.

'I know what happened,' she said to him, hoping for a reaction. 'Do you want to talk?' she said more urgently. At last he looked up.

'They won't allow me in, Roy,' she told him quickly, relieved that he was listening to her. 'You'll have to talk to me here. There are two officers standing next to me. And I've got four minutes left.' To her relief, he got up and came over to the door to talk with her.

*

It was 7 p.m., and the end of a long day. Magda was crouched by her small office fridge surveying the possibilities for a drink, and talking to Madson. 'I haven't got much in here, I'm afraid,' she said. 'There's 7 Up or Coke.' Neither were particularly appealing at that moment.

'I'm not thirsty,' Madson said.

'But I am. I'll have one of these then. You sure you don't want anything?'

'I'm sure,' he said, spreading out some papers he had brought with him on Magda's desk, copies of the correspondence that Jenny had filched for him from Hanley, Gardner, Green. 'Can you look at this?' Madson asked Magda. She came over to the desk with her drink to have a look. 'See here.' He indicated with a pen. 'This reference to "dropping the charge".'

'Against you?' Magda queried. Madson did not think so, for the charges against him had not been dropped. 'So who?' she persisted.

'My feeling is Walter Gardner.'

'Your solicitor?' she said incredulously. But Madson was clear on the point. It was more than just straightforward incompetence that had put him in prison. He had been set up, he was sure of it. He believed that it had been fixed between his solicitor and the police. It must have been in both their interests for some reason. She looked slightly sceptical, but smiled a sort of agreement. 'Am I getting paid for this or is it another *pro bono* case?' she joked, as she sipped her sweet drink.

'Rock salmon and chips?' Madson suggested hopefully.

There was a knock at the door at that point and Lodge put his head round the door. 'Oh, Magda,' he simpered, ignoring Madson. 'You're still here. I was wondering if you'd like a bite of something later?'

'Actually,' said Magda, enjoying the discomfiture of both men, 'we're just leaving.'

Madson got back to the flat to find Sarah and Dominic ensconced on the sofa, demolishing an Indian take-away. Despite their cosy appearance, he sensed that they had been having a row about something, and when they asked him to join them he declined. Just as Sarah was telling him that she got the job, his mobile rang – it was Elaine. He took the phone into his bedroom to talk privately. She wanted to meet him at the office the next day to discuss the case of a black youth named Roy Holt, who seemed to have been wrongly convicted.

Sarah was disappointed not to have talked longer with Madson; she had hoped to talk to him about the new job, and ask his advice about borrowing money for a computer. Dominic seemed to think that she needed an older man to go with her to discuss a loan with the bank manager.

Dominic put his arm protectively around her; he had seen the look that followed Madson out of the room, and he was a touch jealous. 'Come here,' he said gently.

She pulled out of his arms in sudden confusion. 'Not now,' she muttered.

In his poky office Madson was studying the documents from the Hanley, Gardner, Green file. He had sorted them out neatly and added annotations.

Lodge barged in waving a sheaf of papers. 'Busy?' he inquired.

'As usual,' Madson replied.

'Not too busy to take these down to Knightsbridge Crown Court by eleven?' He handed over the papers to Madson, and his curiosity was aroused by the paperwork on Madson's desk. 'I thought you were an outdoor clerk?' he said accusingly. 'Are you working on a case for another partner?'

'Original research.'

Lodge looked extremely put out. 'My understanding,' he said, 'was that you were employed as an outdoor clerk by this firm to perform its business.'

'It's my lunch hour,' Madson said firmly.

'It's ten thirty.' Lodge blustered. 'You know, Madson, I wonder whether you're really cut out for this job,' he started to say, but he was cut short by the appearance of Elaine.

'Good morning. Hello, George,' she said cheerfully.

George looked at her unsmiling. 'Nice to see you,' he said. 'Shouldn't you be in some fetid prison?'

Elaine was unfazed. 'Oh they let me out for dinner parties and celebrity first nights,' she said airily. 'Madson, are you coming?'

'He's got a delivery to make,' Lodge said. 'And on your way back, get me a smoked salmon sandwich on brown bread,' he added.

Wordlessly Madson brushed past him, and followed Elaine to Magda's office.

Donald was peering under the bonnet of a car. Oddly, it was a resprayed version of the one which Berry had recently taken back from Madson. Berry came striding out from his office to see how Donald was getting on.

'He's on his way,' he informed him. Donald lowered the bonnet, looking up at Berry.

'OK?' Berry asked, waiting for confirmation.

'If no one looks too close,' Donald said, grudgingly. He did not altogether feel comfortable with Berry's practice of selling on cars.

'They can't trace it back here,' Berry insisted, reading his mind.

'I thought we had an arrangement,' complained Donald crossly. He had no intention of crossing the line into an illegal business.

'Don't you start.' Berry was annoyed. 'It's a favour, all right? A favour!'

Madson carried a tray of coffee into Magda's office. Magda was talking to Elaine, who had brought Roy Holt's case file for Magda's inspection. 'It's all there. You'll see it if you look through the original case notes. Judge just accepted the police story verbatim.'

'What time are we due at the prison?' Madson inquired as he handed round the cups of coffee.

'Two o'clock,' Elaine confirmed.

Madson thought for a moment. 'I've got to get George Lodge's papers over to the crown court. I'll be at your house by one.'

'Will you come with us to see the boy?' Elaine asked Magda, as Madson disappeared out of the door. But Magda had other commitments. 'Madson can tell me what happened. I have great faith in him,' she said.

Elaine leant towards her with a playful laugh. 'So I hear!'

Magda was instantly alarmed, wondering what gossip was circulating.

But Elaine reassured her: 'I know you think highly of his abilities.'

'That's the reason I sponsored him here,' she confided.

'I also know he's an attractive man,' Elaine teased. 'He's got these incredible eyes, hasn't he?'

Driving with Elaine towards the high gates of the institution, Madson began to feel oppressed. Elaine chatted cheerfully away, filling him in on the boy's background. But the sight of the high walls rekindled dreadful memories.

'It was a shambles,' Elaine was saying. 'Legal Aid assigned a lawyer who drank heavily, and remembers nothing about the case. The judge took every word the police spoke as gospel. Roy had an alibi witness who was never found because nobody believed he existed.'

'Do you think he existed?' Madson inquired curiously. If there was a witness, he could try and find him. And Elaine did think so. She believed in Roy, and was determined to get him a fair hearing. After all, the boy had stayed at school and finished five GCSEs. When he had been stopped by the police he had been going to see someone about a job, but the boy had been in a hot car, with a boot full of stolen video machines. It did not look good.

A guard led Elaine and an uneasy Madson into a sparsely furnished interview room, where Roy was already waiting, sitting on a wooden chair at a table in the centre of the room.

'This is John Madson, Roy,' Elaine introduced him.

Roy knew all about him already. 'You're the one that done eight years, wrongly convicted, right?'

'John's here to help you, Roy,' Elaine broke in; they did not have very long to talk.

But Roy was despondent about his situation. 'Nobody can help me,' he said flatly.

'I promised I'd do everything I could, didn't I,' said Elaine. 'I can't help you if you won't cooperate.'

But Roy simply looked cowed. Madson looked at him. 'Will you take your shirt off for me, Roy?' he asked.

Roy looked suspicious. 'Why?'

'You know why,' said Madson. Elaine appeared confused, but Madson explained that if he had guessed right – it had happened to him once, his first time in Brixton prison – it would explain some of Roy's fears. Roy stood up slowly and unbuttoned his denim shirt, and then pulled up his white T-shirt to reveal a body covered in bruises.

'Who did this?' Elaine was shocked. 'Was it in here, or on the way back?'

Roy began to cry, silent tears falling down his dark cheeks. 'Here,' he said quietly. 'And for nothing, man. I didn't do nothing.' He pulled his shirt back on and sat down.

'What happened?' asked Madson.

Roy proceeded in stages to tell the whole story of his arrest and conviction. He had been going for a job interview on the day of his arrest. 'I was late,' he explained. 'This guy on the estate, he saw me, I thought he was being cool. He says he's going up west, he'll give me a lift. We hadn't gone a mile, these cops drive up behind, lights, you know the routine . . . And this guy just takes off.' He was obviously still stunned. 'He stops the car, says "run" so I run. The cops get me but they can't find this other geezer. Turns out the car's hot and there's like three grand's worth of VCRs and stuff in the boot. I swear to God, man, I swear I never. It was a job interview. I just wanted the job. My mum's not well,' his voice rose as he fought back the tears. 'She needed me and look at me now.' He got up and banged his fist hard against the wall in frustration.

Madson looked at him sympathetically. 'This bloke really exists?' he asked. But this only made Roy suspicious of him.

'You don't believe me, do you?'

'I didn't say that,' Madson sighed.

'I thought you were different,' Roy emphasized. 'She said you were banged up and you didn't do it.'

Madson could only nod that he understood.

This was not good enough for Roy, who was beginning to feel he was going mad. 'Why doesn't anyone believe me? I didn't fucking do it!'

'I believe you,' Madson replied.

But Roy was not listening by this time. 'I shouldn't be here,' he continued. 'I was going for a job interview and I didn't do it!' Roy broke down completely in tears this time, his body convulsed with sobs. Elaine guided him back to his chair, her arm protectively around him. The guards returned to take him back to his cell.

DC Lear had been on the drugs raid with Rourke at Madson and Sarah's flat and now he found himself being interviewed by the police solicitor, Armstrong. To his horror he found that he, as well as Rourke, had been named on the writ that had been issued for wrongful arrest.

'All you have to do,' Armstrong informed him, 'is to swear on oath that the drugs were genuinely discovered in the drawer as described in your report.' Lear squirmed noticeably; he was not very happy with this state of affairs. Rourke had put him in a distinctly uncomfortable position.

'If we lose, what happens?' Lear asked carefully, not wishing to incriminate himself.

'The burden of proof is on the plaintiff,' Armstrong reassured him. 'We won't lose unless they can produce evidence to prove their case. I don't see how they can.'

'This case' – Lear decided to get right to the point –

'it's about Rourke and this Madson, isn't it?' He did not stop for a reply but continued with his train of thought. He had a wife and child to think of, he could not jeopardize their police house or risk a disciplinary hearing. He wanted out now. 'Madson's a brief or something now, isn't he?' He looked up for confirmation.

'He's an outdoor clerk,' Armstrong answered.

'It's him, Madson. It's all about him. If we lose this case there'll be a disciplinary hearing. I can't go through with this vendetta of Rourke's,' he said emphatically. 'I want out now.'

Armstrong looked at him. 'I think you should talk to your commanding officer at the earliest possible opportunity.'

Having failed to secure a bank loan, although Dominic had gone with her to see the bank manager, Sarah had left Dominic sulking in a Charing Cross Road bookshop, and climbed aboard a bus bound for Harlesden. She knew where to go if you wanted to borrow money in an emergency, and this to her mind was an emergency. She was determined to move on in her life. Pull herself out of the hole into which she had plunged with Rob's illness and the corresponding collapse of her career. Now it was imperative to work, and she blinded herself to the risks of borrowing from a loan shark. Dominic had muttered darkly about brutal men and broken legs, which had not helped. She looked miserably out of the window at the drab shops along the bus route.

Madson returned home feeling agitated and distressed. He opened up a cheap bottle of Chardonnay, poured some into a glass, and then looked into the fridge for something to eat. He took out a box of eggs and a packet of butter and began to prepare himself an omelette. As he broke the eggs into a bowl he turned on Sarah's radio, hoping that it would banish the sounds of clanging doors and turning keys, warders' whistles and the loud voices barking orders. He refilled his glass, and drank it down in one. He poured the egg mixture into a hot frying pan, and reached for the wine bottle to top up his glass again just as Sarah walked in.

'Hi.' She greeted him dully; her day had been something of a strain.

'Hi,' he said wretchedly.

Sarah glanced at the Chardonnay. 'Can I have a drink?' She poured herself a drink, and then looked at him. 'You look like you've been back inside.'

'I have.'

'What?' Sarah was startled.

'Just visiting,' he explained. 'Some kid Elaine found, been screwed by the system something rotten. Brought it all back.'

'Shall I make some coffee?' she suggested. 'I think you need some coffee.'

He frowned. 'I thought we had a deal, we wouldn't tell the other person what we thought they needed!'

'Sorry,' she responded with a smile. 'Milk, no sugar, right?'

He turned the omelette out on to a plate, and took another sip of the wine, noticing the flavour for the first time. As she made the coffee, Sarah tried to think what she could do to help him. She was curious about his relationship with Magda; she wondered whether he was able to talk to her about his feelings, about the trauma surrounding this work that he had taken on. Did he have someone to confide in? She handed him a cup of coffee and sat with him companionably. He smiled at her gradually as he began to feel more relaxed. They listened to the music, contented in each other's company.

Sir Ranald looked up at Magda with appreciation as she came though the door wearing a well-cut blue suit, slit at the front to show a glimpse of leg as she walked. He approved of her *pro bono* work and was keen to encourage her; as far as he was concerned she was a smart woman. But he felt bound to bring up the subject of Madson.

'George Lodge wants him out.'

'George never wanted him in,' she retorted.

'Says he's unreliable. I rather like the chap.'

'Me too.'

'Yes, we all know that,' he joked. He was extremely fond of her; she was an asset to the firm. But they would have to deal with George and his complaints about Madson's 'attitude problem'.

The council estate was dreary and bleak. Washing was strung from grey concrete balconies; a mother shouted crossly at the toddler in his pushchair, as she struggled along the pavement; some boys were kicking a football about in the parking lot. Madson got out of his car and looked around with interest. This was the estate where Roy Holt and his mother lived, and he thought someone might know about the youth Roy had accepted a lift from that day. Perhaps he was local. It was worth a try. A dirty football landed at his feet, and a boy shouted over to him to return it. 'What'll you give me for it?' he called, as he prepared to throw it back. It was in his interest to start a conversation. 'Brixton credit card if you don't,' the scruffy sandy-haired boy threatened; he must have been all of twelve years old.

'What's that?' asked Madson with amusement.

'Stanley knife,' the boy scowled, and Madson gave back the ball. He noticed a twitching of the curtains in an adjacent ground-floor flat. 'I wouldn't advise it,' he said. 'I've got a witness.'

'Oh her,' said the boy scornfully. 'She's an old witch. I'm not scared of her!'

An eye appeared in the spyhole in the front door of Mrs Grant's flat. She saw Madson, recognized him from his exchange with the boy and opened the door on the chain. He explained his business and she invited him in for a cup of tea. It was nice to have someone take an interest in her for a change. She did not receive many visitors.

'Vinny,' she said immediately, when he explained about the stolen video machines. 'That's what I heard.'

Madson was staggered that she knew who he was, that she was so sure. Why had he not been found before.

'Nobody ever asked me till now,' she said mildly, shrugging her shoulders. 'You get all sorts around here you know.' She thought about it for a moment. 'Of course he's not from around here, you know,' she confided, replacing a wisp of grey hair that had come astray in her hair net. 'He came with a gang of kids for a few weeks. He lived in north London – Tottenham, I think.'

'And you think this was the bloke Roy's talking about?' he asked, wanting her to be absolutely positive.

'I know it was,' she replied decisively.

A police car was waiting outside Berry's Car Recovery. Berry was outside on the forecourt talking to an officer, trying to fob him off. Two other uniformed officers stood silently surveying some of the cars in the garage. Berry was adamant that he had done nothing wrong. 'This is a con,' he said, his face glowing beetroot with anger. He ran his hand through his ginger hair in desperation. 'Just because I've got form. I told you last time you turned me over. Uncle Donald's got the licence.'

At that moment Donald emerged from the office bearing the licence. He handed it to the sceptical policeman. Leaving him to sort this out, Donald went back into the office area, picked up his mobile phone and called Madson. 'Berry's got the boys in blue on his back,' he whispered urgently, hoping that the police in the forecourt would not hear him. Madson was swift and decisive: Donald should meet him at Hearnley & Partners in one hour.

Magda met Roy Holt in the soulless interview room at the institution. Magda was less affected than Madson by the starkness of the place; she was used to visiting clients in prison. And she had some positive news to impart. There were only three grounds for appealing against a conviction at this stage, and she had been granted leave to appeal on the grounds of a material irregularity: Roy's original barrister had been an alcoholic, and was now in a clinic. At first Roy did not understand what she was saying.

'We've been given leave to appeal,' Magda repeated.

Roy looked stunned; then amazed; then he leapt up from his chair with delight, a different person. He thrust his fist into the air in triumphant salute. 'Yes!' he said.

'It is only leave to appeal,' Magda stressed, in an attempt to calm him. He ignored her, lifting her up and trying to carry her round the room.

'Put me down,' she shouted.

The door opened, and one of the prison guards came in. 'Put her down, Roy!' he barked.

Roy danced about the room, climbing up on the chair. 'I've won my appeal! I'm getting out!' he shouted.

'No, no, you haven't.' Magda tried to explain. 'It's only the right to an appeal. You haven't won anything yet.'

But Roy was no longer listening, he was hopping about in a crazy dance.

CHAPTER FIFTEEN

An air of determination gripped George Lodge as he piled heap after heap of paperwork on to Madson's desk. Short, thickset and thinning on top, his shoulders hunched in petty resentment, he barked orders unrelentingly.

'This brief to Rebecca Rosenblum in Gray's Inn,' he frowned as he pulled out another sheaf of papers and thrust them into Madson's arms. 'This goes to Jack Whittaker – you've been there before; these need to be deposited at the West London County Court by 2 p.m.' He continued in this vein for some minutes, before looking at Madson for a response.

'Right,' Madson agreed, without comment. Though inside he was seething. Yes, he had been hired to do this sort of work as well as the investigative side of the job. But it would surely prove counterproductive to heap so much of it on his plate when he had inquiries to make. George Lodge, he concluded, was a fool. And as far as Madson could see there was no real reason for his prejudice.

Suddenly he realized that Lodge was still speaking to him. He was complaining about Madson's failure to bring him a smoked salmon sandwich the previous day. Well, it was hard luck that the shop had run out of salmon before Madson arrived. There was nothing wrong with tuna fish, and with a squeeze of lemon you could hardly tell the difference. Madson smiled to himself. Lodge slouched out of the office in a fog of resentment.

As Lodge went out, and Madson was surveying the papers with a sigh, Donald came in. He was concerned for Berry's safety. Not only did he need protection from the police but probably also from the man he had been doing the job for. He came straight to the point. 'Gordon's been doing a favour for Mickey Peacock.'

Madson looked up sharply. 'What kind of a favour?'

'Changing chassis numbers, that kind of thing,' Donald explained. Gordon could be so stupid, Madson thought to himself. What would Cheryl do if he got put away again – and the two young boys. Peacock would not stop at one or two jobs, he was a serious criminal and could get Gordon into big trouble.

'I'll go round tonight,' he said to Donald. But Donald still looked extremely worried. He explained quickly that Peacock was on his way over to see Berry as they spoke, and that the police had already put in a rather heavy-handed appearance.

Madson was torn. He looked in dismay at the extent of the paperwork he had to copy and deliver all over town, not to mention the Coleman, Jones & Edwards papers, which had to be collected from the D X. In addition, as Gordon had taken the car back, he had no transport. Together they pondered the various problems that had to be overcome, wasting precious minutes. Finally Donald took matters in hand, insisting that Madson take his car and go and sort out Berry, while he picked up the heap of papers and made ready to take them around London on a bus.

Dropping Donald at a bus stop with explanations of how to get which set of papers to which destination,

Madson roared off up the Marylebone Road towards west London to rescue Berry. He arrived just in time to cross with a rather unpleasant-looking character who must, thought Madson, noting the grimness of his bearing, work for Mickey Peacock. He found Berry in his office, intact and making tea.

Berry was not in the best of moods and he was distinctly annoyed with Donald for insisting that Madson come to give him a talking to. He slammed down two unappealingly grey mugs of tea on his desk and turned to glare at Madson.

'I'm just trying to help,' Madson insisted.

'Well, you're not. You're not helping.'

'Does Cheryl know about this?'

'You must be joking,' Berry spluttered. 'It's a one off.'

But Madson was not going to be put off so easily. 'Who are you kidding?' he retorted sceptically.

But Berry had had more than enough trouble for one day. 'Haven't you got work to do?' he asked dismissively. Then he looked embarrassed – Madson was his friend, after all, and he was trying to help. He pulled out a chair, and Madson drank his tea. He still had a favour to ask of Berry.

'If I was looking for a dodgy video recorder in north London . . .' Madson began.

Berry eyed him suspiciously. Surely he could not think that he was involved in that old game. He was strictly involved with cars, and legit. ones for the most part. 'Are you?' he responded at last.

Madson explained about Roy Holt and how he had been set up. And Gordon was relieved that Madson had moved on to a topic that was less personal. Tottenham, he pondered; he had a few pals who lived up that way – he would find out.

Madson thanked him before he left. 'Look,' he said gently, 'I'm thinking about both of you. You and Cheryl.'

Berry still hedged his bets. 'I know JP,' he said, not quite looking him in the eye. 'But I never gone legitimate before. It's difficult by yourself.'

Thank God for Uncle Donald, thought Madson; at least there was someone who could look out for him. He remembered at that moment that Donald was busy doing his deliveries for him, and felt even more grateful to him.

Madson returned to his office at Hearnley & Partners to find Lodge hopping mad.

'Madson,' he shrieked, 'where have you been?'

'Out,' Madson informed him in a clipped tone as he hung up his coat. He quickly checked his desk for Donald's delivery, but found none.

'Where are those papers from Coleman, Jones & Edwards?' he continued aggressively.

Madson was calm. 'I'm looking for them,' he said, carefully, privately vowing to throttle Donald.

But George was not listening. 'I've just had Jack Whittaker's chambers on the phone. What the hell have you been doing?' He stormed out without waiting for an explanation.

But a question mark hung alarmingly in the air. What had become of Donald and the papers?

Madson picked up the phone and rang Berry in a panic. 'Cool it,' cautioned Berry. 'I don't know where he is. He hasn't ... hang on,' he said as his mobile burbled into life. 'Donald?' he said into the mobile.

Donald, it turned out, had been given a lift from the bus stop by an old friend, and they had peeled off to a poker game at the Three Kings, for a brief respite.

Unfortunately brief had turned into lengthy. 'Calm down,' Berry asserted, having discovered all this. 'He's on the case.'

'By the way,' Madson began to explain. 'About Mickey Peacock . . .'

But Berry did not want to hear him out; he had news of his own to impart. 'By the way, you want dodgy VCRs in Tottenham, try the Golden Cockerel off the High Road. Ask for Arthur . . . Yeah,' he said, taking in what Madson had said for a moment, but dismissing it. 'Well I appreciate it, JP, I've decided to pull out,' he said confidently. 'You'd better get the grapes and chocolates ready.'

Before Berry could turn round, the unfriendly-looking character who had passed Madson earlier at the garage loomed into view, and quickly depressed the telephone buttons, terminating the call. Berry turned to face the man.

'Oh it's you,' he exclaimed. 'I've thought about it. I'm not doing it!' He hurled the phone at the thickset man and, ducking under his arm, made a dive for the door. The man grabbed at Berry, caught hold of his legs, and dragged him down to the floor with a thud. Just then another thug appeared at the door, and he too hurled himself into the fray, kicking Berry in the stomach and winding him.

Lear was packing up his things from his desk, ready to go home for the night, when Rourke walked into the office. After the lengthy talking-to from Armstrong he was not pleased to see Rourke. More than anything he wanted to be moved to another case, another department. But he was just a touch frightened of Rourke, his temper and his vendettas.

Rourke was casual. 'Everything all right with that

solicitor?' he asked, as if it were not of prime importance to him.

'Sure.' Lear was noncommittal.

'You're not worried, are you?' Rourke added, slapping him on the back confidently. Then he went on to explain that he had another job for him to do, which involved tailing Madson.

Lear was furious; Rourke seemed to expect him to go on and on with this pointless investigation, despite the probable damage to his career. He could not comprehend why Rourke could not just leave it alone.

Rourke seemed to read his mind. He fixed Lear with a steely glare. 'Madson's a villain, Jason. He killed his wife.'

'Yeah?' Lear was unconvinced, which infuriated Rourke further.

'He was convicted, wasn't he? He got sent down for life. You want scum like him walking the streets . . .' he broke off, seeing Lear's uncomfortable, reluctant face. 'Has someone offered you a deal? Tell me!' he shouted.

Lear looked away, and finished packing his things. Picking up his bag ready to leave, he shook his head at Rourke. 'I can't go on with this,' he said stiffly. 'I have my family to think of.'

Rourke watched his retreating back, and sighed. Lear had a wife and baby to support, and they had clearly frightened him with some threat of demotion. Well, he reflected, he himself had no such responsibilities, and he intended to go for the jugular. Nobody would stop *him*.

Madson returned home that evening to find Sarah and Dominic unpacking a new Apple Mac computer and printer. He stood by as they set it up, but it did occur to him to wonder where they had got it from. Surely these things cost thousands. 'Great,' he enthused as Sarah began to unwrap the software. 'Where did you get it?'

Dominic made no comment. But Sarah cut in shortly, 'It's mine, I got it out of storage.' She turned back to the software dismissively.

Madson was not put off. 'Storage?' he queried.

'My parents were looking after it.'

'You been down to Bromley, then?' he persisted.

Sarah was cross. 'What is this?' She raised her voice.

Madson, however, was certain that she had told him that her computer had been sold to pay for Rob's heroin habit. Also he knew it was very unlikely she would go to visit her parents.

Finally Sarah whipped out a receipt to show that she had paid for the computer. She had paid in cash. The money had come from Harry Conroy, a loan shark. Madson was first flabbergasted, and then horrified. Somehow he would have to get the money paid back, sooner rather than later.

In the meantime Madson had a phone call from a pub in Tottenham. It was Arthur, a friend of Berry's. He was impressed with the work Madson was doing for Hearnley & Partners, and particularly impressed that an ex con could have turned his life around to such an extent that he was now working from the other side to get people in trouble a fair hearing. Arthur knew a lot of people in the north London circuit; he also knew and disapproved of Vinny. He would be back in touch when he had set something up.

The atmosphere in Magda's office that morning was sombre. Elaine was reading an official letter which had just arrived from the appeal court. Her silence did not bode well. She handed the letter to Magda. 'We lost,' she said bitterly.

Magda glanced at the letter, and added, 'I talked to one of the appeal judges. They felt that although the barrister was ill it made no difference to the verdict.' Magda had done her level best, but they were up against the system itself.

'So if you get a barrister who does a truly terrible job,' Elaine continued grimly, 'that's just bad luck for you.'

Magda looked at her blankly. What more could they do? 'It's bad luck and two years in prison for a crime you didn't commit,' she said flatly. They had done their best and it had not worked. There was no more to be done.

But Elaine persisted: she knew the boy well, having visited him and pursued his best interest for some months. Surely there was still something they could do to win his freedom. 'Did Madson find anything?' She remembered that he had been hoping to trace the missing witness. 'I mean about the boy who gave Roy the lift that day?' she queried, a glimmer of hope reflected in her features.

But Magda could not offer any information on this score; Madson never told her anything about his investigations until they were over.

'Is he in?' Elaine inquired hopefully. She thought he might come down to the young offenders institution with her to talk to Roy.

But Magda had seen Madson briefly that morning, and knew that Lodge had been on at him again. Madson was rushing around delivering papers to other legal firms all over London, and collecting documents from the Chancery Lane DX. He would not be back for some time. And it seemed unlikely that he would have had much chance to conduct any investigations on Roy's behalf.

For once Magda found herself railing against the system. Damn them all she thought crossly, looking across her desk at the dejected Elaine, who wore a worried frown. There was no more that Magda could usefully do on this case, and she forced herself to move her mind on to the next meeting she had to deal with that day.

At the institution that afternoon, Elaine found that once again she was up against the unhelpful attitude of the guards. She had a whole list of visits to make that day in her allotted three-hour visiting period, and she was spending much of her time marching up and down corridors requesting guards to unlock gates.

She found Roy's cell door locked and guarded by Terry, the guard she had dealt with before. Roy, it transpired, was on punishment and could not be visited today. She wondered what he could have done this time. It seemed that they had not been able to find some of the books that he needed for his studies, and he had been told he would have to wait until they turned up or could be replaced. At that he had thrown a complete fit, breaking everything in sight, and had had to be locked up for his own safety – and perhaps the safety of some of the others. They hoped he would cool off after a day or two spent in his cell. Elaine was horrified; she had wanted to tell him personally that his appeal had been turned down, before he received an official letter.

'Surely you can appreciate . . .' She looked at the guard beseechingly. But the guard could not, or would not, allow her to speak to Roy, even through the grille. He had his orders, and there were rules about being on punishment. It was thanks to him, after all, that the lad had not been sent back down to the block.

'I'll tell him,' Terry agreed in the end, but Elaine still looked doubtful. 'What's the matter?' He smiled at her. 'Don't you trust me?'

Elaine looked at him uncertainly, but recognized the hopelessness of the situation. 'You're the one person I do trust,' she said. 'When can I see him?' she asked quickly.

'Sunday.'

She turned to go, 'Tell him I'll be back Sunday. I'm going to see Danny Mawson now.' She strode off down the corridor, moving on mentally to the next inmate on the list she held in her hand.

Outside a twenty-four-hour garage in a broad north London street Madson waited, slapping his arms against the cold air. A flashy black car, its powerful sound system going full blast, pulled up beside him. There was a grinning black youth at the wheel.

'Vinny?' Madson asked.

The window wound down. 'You got the cash?' Vinny queried.

'I'd like to see the stuff first,' Madson retorted. The door was opened for him and he climbed into the passenger seat.

They sped off. However, Vinny made it clear that he would not show him where he kept the goods. The goods would appear when they had a deal in place and the money in hand.

Sitting beside him, Madson reflected that he was a good-looking lad, expensively dressed, exuding self-confidence from every pore.

'You use this car on a job?' Madson asked, as if praising the quality of the car.

'Never,' Vinny confessed easily. 'You get stopped all the time. Learned my lesson!' He smiled brazenly.

'Oh yeah?' prompted Madson, hoping he would continue.

'Yeah,' Vinny responded. 'Got pulled in with a boot-load of stuff once.'

'What happened?' Madson asked curiously, though he thought he already knew.

'Legged it,' said Vinny succinctly. 'They caught some deadbeat, we was both happy, know what I mean?' he laughed. 'You into porn?' he asked suddenly.

'Could be,' Madson hedged, wondering what was coming.

'That's what most geezers want half a dozen VCRs for. Three hundred quid,' he concluded. 'Half before, half on delivery, right?'

'Right,' agreed Madson, seeing that they had reached the spot from which they started. Vinny pulled in, and Madson got out.

'Back in half an hour,' Vinny called after him.

Madson crossed quickly over the road to where Berry was waiting in the garage forecourt with his engine running. He slid into the car beside Berry as Vinny drove off up the road. Stealthily they followed.

Vinny pulled up beside a lock-up garage, jumped out, not noticing that Berry's car had pulled up near by, and slipped inside. Inside was a veritable wonderland of electronic goods piled high up to the ceiling, and as far back as the eye could see. All the goods were new, still in their original boxes, mainly VCRs and computers.

Madson and Berry watched him go in, and waited a few moments. Then Berry with a slight grin pulled out a pair of handcuffs that a policeman might use. 'I always wanted to do this,' he declared happily. 'Ready?' he checked with Madson, and they sprang out and ran towards the garage.

Roy Holt was devastated. He could not believe that it was all over. Mrs Dews had promised him this appeal, and the lady solicitor. They had promised him he would get out. And now they were saying no, he would have to stay here and sit out his sentence. He was innocent, he had done nothing. And nobody believed him. They were all against him. He had nothing. No one was on his side. His shoulders slumped and heaved with the weight of his sobs.

Suddenly he knew what he must do, the only way out. As if in a trance, he began ritually to pull off the sheets and blankets from his bed, twisting them into ropes. There was one way out he thought, almost joy-fully, working methodically – one way to stop the ter-rible pain of desolation and abandonment.

Madson and Berry approached cautiously as Vinny began to load a van with boxes of VCRs. He whirled round as he heard the footsteps approach. 'I told you to wait,' he snapped, as he saw Madson's familiar face. In the next instant he saw the handcuffs in Berry's hand. He put two and two together and took a flying leap over the front of the van, running up the alleyway. Berry leapt after him. 'I'll take the car!' Madson yelled and ran for Berry's car. He raced the car up the cobbled alleyway and managed to cut Vinny off at the top, with-out mowing him down. Berry panted up to them, and snapped the handcuffs on to Vinny with satisfaction.

'You cops?' Vinny snarled. 'Arthur said you was OK,' he added in confusion.

'Not me,' Berry responded flippantly. 'I failed the

written exam.' He looked across at Madson. 'He failed the physical!'

Madson had no time for small talk. He grabbed Vinny's arm and marched him back to the van, demanding to know where he had got the stuff. Then he jammed his face up against Vinny's, 'Remember that kid you were telling me about? The kid who got picked up when you legged it?' he said threateningly.

Berry continued to taunt, and Vinny looked more and more scared by this strange, offbeat pair. Were they business rivals, Vinny wondered? Berry was working out how to distribute the goods in the lock-up to charity when Madson's mobile rang.

'Shut up,' Madson said sharply, as he listened to the phone. It was Elaine, her voice high and quivering with shock and horror. Roy Holt had been found hanged in his cell. Efforts to revive him had failed.

'Forget it, Gordon,' Madson said, snapping off the phone. Leaving them, he walked off, with a heavy heart, back to the car.

CHAPTER SIXTEEN

Magda stretched her arms luxuriously in bed, and watched as Madson returned from the kitchen with a tray of coffee and the morning papers. He sat down on the bed, passing her a cup of coffee and flicking the remote control at the small wall-mounted television; it zapped into life with an item on Christmas shopping crowds.

He took a swig of the hot, satisfying liquid, and had a quick look at the papers. Several of them had headlines on Phil Hartigan, the football star Hearnley & Partners were currently defending. 'The public love him,' Magda commented. But the chief prosecution witness would be giving evidence that day, and sympathy could go either way. She drank her coffee thoughtfully. This was her most prominent case to date, and she would very much like to win it. Reputations could be made or destroyed over a case like this.

She glanced over at Madson, who sat in his bathrobe, having taken an early shower. He looked fresh, handsome, ready for the day ahead. She wondered whether he would be accompanying her to the Old Bailey this morning; he had become very preoccupied with his own business lately. 'Where are you going today?' she inquired cautiously.

'I'm driving you to work,' he said shortly, not looking up from the newspaper he was reading.

'Then you disappear, like yesterday?' she persisted.

He looked at her, slightly irritated. 'I've got a lot to

do.' He did not yet want to discuss the direction his investigations into his former solicitor, Walter Gardner, were taking.

But Magda was determined to support him. 'Why do you have to go it alone? Ranny would give you all the services of the partnership,' she insisted. 'And I want to help.'

'I know,' Madson replied gently. 'But it's for me to do. I have to sort out Rourke alone.' He felt very single-minded about this. He did not want his personal problems, hangovers from the past, to sully his relationship with Magda. At this stage he wanted the two things kept separate. She would have to understand. And for the time being she did.

'You're a stubborn man,' she shrugged, closing the subject.

In a quiet suburban street near Kew, Walter Gardner emerged from the door of his wisteria-covered Victorian home, briefcase in hand, ready to begin his working day. He got into his car, which was parked in the middle of the leaf-strewn semicircular driveway, and began to drive out on to the street. But a blue Sierra, parked unobtrusively on the road, accelerated forward and stopped in front of the drive, effectively blocking his exit.

Gardner looked out of his car window, peering into the window of the Sierra. It was Dennis Rourke. Slowly Gardner got out of his car and went over to speak to him. The front passenger window powered down, and Gardner bent over to look in at Rourke. 'What do you want?' he asked, blustering, wishing that the thug of a man, policeman or no, would leave him alone for good.

'I want you to remember our original relationship,' Rourke drawled rudely. 'I'm the copper, I ask the questions. Have you had any contact with Madson since we talked Sunday?'

'I would've told you,' Gardner snapped in response. He wished fervently that he had never become involved with the man. But he had to listen – he still had a hold over him.

'You haven't been chatting to him?' Rourke asked. 'Cooking up something?' he added unpleasantly.

'Are you mad?' Gardner retorted. 'Of course not!'

But Rourke remained unconvinced. He had put a man on surveillance over the last few days, following Madson. 'Yesterday,' Rourke explained, his man had followed Madson to Gardner's house; he had reported back that Madson had driven to Kew at two o'clock, and had sat outside Gardner's house for half an hour.

'I've no bloody idea why,' Gardner insisted impatiently. He wanted to get back into his warm car, and away to the office.

'He didn't come here for nothing,' Rourke warned maliciously. Gardner glared at Rourke, and then turned and marched back to his car. He most certainly did not want the past dragged up again.

As they walked up the steps of the Old Bailey Magda and Madson were still arguing about the secrecy surrounding the work he was doing on his own case; Magda was also expressing concern that it was affecting the work he was carrying out for the firm. Today she particularly needed him to check some facts for her. Facts that Hartigan's barrister, Belling, might well need to have at his fingertips this afternoon. Madson assured her that he would have the information by then, and went into the Old Bailey with her to greet Sir Ranald and the barrister. Also, being quite a football supporter himself, he was keen to meet Hartigan, and Berry wanted him to get photos signed for Dan and Jeff, who were fans.

They began to move towards the court room.

'I'll get on with checking the time and the rest of that stuff,' Madson whispered to Magda.

She watched him go, wondering if his mind was really on the Hartigan case, and wishing that he would tell her before doing anything which could entangle him further with Rourke.

Berry stood in the forecourt of his car recovery, making notes on a clipboard, as Madson drove up. Donald also arrived at that moment, and Berry beckoned him to join them in the office.

Madson perched on a pile of boxes in the cramped, untidy office, and Berry found what he was looking for, an envelope of Polaroids taken by Donald for Madson. Madson had a look at them.

'Donald's not the greatest since David Bailey,' Berry joked. 'Any good?'

'Yes.' Madson looked serious. He pointed. 'That's Rourke.' Donald had been instructed to take photos of Gardner and the exterior of his house; Rourke's presence was an interesting bonus.

Donald looked perplexed. 'I'm following the guy,' he said, 'but I don't know who's doing what to whom.'

Madson filled him in as he examined the Polaroids more carefully. 'This is Rourke,' – he pointed to the heavy man sitting in the car – 'the bent copper who sent me down, meeting Gardner, my bent solicitor who helped him.' He glanced up at Donald with a serious expression. 'Tell me Gardner's movements.'

Berry could see that this was all going to take some time. He turned and put the kettle on ready to make them all a cup of tea. Donald continued earnestly to fill Madson in on Gardner's movements, carefully consulting his notebook like an old-fashioned policeman giving evidence. 'You could set your watch by him! Last three days he leaves his house any time between eight and ten thirty, leaves the office any time between five and eight. Twice he popped back around two-ish to his house.' He paused to turn the page, and then continued. 'He didn't appear to go out in the evening at all.' Donald looked up from his notebook; that was about it.

'So,' Madson concluded, taking a sip of the tea that Berry had handed him, 'the last three days he hasn't been in his house, say between eleven and one?'

'Yeah,' Donald agreed.

'Right,' said Madson, with a grin of anticipation. Now he was getting somewhere.

The three men strolled out of the office on to the forecourt to have a look at the cars they had available that day. Madson suddenly remembered the photographs of Hartigan which he had got the footballer to sign. He extracted them from his jacket pocket and offered them to Berry. 'Give these to the kids,' he said.

Berry was delighted. 'The boys will be chuffed!'

Donald looked at the images in Berry's hand thoughtfully. 'I heard a story about Hartigan,' he said, scratching his head, 'years ago, before he came to London.' He remembered that he had had a bad reputation with the women – but then so did many footballers, he supposed.

But Madson was interested. 'Do your best, Donald,' he urged. 'Anything about Hartigan might be important.'

'I'll make a call,' Donald offered, not being able to dredge any further recollections from his memory. He felt sure somebody else would remember the story.

'And if you see Walter Gardner and Rourke together again,' Madson added as he got into his car, 'phone me immediately, right?'

'Right,' Donald agreed.

Wendy Anderton QC was giving the case for the prosecution. Philip Hartigan was accused of attacking his estranged wife Mary in the hallway of her home in Oxford, and of beating her so severely that she was now in a vegetative state, from which she would never recover. Hartigan had told the police that he was driving to London at the time, and therefore could not have committed the crime. The prosecution intended to prove that this was a lie, and that prior to the attack he had arrived drunk at the home of Mrs Perrin, their key witness, become even more drunk during lunch, and then gone off to attack his wife.

Belling and Magda conferred in whispers as Anderton put all this to the court. Belling had managed to have a look at Mrs Perrin that morning, and was forced to confess that she looked extremely respectable. 'Classic middle-aged Middle England,' he reported to Magda in muted tones, shrugging his shoulders. 'She'll work well for them.'

'I saw her too,' Magda informed him, noticing with a start that he was rather attractive; lately she had not been noticing such things, and this was, surprisingly, rather refreshing. 'I'm sure you can unpick her at the seams . . .' she murmured into his ear.

Anderton, for the prosecution, was explaining that Hartigan had a house near Oxford and a flat in West Hampstead. On the day of the attack, Anderton said,

Hartigan claimed that he had left his home in Oxford-shire at noon exactly, after making a social phone call to Anne Perrin, and had driven to London in his sports car in under an hour, in time to watch the one o'clock news on television.

Magda and Belling watched with mounting anxiety as Anne Perrin was called and began to give her evidence. She was clearly a strong card against Hartigan. She claimed that on the fateful day he had been drinking heavily, which was obviously likely to make the jury less sympathetic towards him.

Hearnley & Partners had been decorated early for Christmas; golden lights twinkled in the tall tree that stood proudly in reception. Upstairs in his office Madson was on the telephone to the AA trying to ascertain the minimum journey time between Oxford and London on a busy Wednesday lunch time. Would it be possible to do in under fifty minutes, he queried. Lodge stormed in as he was in mid phone call, demanding to know where he had been all morning; there had been no entry in Madson's diary describing his whereabouts, he complained. Madson, continuing his call, looked up briefly at Lodge. 'I'm making inquiries: the Hartigan case,' he said briefly.

But Lodge was not put off. 'You're still the outdoor clerk here. Deliver this to Herries, Morton,' he ordered, thrusting a package at Madson. Madson took it without a word, and continued speaking to the AA patrolman. Lodge left the room, his back rigid with disapproval.

Number One Court at the Old Bailey broke for lunch and Belling steered Magda out into the wide hall. The firm had given Andrew Belling the brief because he was quite capable of reducing witnesses to tears; Magda wondered whether they would require these particular skills. Belling suggested brightly that they discuss his tactics over lunch, but Madson entered at that moment, and Magda became embarrassed. 'Are you free this evening?' Belling queried, oblivious. 'Fine,' Magda whispered; it was only to discuss work, she told herself. Belling excused himself, and Madson quickly filled her in on the expert opinion of the AA patrolman. It would just be possible, he had confirmed, to drive from Oxford to London in fifty minutes at that time of day, though he would have to have been driving very fast.

'I've also been checking case law as it relates to the discovery of evidence,' he said intensely, taking her arm, and steering her gently out of the building.

'So?' she asked, a fraction miffed at being steered so expertly away from the dashing, if rather smooth, barrister.

'Sarah and Dominic did not witness Rourke and Lear's so-called discovery of the heroin!'

She stopped for a moment, taking in what he was saying. 'You're going about this the wrong way,' she advised.

'All I need is points of law,' Madson insisted.

Magda was absolutely sure that this was the wrong approach. It was no good serving a writ on Rourke for planting heroin on Sarah and Dominic with the intention of raising in court the whole relationship between Madson and Rourke, past and present. Madson was determined that this was what the whole case was about. But Magda knew that it was not – it was simply about two kids and an ounce of heroin. Rourke would have the weight of the police force behind him, possibly even a top QC. Her brow creased with concern as she advised him strongly to go and see the Met. legal department, to work out some deal with them. But Madson was not convinced; he wanted revenge. Magda walked away, leaving him to ponder what she had said.

It was not long before Madson was on his mobile phone to Berry, oblivious to Magda's well-intentioned advice. 'Donald's sorted out Gardner's approximate daily routine.' Madson went over the details. 'Now I want to concentrate on Rourke. I have to know where both of them are when I'm at Gardner's. So can you and Donald cover Rourke now?'

Berry was left speculating as to whether his friend had gone mad. 'Follow a cop?'

'Follow a cop,' Madson repeated firmly.

'Sure,' Berry agreed, wondering whether he too was losing his marbles.

At the flat, Sarah and Dominic were also discussing Madson's handling of their case. Dominic was arguing that they should consult another lawyer, for Madson was taking the whole thing personally, and they were facing a serious charge. Sarah was defending Madson and his integrity: 'He's got Magda and that whole firm backing him,' she concluded loyally. But Dominic maintained that Madson's priority was not them, but Rourke.

Sarah had been trying to work, but she found it hard to concentrate when they had not concluded their row. 'Look,' she said, 'I trust him. He cares about us. He's not going to let us go to prison.'

But Dominic was in a mood to hurt, and anyway did not have the same faith in Madson. 'He said he didn't kill his wife either,' he pointed out bitterly. 'Didn't stop him from going down, did it?' Sarah looked extremely distressed by this, and Dominic apologized. He wished Sarah would leave London and its memories of Rob, and start afresh with him in the country. He had been offered the possibility of a recording studio in Devon. Together they could make a new life there.

But Sarah was not placated by his apologies, and she had no interest in a recording studio in Devon.

Rourke himself was being given a hard time. Chief Superintendent Walton was insisting that DC Lear's evidence would not stand up in court. Walton had had Lear in for an interview with Armstrong, and the man had contradicted himself twice.

Rourke for once was concerned: 'It's too late for this,' he frowned. 'We're in court next week.'

'We're in court?' Walton repeated. 'You, Detective Inspector, are in court!'

'I expect the fullest support from you, sir, and the solicitor, and DC Lear, on this matter,' Rourke blustered. He did need them on his side if he was to succeed.

But Walton had already made up his mind; he had been down this path before with Rourke. 'You've got some personal vendetta going on with Madson. That's your affair. It can no longer be our affair,' he concluded, getting up from his seat and dismissing Rourke with a gesture.

Rourke staggered to his feet. 'What?' he said incredulously.

'You'll be provided with the solicitor and the usual support,' Armstrong said flatly. 'But if you go into court to defend yourself against Madson's writ, you don't have my support, and you're doing so at your own peril.'

Madson returned home that evening to find Sarah in a foul mood, and the papers relating to his case unaccountably removed from the table to the floor. Sarah had set out her design papers and the computer on the table. 'What the hell's happened here?' he complained; 'I told you to leave the papers alone. They were all laid out and arranged. You've messed them up!'

Sarah was in a mood to argue; 'I need space too!' she yelled. Then she grabbed her coat from the hook in the hall and flounced out.

At this point, Dominic emerged from the kitchen, where he had been lurking.

'What the hell's wrong with her?' Madson demanded.

'She's worried about the Rourke business,' Dominic suggested nervously, not keen to enlighten Madson further.

But Madson began to calm down and think. 'I don't think she is,' he said. 'She seemed confident I could deal with it. So what's eating her?'

Dominic had found her difficult for some time. Secretly he admitted to himself that she had begun to reject him; she was asking him for more space, and didn't want him to come round all the time.

'Is it me?' Madson wondered aloud.

'No,' Dominic advised, thinking that it might be him, 'leave it, see if it sorts itself out.'

'What the hell is "it"?' Madson demanded.

'Can't help you, man. I don't know.' Dominic shrugged mildly as he let himself out.

With a sigh Madson went over to the table and began to make some space so that he could sort out his documents. As he piled up Sarah's papers, he found a Department of Health pamphlet on nutrition in pregnancy; this, he thought to himself, would explain the moodiness. But he put the pamphlet back at the bottom of the pile, deciding he had better wait for Sarah to tell him when she was ready.

*

There were fresh flowers on each of the tables in the small, old-fashioned French restaurant, and Magda and Belling were sipping red wine at a cosy corner table, enjoying the chance to relax after the drama of the day. Anne Perrin had been very convincing in her testimony, and Magda was concerned. 'I think the jury like the Perrin woman,' she said.

Belling did in fact agree that she had been a very convincing witness, but he thought it a pity to ruin a jolly evening by saying so. But Magda persisted. Reluctantly he looked at her. 'At the end of the day,' he reflected, 'we'll have to put our boy in the box.'

'I don't like it.' Magda frowned as she leaned towards Belling, and he took advantage of her concentration to glance discreetly down at her cleavage. 'He's quite moody, temperamental.'

A crisp waiter arrived at their table, and Belling swiftly ordered for both of them. He did not want to break the intimacy with Magda.

'If Anderton provokes Hartigan, who knows where it could lead to? He's no rocket scientist.'

'Well,' Belling advised, impatient to get this part of the evening's discussion concluded, 'can you doublecheck those timings? The prosecution seems very agitated about them.'

'I'll set Madson on to it,' Magda said. As she mentioned him, she pictured him in her mind, studying intensely, hunched at his desk; in her imagination she traced her fingers over the laugh lines on his face. She began to wonder where he was this evening, whether he was all right.

Belling eyed her with a frown. He could not quite read her expression, though it was clearly something to do with this Madson. But he was only an outdoor clerk, it was impossible, thought Belling.

*

Early the next morning Madson was up and going through the Hartigan file in Magda's large, bright office. Magda was already in court with Hartigan and the defence team. She had telephoned him early, asking for him to make some rapid checks on timings. Mrs Perrin had insisted that she had been on the telephone to Colfords, an electrical appliance shop in Oxford, just before Hartigan had arrived for lunch. Could this be verified?

As he sat deep in concentration, with a long list of points to check through, the door swung open and George Lodge strode in in a bad temper.

'What are you doing here?' he demanded.

'Working,' Madson said.

'This isn't your office!' George insisted.

Madson looked up from the papers and explained, 'I'm going through case files.' He indicated the thick Hartigan file.

But Lodge was not listening to him. He thrust a large manila envelope towards Madson. 'You're an outdoor clerk. You don't sit in Miss Ostrowska's office,' he spat, consumed with jealousy. 'Take these papers to Denson, Miller & Company now!'

'No.' Madson returned to his list.

'What the hell do you mean, no?'

'George,' Madson said quietly.

'Yes?' Lodge was puzzled.

'Piss off.'

Red in the face, Lodge departed without saying a word.

CHAPTER SEVENTEEN

Lodge stood in Sir Ranald's office confronting a startled Sir Ranald, 'Piss off?' he repeated in some confusion. 'He said that? Piss off?'

'Yes.' George glared. 'It's an outrage!'

'I'll talk to him,' Sir Ranald agreed calmly, wondering if they were all suddenly back at school; his eye moistened as the fond memories of his alma mater came flooding back. He looked round to find Lodge still belligerently standing his ground; he was not going to be easily deflected.

'I want more than that,' George persisted. 'He goes, or I go.' Having thus thrown down the gauntlet, he paused dramatically, expecting a suitable response.

But Sir Ranald had no patience with this type of petty behaviour. 'I'll deal with it,' he said shortly.

'Did you hear what I said?' George asked incredulously.

As George finally departed from his office, Ranald sighed; he had no wish to take on the mantle of headmaster.

While Donald went off to follow Rourke round the police stations of west London, Madson and Berry headed over to Gardner's house. Madson hoped that Berry would be able to supply him with sufficient professional knowhow to get him in unobtrusively. He had already noted that there was an alarm on the house, and had no idea of how to get past it undetected.

The two men sat in Madson's car across the street from Gardner's house, taking in every detail of the prosperous exterior. Through the overgrown foliage, Berry could clearly see the red alarm, prominently marked 'Cordell Security'. Madson ran the whole story past Berry. When Jenny had broken into Gardner's office and stolen – 'Borrowed,' Berry corrected – Madson's original case file, there were letters in it, correspondence between Gardner and Rourke. Madson looked at Berry to make sure he was taking in the full implications of this connection. There was one letter, Madson explained, that had said something about 'dropping the charge'. Having spent a considered amount of time studying these letters, Madson had reached the conclusion that it was not referring to dropping the charge against him. These letters referred to Rourke dropping a charge against Gardner. Berry's astonished expression showed that he was following Madson's train of thought; the light had begun to dawn.

'But there was some correspondence missing,' Madson continued. 'Gardner mentions this letter from Rourke, and another letter from him to Rourke. The letters weren't there.'

'OK . . .' Berry wondered what other revelation was to come. In his world there might have been somebody given a good kicking, or beaten up, but this type of calculated assassination by educated men was quite a shock – a kind of fraud, he thought, based not on money but on callousness and hatred.

'I think the missing correspondence could be here,' Madson concluded, looking at Berry for his advice as to how best to get into the place.

'According to my panel of experts,' he began seriously, 'Reg Hill and brother Mick . . .' – a smile played briefly around his mouth – 'the Cordell Security alarm system is dead basic. Not a phone-through job, just contact points, infra-red, bells, etc.'

'So how do I get in?'

Berry looked pleased with himself; he had done his homework, and anyway he was familiar with good old-fashioned breaking and entering.

'Check how far this is from the local nick,' he began.

'Three miles.' Madson had checked that only this morning.

'Take a pickaxe, rubbish a door at the back, run through. There'll be a control box near the front door; pickaxe that. Get out of there. Drive off fast, couple of miles. Drive back half an hour later. See if there's activity. If there is – you've had it. Drive on. If no activity, you're in!'

'Right,' Madson nodded, taking this is in and digesting it rapidly. Thoughtfully he turned the key in the ignition and drove away, hoping fervently that he would be able to pull it off.

Donald was waiting for them, jumping with excitement, as they reached the entrance to the recovery garage; Berry wondered if he had been drinking.

'I've remembered. I've remembered!' he smirked at Madson. He had indeed been drinking that lunchtime, having discovered the favoured watering-hole of Brian Fenton, the physio who had treated Hartigan in his second-division days. The three of them wandered over to the office as Donald filled them in.

Fenton was a drunk, but none the less Donald had managed, with the help of fifty quid slipped into the man's pocket and a few shots of whisky each, to extract the half-remembered story from him. In a pre-season tour of Germany in 1990 Hartigan had got himself involved with a girl in Hamburg. One night he had beaten her, and she had been taken to hospital half dead.

'Cops?' Madson asked, wondering whether there would be witnesses. But Donald assured him that, as far as he knew, it had all been hushed up, no charges brought. The club had paid over a suitcase full of money; they did not want their biggest asset rotting in a German prison for years.

Having repeated the story, Donald collapsed into Berry's office chair, dragged his feet up on to the desk, brought them to rest neatly on a pile of invoices and promptly fell asleep.

That night Sarah sat morosely working on her computer as Madson banged about in the kitchen making himself a sandwich. He then opened the fridge and pulled out a carton of milk. Pouring the milk into a glass he looked speculatively over at Sarah. She did not react to his attention, continuing to type, though she did not appear to be deep in concentration. She seemed, rather, to be avoiding his eye.

Finally she gave in and looked over at him. 'How's the footballer case?' she asked, in a manner which did not sound particularly concerned.

'I thought you weren't interested,' Madson observed, annoyed with her mood; he did not see why he should make things easy for her. Sarah read his expression and apologized. She knew she had been giving both him and Dominic a hard time. But her mind was in such turmoil, she had not known how to begin to talk about what was happening to her body. It was all so complicated, so confused. At last she took a deep breath and told him that she was pregnant. He took it in his stride, having guessed already, but he wondered whether she had told Dominic.

Before Madson could begin to ask how Dominic was taking it, she was in his arms, weeping with relief at having begun to share her secret. Between hiccuping sobs she slowly filled in the details for him. She knew it would appear that Dominic was more likely to be the father but, she explained through her tears, a couple of months before he had died she had spent a few nights with her husband, and despite his weakness and dependency on drugs they had made love. Now she felt instinctively that Rob was the father of her child, but she was confused, and scared, and could not bring herself to confess all this to Dominic, so she had pushed him away.

Madson stood silently rocking Sarah in his arms. She raised her head and looked into his eyes. He smiled at her, patting her arm, comforting her, and thought what a miracle life was: he had lost his son, but perhaps was to have a second chance, as a grandfather.

Striding towards the door to the main courtroom at the Old Bailey – he had planned to get there for that morning's session before Belling cross-examined Anne Perrin – Madson met Magda coming out to look for him. She was hopeful that he might have uncovered information they could use to discredit Perrin, who was turning out to be a strong witness against Hartigan. They sat down on a bench in the hallway to talk. Madson produced a Xerox copy of a phone log triumphantly from his briefcase, knowing she would be pleased. She looked at it with interest as he explained that Perrin had said early on in her testimony that she was phoning a local repair shop as Hartigan arrived at her house for lunch. Having checked with the shop, Colfords in Summertown, Oxford, Madson had discovered that they had logged the time of her call. Madson pointed to the time of the call on the log in Magda's hand; it said 10.45.

'She said midday.' Magda was aghast.

Madson was pleased at the response he got for that gem of information. But then he went on to tell her the story he had gleaned from Donald about Hartigan's behaviour on the 1990 tour of Germany – how he had beaten up a girl and the incident had been hushed up. It was horribly similar to the events they were dealing with now.

'We have been retained by Hartigan to present a defence,' Magda reminded him in a disapproving voice. 'This information doesn't help.'

Madson, however, had wanted her to know that this was the calibre of the man they were working to defend. 'Anyway,' he added. 'If I've found out, maybe the prosecution will.'

Magda hoped fervently that they would not. However, the telephone log could be useful. Andrew would be keen to show that Perrin could be mistaken in her testimony. She went back into the court to make Belling aware of it as soon as possible.

It was just after eleven o'clock and raining when Madson stopped his car near the side of Gardner's house. He sat in the car for a moment glaring intently at the grey facade, but there was nobody about. Carrying a holdall, Madson walked quickly up the driveway and rang the front doorbell. To his relief there was no response, and he turned to go round the side of the house and through a little courtyard to the back garden, which was screened from prying eyes by tall trees and shrubs.

At the rear door Madson stopped, dropped his holdall and quickly glanced about. Still no one. High above the door he noticed another red Cordell Security alarm bell mounted on the wall. He took out a heavy panel beater's hammer Berry had given him. Raising it high above his head he brought it down hard on the Yale lock of the kitchen door. Not only did the lock shatter, but the door splintered with a dramatic crack and fell open. The alarms began to scream and the red lights to flash on and off. Madson rushed through the house to smash the alarm itself, and having done that, fled through the rear door and back up the driveway to his car. He hurled himself into it and roared away. He had never before done anything like it.

For the next half hour Madson sat chain-smoking in a back street in Chiswick. He saw no one, and so far as he could tell no one saw him. He threw the stub of his last cigarette out of the window and drove hastily back to Kew to survey the scene.

Nothing seemed to have moved or changed. There was no sound of the house alarms, no flashing lights, no police, not even a curious neighbour peeping through a gap in the curtain as far as he could make out. Stealthily he went into the house and began to search the large, high-ceilinged living-room. There were proud ancestral portraits, a bookcase, a small antique desk, but, so far as he could discover, no legal files or papers. Methodically he went through the entire house room by room. Climbing up to the second floor, he emptied every drawer and checked every cupboard; even the odd suitcase under the bed was pulled out but found to be useless.

There was so much at stake here, so much to lose if he were discovered. He was sure Gardner must have kept files, records, as all solicitors did, and these particular records were personal; they had not been kept with the other papers at the office, it would have been too risky. They had to be in this house. Looking up he suddenly spotted a folding ladder going up to an open hatch. He pulled down the ladder and was soon inside the loft.

In the gloom of the unlit, unconverted loft space, Madson looked about under the cobweb-strewn rafters for the files he had come for. He pushed aside rusting, old-fashioned bicycles, tea chests, boxes of crockery, a violin case. Right at the back he found a clear area, containing a row of four small steel filing cabinets, each one marked with handwritten dates on pieces of yellowing paper. With trepidation he opened the one marked '1987–89'. He had first met Walter Gardner, the greying regulation solicitor, in 1987. There was nothing special about him, though he had got others off; not the top league, but trustworthy, or so it had seemed. In 1988 Madson had been sent to jail for life. With a set face he began to pull out the correspondence for this period and read it on his knees by the light from a tiny loft window.

An hour later Madson gathered up a sheaf of letters and skipped down the ladder to the upper landing. At the top of the main staircase he stopped sharply as he caught sight of a malevolent Gardner, his small eyes piggy with hatred, his weak chin quivering as he levelled a double-barrelled shotgun straight at Madson.

Briefly, Madson regarded him in silence. 'Still thriving, eh? Doing your bent deals?' he said bitterly, his voice returning. But Gardner had the gun. He waved it at Madson, indicating the living-room.

'Save it all for Rourke. He's on the way. Go in there.' Seeing no alternative Madson began to descend the stairs and move towards the living-room.

Gardner gestured for Madson to sit opposite him, on a yellow velvet sofa. Warily Madson sat down. 'What was the deal between you and Rourke over my trial?' he asked, thinking that Gardner might be shocked into revealing more details of the incident before Rourke, probably the cleverer of the two, arrived to shut him up.

'Shut up . . .' Gardner snapped, not intending to fall for that sort of thing, and wishing fervently that Rourke would not take too long to turn up.

'I'm glad Rourke's coming,' Madson continued, ignoring Gardner's glare. 'Maybe he'll confirm some letters I've just read, 1987. These.' He pulled a batch of letters from his jacket pocket and waved them aggressively at Gardner. 'You were a solicitor with his hand in his client's till. Fraud. And Rourke was investigating you . . . about the time I was arrested. Then he stopped investigating you.' Madson stopped talking hoping Gardner would confirm what had happened. Instead Gardner clung more ferociously to his gun, pointing it with renewed fury.

'Give me those!' he yelled.

'No,' Madson replied firmly, wondering whether the gun was actually loaded, and even what the extent of the damage might be if it went off. Quite a lot he imagined, though he did not think for a moment that Gardner would actually use it.

'Give me those letters.'

Madson shook his head. 'Go on,' he dared him. 'Shoot me!' Madson had served eight years in prison because of this man, who had let another man go down rather than face the music for his own misdeeds. Madson had even found a copy of the writ that Gardner had been served with in November 1987. But he had never gone to court. And soon after Madson had gone down, delivered by his own defending solicitor. It would be unbelievable, he thought, if it were not true. Gardner continued to wave his gun ineffectually, threatening Madson that he would be sent straight back to jail for burglary. In reality they both knew that the game was up. But they waited tensely for the joker to turn up, DI Rourke; with his spluttering hatred, no one could be sure of his reactions.

Suddenly the door opened, and Rourke stood squarely in the doorway. His whole body was bursting with barely restrained anger. Ignoring Madson, he glared at Gardner.

'What are we going to do with him?'

In reply Gardner merely shrugged nervously, and began to mutter that he did not know.

'Shut up,' Rourke snapped, turning his attention now to Madson.

Madson looked at him coolly. 'It's not what you are going to do to me. It's what I'm going to do to you.'

'You threatening me?' Rourke replied. 'You must be more stupid than I thought.'

Madson glared back at Rourke, standing his ground; he was not scared of Rourke or of the gun. This was the moment he had been waiting for all these years, the moment of truth. He knew that Rourke had hated him even before the night of his wife's murder. It was unreasonable that Rourke should feel such passionate hatred for someone he hardly knew. Perhaps they were just too similar, perhaps Rourke was jealous because Madson had the integrity to live his own life, make his own decisions, while Rourke himself lived under the constant pressures and strains of the rules governing the police force. Certainly he always looked like a pot about to boil over; continuous repressed rage had taken its toll. Madson wondered just how closely Rourke had identified with him – perhaps so closely that the lines had blurred, and Rourke was now raging in frustration at his own image. It was the look in Rourke's eyes that frightened Madson; he looked like he might well be capable of using the gun.

Donald pulled up outside Gardner's house; as instructed, he had been following Rourke for some time. And by all appearances, he thought, noting the three cars parked along the street, belonging to Madson, Gardner and Rourke, it was a good job he had. He had already called Berry on his mobile. Now he waited for Berry to arrive before taking any action.

Donald got out of his car as he saw Berry drive up the street. Berry parked and leapt out to join him on the pavement. Together the two men strode like the cavalry up the pathway to the front door. They paused for a moment, listening to the raised voices from inside.

'Why?' Madson was asking.

'You were a thug,' Rourke retorted. 'We'd got you under arrest. We'd got all the paperwork done. All ready to go to the CPS. You know, why waste good paperwork?' he said almost flippantly.

Madson's strained voice could be heard clearly. 'But I didn't kill my wife, you knew that . . .'

Donald and Berry listened in growing dismay as Rourke at last revealed who had murdered Elizabeth Madson. A young lad, eighteen years old, a drug addict; he had been picked up that night, burgling a house in the next street. The bloody knife had been found in his pocket. The explanation was so simple, so terrible in its own terms, so poignant. Berry decided it was high time to go in.

Donald and Berry loomed large in the doorway. Rourke, Madson and Gardner were staring at each other in shock, Gardner still holding the gun.

'Who was he, this kid?' Madson turned to Rourke,

devastated. It was such a simple explanation, not what he had expected, the horror of it almost took his breath away.

'Robbie Salter,' Rourke told him, enjoying Madson's grief.

Incredulous, Madson wondered for the first time whether Rourke was psychotic. Then he put this from his mind and concentrated on Salter. 'Where's Salter now?'

'Hanged himself in Winson Green Prison, 1991 . . .'

Madson stared at him, with wide, blank eyes. All his years of suffering had been for this, this hatred, this bumbling stupidity. It was hard to take in.

'Come on,' Rourke said, disregarding the presence of Berry and Donald. 'You're going back to prison.'

Madson looked at him sharply. 'No, not me you,' he said, lifting his hand to show the papers he held.

'He found my papers,' Gardner explained in a small, scared voice. 'My notes from years ago about meetings we had. Papers about you and my fraud case.'

Rourke looked at him in disbelief. 'You stupid bastard!' He turned to Madson. 'Give me those papers!' he demanded, grabbing the gun from the terrified Gardner, and aiming it squarely at Madson.

Madson glared back at him, quickly recovering himself; Berry and Donald were there after all. They took a step forward as if to acknowledge this.

'Now you have to decide whether you're going to use that gun. And murder me, in front of him, here.' There was a moment's silence. Then Madson continued, 'Two shells in that gun. Three of us. And now, we walk. With these papers.' He got up slowly, aware of the gun, and began to walk towards the door.

Rourke was not finished yet. He wanted the papers back, and he knew how to get at Madson. With a nasty glint in his eye he mentioned Sarah and the drugs case. He could get her put away for years, he said nastily, she would be thirty before they would let her out of Holloway, her life ruined. If Madson handed over the papers, he could have a word, get the case dropped.

The two men stood on the faded Persian carpet, apparently locked in combat. Then Madson gave way, he agreed to the terms. If Rourke got Sarah off he could have the papers, and save himself from certain prosecution. Madson walked towards his old rival holding out the papers. He handed them over and then, when Rourke glanced down at them, he drew his fist back and smashed him in the jaw, sending him reeling back and then crashing to the ground. All the aeons of pent-up frustration were in that powerful punch.

Rourke lay on the carpet, temporarily unable to move, and Madson bent down and took the papers back.

'Soon as I hear the case against Sarah is dropped you get them back. But I keep the photocopy, OK?' Without waiting for a reply he turned and, flanked by his good friends Gordon and Donald, marched out of the door.

Much later in the day Madson dressed sombrely for the Christmas party at Hearnley & Partners. In his hand he held an envelope containing his resignation, which he intended handing to Sir Ranald. For him, certainly for the time being, it was all over, he had no other desire but to get away, to escape from the terrible revelations. He had kept himself going in order to find out the truth from Rourke. Now that he had, he found it unpalatable.

Magda telephoned, wondering where he had got to and filling him in on the success of their defence of

Hartigan. The jury had found in his favour, and he and Belling would be joining them for the celebration that night. She was so pleased and talkative herself that she did not notice how unusually silent Madson was. She rang off cheerfully, looking forward to seeing him later.

Madson climbed the broad steps of Hearnley & Partners slowly that evening; in reception he brushed past the enormous Christmas tree and the drunken George Lodge, who was dressed in a red Father Christmas outfit and full of seasonal bonhomie. Lodge handed him a drink and wished him Merry Christmas, adding to Madson's disgust that he was willing to forgive and forget. Madson climbed the stairs, still in his dark winter coat, and was forced to push past Hartigan, who was celebrating his victory with two svelte girls draped across him, lipstick everywhere.

Upstairs he handed the letter to a startled Sir Ranald, and hugged Elaine, saying he would not stop, but he would speak to her later in the week. She looked at him with concern, realizing that something important had happened. She kissed him on the cheek and let him go, knowing that he would tell her when he was ready. As he went to go back down the stairs, Magda came out into the hallway to speak to him. She saw the intense look on his face, and wondered whether it was over. She leant against the top of the banister, gorgeous in her olive-green velvet dress. He stopped to look at her, and smiled at her beauty.

'Are you leaving?' she asked.

'I was going to tell you . . .' he saw her hurt, but could not explain at that moment. 'We're grown-ups, Magda . . .' he said ineffectually.

'Exactly,' Magda said harshly. 'And grown-ups talk about their feelings. When did you ever ask about mine?

What are my hopes, my fears, am I hurting inside? You slept in my bed, John, but you never knew me.'

Madson could see the tears in her eyes. 'I haven't had a relationship in eight years,' he said gently. 'Maybe we expected too much of each other.'

'I thought I was helping,' she murmured sadly.

'You were.' He kissed her softly on the cheek, and she watched as he made his way down the stairs and out into the night.

His collar up against the wind, Madson made his way along the Embankment, striding through the dead leaves towards the lights of Westminster Bridge. He stopped and looked up at the sky, realizing that, for the first time since his arrest eight long years ago, he was truly free.